the wishing Box

the
wishing Box
a Novel

dashka
slater

CHRONICLE BOOKS
San Francisco

acknowledgments

This book has been fortunate enough to have had many perceptive readers and critics at various stages in its development. Particular thanks should go to the members of my writing group, Mike Behrens, Toby Brothers, Dave Harrach, Susan Pagani, and Michael Welch, who patiently read draft after draft, and to Linnea Due, Dori Appel, Philip Slater, Scott Slater, Wendy Slater, Felicia Eth, and Jay Schaefer. I also owe a special debt to John Raeside, my editor at the *East Bay Express,* who let me take a leave of absence to rewrite this book and who has taught me much about narrative.

Text copyright © 2000 by Dashka Slater.

Library of Congress Cataloging-in-Publication Data:

Slater, Dashka.
          The wishing box : a novel / Dashka Slater
p.   cm.
ISBN: 0-8118-2606-6
I. Title.
PS3569.L2618W5   2000   99-13147
813'.54—dc21   CIP

Printed in the United States.

Designed by Jeremy Stout

Distributed in Canada by Raincoast Books
8680 Cambie Street
Vancouver, British Columbia V6P 6M9

10 9 8 7 6 5 4 3 2 1

Chronicle Books
85 Second Street
San Francisco, California 94105

www.chroniclebooks.com

■ For *Milo* ■

*P*rologue (Julia)

My grandmother was doing the breaststroke in the YMCA's steamy haze. Her face was cupped by water; water spread away from her. She cut onions this firmly but never with this much pleasure. Her legs extended out and she sailed, gliding.

My grandmother's eyes were open as she swam. She watched bubbles roll along her arms: tiny fish scales, blue coins, disappearing when she surfaced. Head down again, she saw her shadow on the tile below, ascended and saw herself undulating on the thin underside of the water's surface. The reflection of her arms, silver and shimmery, curved down as she reached up and through them and drew a muggy breath.

Then she was down, immersed again, pulling the water close and releasing it. She was mother of water, cradling it, father of water, abandoning it, tilting up her face for a morsel of air and then bringing her face down as if returning to a conversation.

As she swam she sometimes turned her head and watched the other swimmers glide back and forth like fish in an aquarium. She could see the headless sidestroking bodies of ladies who kept their hair dry, and the frothy wake of girls who swam with abandon. She watched their shadows on the bottom of the pool, vague as cloud-shadows. But then she noticed something strange. My grandmother skipped a breath and stayed underwater to stare. It was the shadows of their long wings that attracted her attention.

The pool was filled with angels, washed pale blue by the water's light as they glided between the black lane markers.

When my grandmother lifted her head, blinking to clear the haze from her eyes, she saw her father sitting at the edge of the pool, his feet dangling in the water. She swam to him. He leaned down and peeled the rubber bathing cap from her head and then reached for her hair and slowly unraveled the braid she had done in the locker room, without a mirror. When he finished, she sank back into the blue-gold water and her hair fanned behind her and around her, like a mass of words that are finally spoken.

"But how do you know what he did?" I asked my aunt Simone. "You weren't there. You weren't in heaven."

She was brushing my hair into a ponytail for the funeral.

"I didn't have to be there," she explained. "Irma was there and she told me how it happened. Last night I went into my room and she was there, by the altar, drinking from the glass of water I left out for her. I said, 'Mama, what are you doing? You had a stroke at the Y today and died.' And then she told me what happened."

"I don't believe you."

"Well, you should. Because she came back from heaven so I would tell you. She said you wanted to know the truth about things."

In the mirror I could see the reflection of Aunt Simone, hairbrush in hand. The room spread away behind her: the four-poster bed, the chest of drawers, and the small altar by the window, fumy with lilacs and scented candles. A half-empty glass of water rested on the windowsill.

$\mathscr{A}$n Ill Wind (Simone)

Their father left in a gust of wind. That was when Julia learned that things can change, very suddenly, and for the worse. That day the wind blew the lids off garbage cans and lashed the windows with tree branches. It was the wind that brought Lisa's cold, an ill wind that blew evil spores into her sinuses. I knew I could not cure all that the wind would do, but I could at least unstop my little niece's nose. I brewed a tea of sage and chamomile and sat at the kitchen table and watched her drink it down.

It was a Sunday in April, the first warm cusp of spring. Julia was seven, Lisa five. Of the two, Julia was the milder in temperament. At seven, she already suspected that our lives are not ours to govern. Her child's ear was still keen enough to hear the rustle of Fate's body slithering through time, and the sound distracted her, giving her eyes their dreamy blear, and her small mouth its ruefulness. I tried to teach my nieces what I knew about the world, that time is porous and fate indifferent, and that we may know the future as we know the past. But Lisa was a willful child who never wanted to hear that her destiny had already been written. And Julia was cursed with a tendency to see both sides of every question, so that while she believed me, she also believed that I was wrong.

I baby-sat for them that Sunday while their mother went out shopping. My sister Carolina was thirty-five by then, but age can only instruct a willing pupil. She was still as foolish as a girl, and as prone to fads and lavish disappointments. Her obsession then was the MG Midget she'd bought for cheap from a Lithuanian mechanic, and she insisted on driving it to the market, despite the fierce wind. As I set Lisa's cup down on the table, it held a ripply picture of Carolina being swept from one side of the road to the other, like a spider under a broom.

Water reflects much more than light if you know how to read it, but it takes a clear eye and a patient soul to make sense of what you see. I have the patience, and my eyesight is better than most. At sixty I can still thread a needle or find a button on a parquet floor, and when I look into a vessel of water, I can sometimes see the future or the past, or even things in the present that are far away. But this second vision, this window into time, has grown cataracted with memory. Sometimes I can't tell what I remember and what I've dreamed, what I've foretold and what I've only feared. When I look back at that augurying cup of tea, I can't remember if I understood what the picture of the wind was telling me. I only know that the steam from that cup fogged my spectacles and I had to untuck a corner of my blouse to wipe the lenses clear.

The girls were restless and edgy from the wind. They were bored with their toys and dolls, and as I sat trying to coax Lisa into drinking her healing tea, they kicked each other under the table and thought I didn't notice.

"I have a surprise for you," I cajoled, hoping they could be distracted. "Picture books."

I was still a librarian then and I liked to bring my nieces books from the discard shelves. Carolina never approved of my selections, but that was because I refused to pander. That day I brought them a book on Renoir and one on Caravaggio, an illustrated home-plumbing book, and a medical treatise on rashes with seventy-five full-color photographs of hives, blisters, whelks, and shingles. I had no use for storybooks, with their mincing illustrations of insipid infants and simpering beasts. Such sugarcoating only teaches children to look at the surface of things. I wanted my nieces to discover the story on the lips of Caravaggio's insolent saints, the message written on the thighs of Renoir's blowsy nudes. The serpent Fate slithers between the lines, and if you want to find her, you must visit where she lives.

Julia could have found her if she wanted to. She was the kind of child who would stare at objects until they blurred into a corona of light and then turned crisp again. It was hard for her to decide which vision was the truer one. When she looked at the photographs of raging urticaria and furfuraceous rashes, she teetered between repulsion and captivation. The pimples and rashes were disgusting, but she found that if she watched the inflamed pustules long enough, they became an auburn landscape of snowcapped mountains. It was only Lisa who was certain what she was seeing. "Ew, gross!" she squealed as she looked over Julia's shoulder. "I bet you could die from that."

By afternoon Lisa had turned feverish and I sent Julia outside to play in the wind. I sat at Lisa's bedside and watched Julia through the window. The wind felt to her like a cold muscle, pressing against her, blowing her hair in front of her face. It made her want to dance and do funny walks. She stood straight up with her arms spread out like wings. She waltzed along the sidewalk the way her daddy had taught her, ONE-two-three, ONE-two-three. The wind blew behind her, propelling her along, whipping her skirt between her legs. She thought it was friendly then. But when she tried to run against it, it blew her back and tipped over the mug of hot chocolate she had been allowed to bring outside, her favorite mug, with a picture of a bumblebee on it.

She saw then what kind of wind it was, a cruel wind, a careless wind, like certain neighborhood girls who played too rough and broke her toys without even noticing. The wind seized trees by the neck and shook them, knocked potted plants off windowsills. Nothing would stay still. A tricycle sailed down someone's driveway and capsized at the curb. She watched the big front wheel turn slowly in the street and felt sorry for the tricycle, sorry for the trees, sorry for the shattered mug and the cocoa seeping over the concrete. At last she sunk down on her own front steps and huddled against the darting, flickering air, seeing how the wind could turn you against yourself.

I was about to go outside and fetch her in when I saw her father walking down the street, his hands in his pockets, his black hair blown straight up. He smiled at her, a guilty, bashful smile, and she stood up, her heart full of pleasure. The two of them were like two versions of the same letter, capital and lowercase. They didn't look alike, but they meant the same thing.

"Your hair's standing on end," Julia told him.

"Is it?" He smoothed it with one hand. "Something must have scared me."

She waited for him to tell her what—a monster maybe, or a robber. He liked to tell her stories about the exotic characters lurking inside the green-and-white clapboard houses of working-class Watertown, the adventures he had when he was walking home. But now he just leaned down and tousled her hair as if she were someone else's daughter.

"Your mama home yet?" he asked. When she shook her head, he went inside, leaving Julia standing in the wind.

Late that night she woke up, afraid of the wind's yammering. The house cracks wailed and skirled. There was a rushing noise as if a great dam had broken and a clanging as some metal thing blew down the sidewalk. She lay still, listening, trying to tell apart the noises. Something slogged against the back door, jarring the windowpane. She held her breath and pressed herself flat against the sheets, trying to be invisible. Knock. Knock. Knock. Whatever it was, it wanted in.

At last Julia leaped out of bed and climbed the stairs to her parents' bedroom. "There's someone trying to get in," she whispered.

Julia's father opened his eyes and put his fingers to his lips. The pounding continued, slow, then fast, then slow again.

"Let's go see who it is," he said quietly and got up, pulling on the bathrobe that was slung over the doorknob. Julia crept behind him, tailing him as he padded down the stairs and through the dim, chilly atmosphere of the house to the back door. He listened for a moment and then pushed his daughter back with one hand. With the other, he quietly undid the bolt and jerked open the door.

When he saw what was out there, he laughed, the chuckle of a man who was used to being fooled. His boots were tied together at the laces and strung by a hook on the back-porch roof. It was they who'd been trying to get in, his brown leather work boots, kicking at the back door in the wind. Julia's father lifted them from the hook and tossed them over his shoulder.

"Christ, it's really blowing out here, isn't it, Princess?" he said and walked down the back steps to the anemic lawn. Julia followed him, the grass cold on her bare feet, and stood beside him with the wind stinging her eyes. "Chilly?" her father asked, and he put his arm around her shoulders. With his arm strapping her close to his body she didn't mind the wind, and she watched the flailing trees with sleepy fascination.

"Look," her father said. "The Farringtons' sheets have blown off the line."

A pair of sheets, yellow and printed with daisies, wafted across their neighbors' yard like ghosts. They lurched and twisted and got snarled in the bushes, but one pillowcase inflated like a balloon and was borne over the fence.

"Good-bye!" sang Julia's father. "It's off to travel the wide world. Imagine—that tattered old pillowcase is going to fly all over Boston and out to the sea."

He lifted his daughter into his arms and carried her back up the stairs.

"It's a good thing I held you tight out there," he said as she lay under her blankets. "Because otherwise you could have blown away. You might've flown away with the pillowcase, up over all the trees and houses with your nightgown full of wind like a sail. You could've gotten tangled up in telephone wires and had to stay up there till the morning. We'd have had to call the fire department to get you down."

He grinned at Julia and she shut her eyes, nearly dreaming.

"Maybe you'd just have kept going, blowing and blowing out to the harbor. You'd look down and see the boats and the big green waves underneath you. And the people in the boats would think you were a bird, a white seagull. You'd just be flying all night long, far, far from home with nothing above you but the big black sky and the little yellow moon and nothing below you but the cold green sea and no one for company except the pillowcase that came sailing with you. And when you got sleepy you'd rest your head on the pillowcase because it would be full of air like a balloon and you'd lie there on your bed of clouds and spin around in the blustery wind . . ."

While Julia was dreaming of flying and Lisa lay sniffling and Carolina dreamed of wearing a lace dress with green buttons, Bill Harris put on his boots and went out the front door. Julia never knew if he was already packed before she came fearfully upstairs, or if her fear of intruders put him in mind of certain real dangers and gave him the idea of leaving. Maybe it was the flying pillowcase that made him think of it. The next morning Carolina told her that the wind had blown him away, and for a long time that was what she believed.

ℳake a Wish   (Julia)

Aunt Simone would argue that there was no beginning. Everything that happens, she says, happens because of something else. Every reason has a reason. Try to put your finger at the start of a story and you'll find yourself up to your elbows in history.

But every time I try to understand the events of the past few months, I come back to the night before my son's seventh birthday. I must have been thinking about my father that night, because I was always thinking about him. His absence was something I carried with me, a mossy depression in my chest like the hollow of my solar plexus. And as I thought about Steven becoming the age I was when my father left, I wondered what it would be like to follow in his footsteps.

Steven was sleeping in his sky blue room, surrounded by the litter of his life as a little boy: toy cars, action figures, books and crayons, the shells and rocks he gathered at the beach. I stood over his bed and breathed in his smell of dirt and apricots. Asleep, he looked contemplative, as if considering the implications of his own dreams. I kissed his cheek.

"Good-bye, Steven," I whispered.

Then I went out into the hallway, put on the oversized man's suit jacket I use as a coat, and went out the front door, locking it behind me.

I went down the steps carefully, listening for a sound from him. The night was moist and blue and unremarkable. Nothing reproached me besides a loose board on the third step, and it only did so weakly. I breathed and breathed that outside air, smelling of night-blooming jasmine and fog. Somewhere down the street, someone was having a party. I could hear the tugging of a bass line, daring me to be the daughter of that wayward man who left his children in the middle of the night.

Down onto the sidewalk. My shoes on the pavement, snap-snap-snap. Past the college-student house next door with its line of Heineken bottles on the front porch. Past the house with the barking golden retriever, now safely inside and asleep. I made it three doors down, to a stucco bungalow with a riot of roses flung across its front fence. And then I stopped as if winded, tore off a browning white rose as a trophy, and bolted back to my front door before Steven could wake up.

The next day I told Lisa what I had done. She looked at me and shook her head. "You couldn't leave Steven in a million years," she said. "You wouldn't even let me hold him until he was three months old."

It was true. When Steven was an infant he'd seemed too precious, too miraculous to rest in someone else's hands. Maybe it was the legacy of having been left when we were young, but Lisa and I both had a tendency to love too fiercely. Lisa loved men so rashly that they fled in panic, and I loved my son so well that grown-up men rarely sustained my interest. And so we lived alone and palled around together, not because we were much alike but because we were used to each other and shared a common history.

"Do you think we're like him?" I said as the two of us stood in her immaculate kitchen, mixing the batter for Steven's birthday cake.

"How should I know?" Lisa said. "I don't even remember what he looked like."

I remembered. As I measured cups of flour, I could picture his face as it looked the last time I saw him. Dark straight hair, green eyes, a blunt face like a prizefighter's. Soft, flexible baby lips that hung around the edges of his teeth when he smiled. A smile that didn't commit, only slunk halfway up his face on one side. I remembered his lips coming together before he began to tell a story, the story gathering energy inside his mouth before he set it loose.

Lisa was cracking eggs into a bowl. From the way she crushed the empty shells with her hand, I could see she was still mulling my question.

"Mitch says that you and I are the victims of a childhood trauma," she said after a pause.

I sighed. Up until two weeks ago, Mitch had been Lisa's boyfriend. He had left her abruptly after seven months of honeyed loving, and she had been introspective and sulky ever since. Somehow every topic of conversation seemed to circle back to Mitch's parting shots.

"Everyone's the victim of something," I told her. "I'm sure Mitch had something bad happen to him when he was a child that would explain how he became the kind of asshole who psycho-analyzes his girlfriend while he's breaking up with her."

Lisa was silent and I knew I had gone too far. Her hands were chapped and spotted with small cuts and burns, the tokens of her work as a chef at a local bistro. Lately it seemed to me that all of her was scabbed that way. I couldn't open my mouth without nick-ing one of her tender spots.

"I'm sorry," I said. "He's not an asshole. I just don't think it was a very helpful thing for him to say."

Lisa brushed the hair back from her face. "But don't you worry about Steven?" she asked, her whisk slitting open the yellow egg bellies and marching them around the bowl. "About him not having a father?"

"Steven's doing just fine, if you hadn't noticed."

"Aw, get off your high horse. No one's criticizing Steven. I'm just thinking about what Mitch said. That I didn't learn to love properly as a child."

I shook my head. I hated psychology. I hated the way it pre-sumed that you could undo the events of the past just by naming them. Of course Lisa and I were shaped by our father's disappear-ance. But our natures were hardened now. Fired, glazed, and set out for display. It was too late to put us back on the wheel.

"Can we talk about something else?" I pleaded. "Did I tell you that Steven's completely hooked on rap music? He can do all the dances they do in the videos. You won't believe how graceful he is." I tried to show her how Steven moved, supple as a blade of grass, but it wasn't a talent he'd inherited from me.

Anyway, Lisa wasn't paying attention. She had her hands on her hips, like a squat two-handled jug. "The thing is, is I think he's right," she said. "I think I am the casualty of a childhood trauma." She took the flour mixture out of my hands and began folding it into the other ingredients. "I don't know. I just wish he'd come back."

"I think you should find someone who loves you the way you are."

Lisa's spoon kept moving, obscured by the flour's hazy fall. "I don't mean Mitch," she said. "I mean Dad." Then she put the bowl down on the counter. "I mean, don't you? Just so we could figure it all out?"

Steven's face opened like a flower when he saw the cake, its candles all aflame.

"Make a wish," I prompted.

He blew until the candle flames bowed down and disappeared. We all applauded, even Aunt Simone, who doesn't approve of wishes.

"What did you wish for?" Lisa asked as he tucked into the first slice.

Steven pressed his lips together, chocolate leaking from the corners. He knew the rules. Don't tell or it won't come true. Hold it in, hold your breath. Wait. But I knew what he'd wished for. The Oakland A's looked like they were going to make the play-offs, and Steven was baseball crazy. All he wanted was for them to win the World Series, a gift I gladly would have given him were it in my power. Instead I gave him a green satin A's jacket, a slightly dog-eared Rickey Henderson rookie card, and a promise that I would find us tickets to a post-season game. That was good enough for Steven, who danced around the room in his new green jacket singing "Oakland A's, Oakland A's, Oakland A's."

Lucky for me he was still little enough not to mind me kissing him on impulse. When he sat back down at the table, I leaned over and kissed his head, and he edged his chair close to mine and slung his arm around me.

"Seven years old," I murmured into his hair. "I can't believe it. I still think I'm the one who's seven."

I felt Lisa's eyes on me and looked up to see her frowning, the cake knife in hand. *Childhood trauma,* her eyes seemed to say. I shook my head as she offered me a slice.

"No thanks," I told her. "I think I had enough while we were cooking."

I let the birthday boy plan the evening, and he insisted on dancing and baseball. My friend Dawn came over when she got off work, and the five of us watched the A's game. We rooted so passionately for Jose Canseco, the A's handsome right fielder, that Steven blushed for us and told us to stop. When the game was over, we tuned the radio to the soul station and Steven climbed up on the sofa and demonstrated the latest dance moves, barking out instructions while Lisa, Dawn, and I shimmied below. Aunt Simone watched it all from a chair in the corner, her face inscrutable.

She had dressed up for the party in an orange Chanel suit that would have set off a bidding war at any San Francisco thrift shop, and she had given her bouffant an extra coating of silver hairspray. She glinted as she watched us, but I couldn't tell if the gleam came from her metallic hair, the rhinestones on her spectacles, or her own steely pupils. When I was a little girl, my father used to make fun of Aunt Simone's mincing high-heeled walk and prominent front teeth, and her habit of painting her black hair silver. But I stopped laughing at Aunt Simone after he left, and I was glad when she followed me and Lisa to California. We needed someone around who could tell us the truth about things.

"Come dance!" Steven called to her as he shook his little hips across the sofa.

Aunt Simone shook her head. "If I dance, who will watch you?" she asked. "Every performance needs an audience."

I thought about that as I kicked and hopped in imitation of Steven's complicated steps. I would have liked to be watching us: heavyset Lisa lumbering arhythmically; Dawn, tall and angular, her hips stabbing from side to side; me, small and spiky-haired and a little too worried about the steps; and conducting it all from Lisa's oatmeal-colored sofa, my green-eyed and graceful son. I thought he was lucky to be growing up in the company of women, no matter what Lisa said.

By the time we were done dancing, Aunt Simone was dozing in her chair, and Steven had a telltale pinkness around his eyes that told me he was ready for bed. "We're tired," I told Lisa and Dawn, and knelt by Aunt Simone's chair to wake her up.

"I was dreaming," she said when I whispered her name. She reached up to her face to rub her eyes and succeeded only in dislodging her spectacles. "I saw my mother when she was still a young girl in Mexico."

Normally I would have been interested in Aunt Simone's dream, but it was late and Steven had school the next day. "Do you want me to take you home?" I asked her.

"Thank you, dear." She stood up and smoothed her skirt and waited for Lisa and Dawn to kiss Steven good night. "Do you know," she said as we walked to the door, "when my mother wanted to make a wish, she used to lock the Virgin Mary in a box."

I nodded and began rummaging around in the coat closet for Aunt Simone's raincoat and my leather jacket.

"Blackmail," Aunt Simone went on. "The people from her village used to torture the images of saints until they got their way. Some Christians, hmm?"

I was about to ask her what had made her think of saints and wishes, but Steven shuffled closer to me and rubbed his face against my stomach. "Time to go," I said, and then we were on the landing, looking back at Dawn and Lisa waving on the threshold.

"I'll call you tomorrow," Lisa said and tucked her hair behind her ears. It was a gesture she only made when she was trying to be crafty. If I hadn't been thinking about getting Steven home to bed, I might have thought to worry.

I had trouble concentrating at work the next day. Something was up, some current of change. As I sat at my desk trying to focus on the book I was editing, I felt as if a light breeze were sighing across the nape of my neck, rousing my skin to gooseflesh. In retrospect, I suppose it was a warning, but at the time it felt thrilling. I was tired of my life the way it was. It was 1989. I was twenty-nine, I had no career ambitions to speak of, no relationship, and no clear idea what it was that I wanted from my future. I was ready for something to happen.

It's hard to avoid thinking about your future when you work at Enhancement Press, an imprint devoted to books about self-improvement, self-fulfillment, self-contemplation, and self-actualization. Is your aura limp and lifeless, your inner child fretful, your spirit guide disoriented? Enhancement Press had all the solutions on hand, in paperback, with a photograph of the tan, self-satisfied author on the front cover.

At the moment, I was copy-editing the latest book by Shantra Maloney, whose seminal tome on the power of positive thinking *I Am, I Can, I Do* was still one of our best-sellers. As far as I could tell, Maloney was possessed of only one idea, which she faithfully regurgitated into a new manuscript every year. "Every day we have many thoughts," she wrote this time around. "You maybe think to yourself, 'I don't have enough money' or 'I am fat' or 'I think I will go outside and breathe the fresh air in my beautiful garden.' You probably think that you are thinking these thoughts because they are true. But the truth is that they are true because you are thinking them!"

Here I stopped reading long enough to wonder why it was that all of Shantra's books sounded as if they had been translated from the original Croatian.

"Thoughts are much more powerful than you think," she continued. "Every war, invention, or work of art began as a thought! Everything that happens to us is something we first created in our minds. That is why you must learn to take complete responsibility for your positive future by using the power of your thoughts."

I tried using the power of my thoughts to make the manuscript burst into flames, but it didn't, so I continued through the perky sentences, fixing punctuation and grammatical errors and marking where the text should be italicized and whether the headings should be centered or flush left. When I was done with the chapter, I leaned back in my chair and looked up at the sign over my desk. It said, I AM RELAXED, CHEERFUL, AND READY TO ACHIEVE. Ralph Kaffey, my boss and the founder of Enhancement Press, had made me write it on a three-by-five-inch index card and tape it over my desk one day when I had come into work hungover and in a bad mood. It was supposed to help me cultivate a better attitude.

Ralph was a pudgy man with small, heavy-lidded eyes, thin lips, and strangely prominent jowls that made him look like an overfed iguana. His philosophy was a mixture of New Age and Dark Age, and he had started Enhancement Press for the purpose of publishing his own treatise on employee management, *I Love My Job, My Job Loves Me.* His method relied on the copious use of affirmations. His nagging little messages were everywhere in the office. The one over the kitchen sink said, I DO MY SHARE TO KEEP THE OFFICE CLEAN. The one over the xerox machine said, I TREAT OFFICE PROPERTY WITH LOVE. Above the window in my office was one that said, LIGHT COMES FROM WITHIN. That was to remind me to keep the shades drawn. Sunlight gave Ralph a rash.

I was just about to yank down the affirmation over my desk and tear it into pieces when the man himself wandered into my office, gnawing on some kind of vegan burrito. He positioned himself behind me and stared at the manuscript on my desk. "How's Shantra's new book coming?"

"It's a lot like her last one," I said. "Except even less well-written."

"Better fix it the fuck up," he said. "She's gonna be on *Oprah.* We need books in the stores."

"Okay." I waited for him to leave. He didn't. He placed one large buttock on the edge of my desk and stared at me for a long moment, chewing.

"You asked about my season tickets the other day," he said at last. "Want to see an A's play-off game?"

"I want to take Steven," I said, not sure what exactly he was offering. I was pretty sure he didn't want to go himself, since he'd bought the tickets as a tax write-off and usually sold them to his staff at a 15 percent markup. "Steven would completely flip if I could take him."

"Makes the tickets a powerful motivator," Ralph said, licking a dollop of salsa from his upper lip. "You can have 'em if you can have Shantra's manuscript ready for the printer two weeks from Monday."

"Two weeks? I thought it wasn't going to the printer for another month."

"Life is full of surprises, Julia," Ralph said. "Maybe you could surprise me by not questioning every fucking thing I say."

"I can't get it done in half the time. It's impossible."

"That's negative languaging, Julia," Ralph said. "When you use a word like *impossible* all you do is convince yourself that you can't succeed." Then he took an index card from his back pocket and wrote in block letters, I AM THE CAUSE OF MY SUCCESS.

"Something to think about," he said and pinned it on the wall above my desk.

Lisa stopped by late that night, after her restaurant closed. She sat down at my kitchen table and unwrapped the foil from the dinner she'd brought with her. "Try this," she said, offering me a forkful of something blue. "It's a crabcake made with blue cornmeal. Excellent, if I do say so myself."

I shook my head. Steven and I had eaten packaged Welsh rarebit for dinner and I was still feeling overcheesed. "How's the restaurant doing?"

"Great. We got reviewed again in the *Chronicle,* and they said if anything, we'd gotten better." She smiled, her face still rosy from kitchen heat. "The restaurant is the one thing in my life that's going great."

"Good," I said. I was jealous. It didn't seem fair that Lisa should be tooling along on the career path of her dreams while I was being affirmed to death at Enhancement Press. "I'm glad one of us is enjoying work."

"Why? What did Ralph do today?"

"Just the usual lesson on the power of positive thinking."

"Poor Julia." Lisa reached across the table to pat my hand. Then she leaned back and rubbed the sides of her arms as if she were cold. "Do you ever wonder, though, if some of that stuff might be true?"

I stared at her and she made a great show of hunting down a morsel of crabcake that was hiding under a leaf of escarole. "I don't mean affirmations, exactly," she said without looking up from her plate. "I just mean changing things with your thoughts. Or whatever. Wishing for things."

I kept still, feeling fear rake its jagged edges over the layer of muscle just below my skin.

"Look," Lisa said. She put her fork down and began rummaging around in the African basket she used as a purse. After a moment she pulled out a little ivory-colored statue. "Do you remember what Aunt Simone said last night? Well, I ran across this at a junk shop on my way to work today. It seemed like a sign."

She pushed the statue across the table and I picked it up. It was a plastic Madonna, arms folded in prayer. I peered at its bland little face. Eyes downcast, the Virgin revealed nothing.

I handed her back to Lisa. "A sign of what?"

"I think we should try it," she said. "Wishing for something."

"Why?" I felt cross. It was bad enough having to listen to this kind of talk at work.

"I don't know. Just for the hell of it. What if we wished for Dad to come visit us? Just to see what would happen." She grinned at me, pink-faced and earnest, wheedling. "Come on, Julia, what could it hurt? The worst thing that could happen is it doesn't work."

"The *best* thing that could happen is it doesn't work," I corrected. "What if he's dead? Haven't you read 'The Monkey's Paw?' Do you want a decomposing corpse to come knocking on your door, because I certainly don't."

Needing to do something, I filched a piece of sautéed summer squash from Lisa's plate and popped it in my mouth.

"So we'll phrase it carefully," she said. "Wish for him or his personal effects, whichever would be less disgusting to look at." She reached back in her bag and pulled out a little metal index card box. She put the box on the table and stood the tiny Madonna next to it. "Let's just try it. Please?"

Standing on the Formica kitchen table, the Madonna looked like a misplaced chess piece. I felt a sudden loss of gravity, as if the earth had moved out from under us and we were suspended in midair with the table floating between us.

"Fine," I said. "Go ahead. I won't stop you."

Lisa smiled, her face broad and satisfied. The box and the Virgin were in front of her like ingredients set out for a cooking show. She opened the box and put the little statue in it.

"Holy Mary, Mother of God," she said in a ponderous voice, "we are locking you in this box and we won't let you out until you grant this wish. Send us our father, if he's alive." She looked up at me and smiled with just the corners of her mouth. "If not, send us his personal effects. That is our wish."

She shut the lid of the box and locked it with a tiny key.

"There," she said. "That ought to do the trick."

"I can't imagine that a plastic statue is going to care about being in a box," I grumbled. "She probably *came* in a box."

"She's more than plastic. I went to St. Francis de Sales Cathedral and dipped her in holy water," Lisa said, her chest inflating a little with stubbornness. I didn't bother asking when she'd started to believe in things like holy water. I just shook my head and got up to put her empty paper plate in the trash, leaving the box sitting on the table. It seemed full of promise and evil, like the one Pandora opened.

"Take it with you," I said from the garbage can, not wanting to touch it.

"Let me leave it here. I don't want to be tempted to let her out."

"Fine." I didn't see what could tempt her, but I wasn't going to make it into something more than it was by arguing. I scooped up the box and put it in the spice cabinet behind a wall of cumin and oregano jars. Then I shut the door, leaving the caged Madonna in spice-scented darkness.

$\mathcal{T}$he Laws of the Past (Simone)

I wasn't born knowing how to tell fortunes, I learned it. It's not a talent, it's a skill like plumbing or using the Dewey decimal system. If you know how to read, you can learn anything. Everything I know I learned from a book.

My father was a professor of anthropology. Thin and tall as an icicle and with a heart about as warm. I looked up at him when I was little, and it was like standing at the foot of a ladder. At the top of the ladder was his head, blond on top and red below. I could see he and I had nothing in common. I was little and dark and liked observing more than talking. His voice was like a cannon and it was always firing. He thought he was so clever, but he didn't fool me for a minute.

The only useful thing he taught me was that books could be my teacher. When he was home he spent almost all his time in his library on the third floor. The walls of that room were solid books. I used to think the walls *were* books and if I took a book off the shelf I would be able to see through the gap into the next room. I was right. He did use books as walls. And once I learned to open up those books, walls did become transparent.

I learned how to read as soon as I was able. My father taught me. He was trying to teach Carolina—she was his favorite, selfish like him. Where I was sallow and knock-kneed, she was a fat plum of a baby with thick black hair and eyes that only knew the answer *yes*. She and I never had much to say to each other. I took care of her as an older sister should, but we were born into a war and in a war you choose sides. Carolina had no use for losers, so she chose Papa. Her first word was *Papa*, and after that she repeated everything he said to her. The only thing she ever took from our mother was the pronunciation of her name. It was a family name, and our aunt and great-aunt Carolinas pronounced it like the state. But my sister liked the way it sounded when my mother said it, and to this day she'll correct you if you don't pronounce it the Spanish way, *Caroleena*.

Papa never got tired of talking about how clever she was, and when she was four years old he decided to teach her to read. I was about to start first grade, so he let me tag along. It was the first and only time I ever beat Carolina at anything. She did well for such a little thing, and Papa gave her a dozen kisses every time she spelled a word with the wooden alphabet blocks he laid out on the floor of the library. As for myself, I simply paid attention. I knew too much to want to win any favors from him. But when he asked me a question, I knew the answer. What sound does *F* make? *Fffff*, I showed him with my lip against my teeth. What is this word? *Doll*, I said, and I didn't prance around to show how pleased with myself I was the way Carolina did. How do you write pony? P-O-N-Y. I ate up his lessons like they were birdseed and I was a little chickadee. He nodded to show that I had the answer right, but he never bothered to praise my progress.

By the next fall, I was bored with Dick and Jane and all the empty-headed primers we read in school. When my father was at the university, I snuck into his study and opened up his books. That was the first fortune-telling I ever did, and I still do it every morning after my tea and toast. You choose a book at random, open it up, and the first sentence you read is your fortune. In my father's library I took Bertrand Russell's *Problems of Philosophy* down from the shelf. I opened it and read, "We have therefore still to seek for some principle which shall enable us to know that the future will follow the same laws as the past."

That was my first lesson, and like a fortune tucked into a cookie, it was a lesson within a lesson. The first lesson was that it was my destiny to know the future, to find the principles that would make the future as easy to read as the past. That lesson was wrapped inside another, which was: I could find those principles in books.

Scientists, my father used to say, can find out about the past from objects in the present. An anthropologist digs up a stone tool and learns about an ancient people. The kind of rock tells him where those people traveled; the marks and chips on its surface tell him how it was made; the shape of its handle tells him how it was used. These in turn tell him more things: how much knowledge of tool-making those people had, what they ate, what they did for sport.

An object holds as many clues to the future as it does to the past. I could tell your fortune with a paintbrush, a piece of lint, a credit card if I had to. Better, of course, to use the palm of your hand, but such things are not required. I told the fortune of a man who had no hands, nor feet either, and he was glad I did. I looked at his tongue and I saw true love waiting for him. My own future isn't quite so rich. Long ago, I flipped through the pages of my life and saw that no man had marked his place in it.

I tell you all this so you understand how I know what I know. It has nothing to do with magic, nor with wishing, either. Long ago, before the sun rose over the earth, everything was soft as the flesh on your arm. Trees, rocks, everything. Spongy, flexible. Then the sun rose and everything in the world baked like pottery in a kiln. Hardened. In the old days, the past and the present and the future flowed independently, three separate clay rivers. But when the sun rose, they dried into one thin hard stream. This is a story to tell you why the world is the way it is. There is no past, present, future. Everything happens at once. And that is why the future is easy to see, and the past, too. It's all happening right now. I shut my eyes and open my ears and I hear it, like a story someone is telling me.

I open my ears like the stubby wings of a common bird, a sparrow or starling, say, and I ride the jetstream of time backward and forward. Today I am sliding backward, back before I was born. I want to show you why I decided to see the future. Don't be fooled, the way my nieces were—you can't change the future any more than you can change the past. But listen to the story of my parents and you'll understand why it's worth finding out what's in store for you.

At the pyramids in Mitla the anthropologists called my father Goose. His name was Angus, but it sounded like Goose when Mexicans said it, and he looked like a goose as he walked through the ancient city, his neck way ahead of his body. He was just out of college and everything excited him, every piece of chipped stone, every pot shard. He liked living cultures more than dead ones and stole down to the village below the site whenever he could, but the archaeologists were paying him to stay among the pyramids and help catalog the artifacts. He spent the mornings in front of a type-writer in a palapa office, logging identifying notes onto a stack of index cards. When the sun grew hot and the senior members of the dig retreated into the shade for their afternoon siesta, he left his typewriter and climbed among the ruins' giant rocks, his fair skin turning pink in the sun.

In the evenings, Indian girls came from the village to sell din-ner to the men at the site. They were the sisters and daughters of the men who were hired to haul the fallen rocks back into position, small barefoot girls with wide hips and strong legs. At seven o'clock you could see them walking up the path toward the ruins, their crimson skirts and blue head scarves a bright spot of color in the dust. My mother, Irma, was one of those girls. She had a round face with a high curved forehead and wide, cinnamon-colored lips. She and her friends carried baskets of cooked food and fruit wrapped in leaves and corn husks. They weren't allowed into the city of their ancestors, so the men came down the path to meet them, wiping the ancient dust from their hands as they walked.

Angus was the tallest man she had ever seen, and she had seen plenty of Anglos since anthropologists began coming to Mitla. He was sitting on a rock, rolling a cigarette. He watched her carefully as she handed him an orange from her basket and put the coin he gave her into the pocket of her apron. Then he reached out and grabbed her wrist.

She didn't flinch, just stood looking at him with her other arm curved around the lip of the basket that was resting on her hip. Even though he was sitting and she was standing, they were nearly at eye level.

"What is this from?" he asked. His fingers stroked the long cut that traversed her left hand.

She looked down at his fingers and laughed.

"From cutting fruit." She mimed the motion of the knife slipping. Then she pulled her hand away and hoisted the basket back onto her head. He watched her as she walked toward the other men, one hand stabilizing the basket, her blouse pulled tight across her breasts.

After that he asked her a different question each time she came up to the site with a basket of food. First he asked her about the local markets, what food people ate, and where it came from. Later he asked her about Mitla. She told him that long ago, Mitla had been the center of the world of the dead, before the sun rose over the earth. In those days the heavy stones were soft and light, and even though the ancient ones were tiny as babies, they piled them into monuments. She told him about the souls of dead people, how they grow hungry from travel and angry if they aren't provided for. How sin makes the soul heavy and weighs down the bodies of the dead.

The truth was, she liked to talk. She couldn't linger for long or she wouldn't sell any fruit, but she blurted out the answers to his questions in one breathless sentence before turning to the next customer. Most of the time he only understood half of what she said; she spoke Spanish with a thick Indian accent, and Zapotec phrases kept sneaking into the torrent of words.

"Do you talk so much at home?" he asked her, and she told him that she didn't speak a word until she was two years old. Her parents were afraid she'd grow up mute, so they gave her water that hens had drunk from, which always loosens a stuck tongue. "Maybe they gave me too much," she said, laughing.

After a few weeks my father wasn't thinking as much about the dusty stones of Mitla as he was about Irma's dusty calves. Once she came up to the site with a jug of pineapple juice. As she poured it into a mug for him, a drop landed on her leg and a shiny streak of brown skin opened in its wake. Suddenly he wanted all of her revealed to him, not just that one wet streak.

He liked that Irma knew more than he did about something he was interested in, and for the first time what he was interested in was another person. He thought about her as he lay on the hard mattress in his hotel room overlooking the main square of the village. Her body was dense and round like the stone idols in the ruined city. There was a whole culture bundled up in that body, a whole history of tribal legends and customs. He stayed up all night reading about the ancient Zapotecs, finding questions to ask her on every page. He had never needed much sleep, or food either for that matter, but now the lack of it gave him a new awareness of his height. When he walked the ruins during siesta, he felt himself teetering, even on the flat grass field where the ancient Zapotecs played ball. He attributed his vertigo to the heat, and to love, and to exhaustion. But often when we are struck by the hand of Fate, the blow sends us reeling.

He wasn't the only one off-kilter. My mother, as she walked down the path that led from the ruins to her parents' house, felt her body fading into lightness. She weighed nothing. It was all the talking she had done. In truth, she didn't talk much at home. There wasn't time for it or room—her two older brothers and four older sisters did more than enough talking. And her sweetheart Eligio, whose family lived next door to hers, talked so much that she couldn't get a word in edgewise. Sometimes she nearly fell asleep to the sound of his voice droning on and on like the legs of a cricket. Only during those few minutes at Mitla could the words fall away from her. Later she told me she believed that talking was her mistake. Words kept inside were a ballast, steadying her. Without them she was knocked off course. She didn't understand that we are all on one course from the beginning, so she blamed herself instead of blaming Fate.

They got married. Why should I bother telling about the meetings between my father and her father, the disapproval of my father's colleagues, the excitement of my mother's parents, who could think only of American riches? What is there to say about Eligio, who was taken by surprise? Irma and Angus were married in the village church, with all the days of ceremony and feasting before and after, the blessings and the dancing and the gifts of turkeys and chocolate and cigarettes and the men getting drunk on tepache and mescal.

It was my father who insisted on the whole long rigmarole; he wanted to see how it was done. It was halfhearted, even the blessings. No one likes to have their customs on display, and my father's curiosity was embarrassing to everyone. Eligio got drunk and danced by himself, murmuring all the while about the fickleness of love. Of course, he promised to murder my father, but he had too gentle a spirit to carry it out.

My father's parents weren't invited to the wedding. He wrote them a letter afterward, knowing that they would be angry that he had married a peasant, and that his having done so in a Catholic church would nearly kill them.

He told Irma they would stay in Mexico. His idea was that he would study the Zapotecs, and she would be his translator and informant. He could teach her to read and then to type and she would type his notes for him. They moved into a hacienda-style house where she slept in a bed for the first time in her life. When they made love, the bed moved with them and the sensation made her laugh. She laughed the whole time he was inside her. Not because it was her first time; she had gone to meet Eligio in the fields more than once. But making love with Angus was different than it had been with Eligio. Eligio talked the whole time, commented on the smell of the bean leaves dying back into the fallow earth, the sound of the wind tumbling down the sides of the mountains, the feel of her hands pressed against his back. Angus was quiet when they made love, and she was so much shorter than him that her face was buried in his chest. He raised himself up on his elbows and looked down at her and she craned her neck back to find his eyes, but the distance was too far for their mouths to cross, and they made love without exchanging a single kiss.

Six months after he wrote them about his marriage, my father got a letter from his parents. He picked it up at the post office in town and brought it home without reading it. He was angry that they had taken so long to write and angry that they had written at all; he was always aggravated by the people who were close to him.

Other people's desires slowed him down, tripped him up. He preferred to do exactly as he pleased and thought the world would be a better place if everyone else did the same.

"Why don't you read it?" Irma asked him when she found the letter on the dining room table.

He shrugged and let his eyes cloud over with preoccupation, as if he were too busy to give the question much thought. "I know what they have to say," he said without lifting his head from the book he was reading. "I've heard it my whole life."

Every morning my mother placed the envelope next to her husband's plate, and every day it lay there unopened, growing spotted with the fallout from his breakfast.

After a week went by, she opened up the letter. She didn't know the story of Pandora, or of Eve and the apple, or of Bluebeard's wife, but she knew that it is men who run away from Destiny, women who know they cannot run and so demand to know its name.

The handwriting was thin and spiky. Irma had only learned the fundamentals of reading and her command of English was sketchy at best. The evil in the world flew out of Pandora's box in a rush and a torrent, but it took all day for my mother to decipher her father-in-law's letter. I have it still, so I can tell it to you exactly. My mother saved it as a keepsake so she could always remember how things fell apart.

My Dear Boy,

There is no point in telling you our reaction to your letter. You knew what it would be when you made your decision and no doubt hurting us was your intention. If it was, you have succeeded. Your letter made no attempt to spare your mother pain and for her sake I have had no wish to answer it. But we have had news which requires me to swallow my disappointment and write to you.

Your mother is very ill and my opinion as a doctor is that she will not last the winter. She has cancer of the stomach and it is spreading quite quickly through her body. In spite of everything she would like to see you before she passes on. I cannot vouch that all will be forgiven; only the Lord can truly forgive. I can only tell you that if you come now you will be welcome in our home and your wife will be welcome also.

When Irma showed him the letter, my father knew he was trapped. There was nothing to do but go back and pay his respects to his dying mother. They left a week later, stopping in Mexico City long enough to buy my mother a pair of shoes and two wool dresses, a blue one for every day and a black one for the funeral.

The train ride to Boston took almost two weeks. Irma spent most of the trip with her nose pressed against the glass, watching the color fade from the landscape as the train hurtled north. First the green dwindled away from the edge of the tracks, and then the blue seeped from the sky. Finally even the brown was gone. By the time the train pulled into Boston's South Station, everything was white.

Do you see now? My mother was a fish, the letter was a dangling worm. She swallowed it and it wriggled from her belly to her chest and wrapped itself around her heart.

Three months they were supposed to stay in Cambridge, but that mother-in-law liked dying so much she didn't want to stop. She spent all winter dying and all spring and summer. My mother cared for her like an angel, not out of selflessness but out of habit. She had worked hard all her life. She didn't know that working hard would make her in-laws treat her like a servant.

In the fall, Irma discovered she was pregnant. As she emptied her mother-in-law's bedpans, she was thinking about the baby taking its first breath of air in her mother's house. Air that smelled of coffee and chickens and dust, not the air of ice and sickness that she was breathing now. In Mitla you clean the afterbirth, seal it in a clay jar, and bury it near the house; otherwise the baby will go blind, or worse. My mother dreamed she was in the garden behind her in-laws' tall Victorian, placenta oozing from between her legs. Sometimes she had her hands cupped between her thighs and the warm pulp spilled over them and fell into the snow. Other nights she held the afterbirth in one hand and with the other she was digging, her fingernails clawing at the frozen earth and never denting it.

My father's mother died in February 1929. Irma was five months pregnant. When she found her mother-in-law sitting in a rocking chair by the window with a shawl over her knees and no life in her chest, she felt the weight of her dreams lift. She set a tray of food and water on the nightstand so that the dead woman's soul could gather provisions for the long journey to the world of the dead. She was happy then. She thought she was finally going home.

But first they had to wait for the funeral and the burial and for the will to be read. And then my father decided she was too far along, she shouldn't travel, and besides, it was better to have the baby there where there were doctors. And then the worm slid down into Irma's womb and wrapped itself around the baby's throat. She lost the child in her seventh month.

And then she was too sick to travel. After that my father was teaching for the summer at Harvard and had to wait until the fall to leave. By that time my mother was pregnant again. And then it was: You can't travel while you're pregnant, you've already miscarried once.

This time I was the baby in her womb. I looked up and saw the worm. The worm was the future: cold, coiled, and hard as clay. I saw the truth: She was never going home again.

When I was a baby floating in my mother's womb, she called out to me and I answered. Not in her own language—what language does an infant, a pre-infant, speak? No language but the language of love, and that is the language I spoke to her. I shouldn't have, but what did I know? I was an embryo, a tiny limbless thing. I thought you speak when spoken to. So when she called out "Mama!" in a voice full of longing, I answered with love, my fleshy, transparent heart pumping out love love love in answer to a name I didn't know did not belong to me. She was lonely and afraid, cold, longing for her mother to comb out her hair. She cried out and there was no one but me to answer.

She was alone in the house all day. Her husband and father-in-law both worked until evening and then studied at night, sitting in the living room with a pile of academic journals and a decanter of Scotch between them. Irma spent the evenings upstairs in her bedroom talking to me. After nearly two years in Cambridge she had plenty of betrayal to report. Angus had never finished teaching her to read, never taught her to type his notes. He didn't ask her to tell him about Mitla anymore. The books he read after dinner weren't even about Mexico. There were no jobs at Harvard for a Zapotec expert; what they needed was someone who knew about the tribes of central Africa. When my mother looked at the books piled on the living room table, she saw photographs of dark-skinned strangers. He had abandoned her for another culture.

I was too smart, too active to be confined in the squishy fetus body. I hovered outside of her for all nine months, scouting out my future world. I only slipped in at the last moment, as my infant mouth opened to breathe its first breath of air, which was not laced with the smells of coffee, dust, and chickens, but with the hospital scents of ether and isopropyl alcohol. I soon grew tired of my clumsy babyskin as well. Irma tied an amulet around my neck and tucked peppercorns among my clothes to keep my soul inside my body. But my father snipped the amulet and shook the pepper out of my diapers and so my soul came and went as it pleased. What a stupid baby, my father said as he poked my stomach and I stared vacantly back at him. Little did he know my soul was hovering by his shoulder, looking at him closely and not thinking much of what it saw. I followed him around the house and watched him settle in. It was obvious he didn't intend to go to Mexico again. That was when I decided it was better to see the future before it comes.

The future isn't for everyone. Some people like to be surprised. But if my mother had known my father would betray her, her heart would have only been broken once and not a thousand times. On the day she died in the YMCA swimming pool, she was still planning to return to Mitla. She wanted to see Eligio, although I had told her he had married long ago. She wanted to see her parents and the dusty road she used to climb on her way to the ruins. She never learned to accept what comes. It's hope that hurts, not the lack of it.

Did I tell this to my nieces as they were locking up the plastic idol? Julia at least already knew what I thought, and I try to avoid repeating myself. My philosophy has always been to leave well enough alone. Those who think they want to know will ask, and if I think they really want an answer, then I'll give them one. Most people are only asking for more hope.

Anyway, they were fated to start it all up again. Something was in the air, a kink in the hard river of time perhaps, a soft spot like a baby's head. I could feel the wind blowing time back and forth. I could feel them all remembering.

ℭhe Sombrero (Julia)

She was trouble. Silent, trapped, and tucked behind the spices, she was like the high-pitched whine of electricity that sometimes kept me from falling asleep at night. A noise right on the edge of my hearing, needling me.

Lisa couldn't resist taking out the box every time she came over. "Mary dear?" she crooned. "Is it dark in there? Are you frightened? It's nice and sunny out here, Mary. Give us our wish and we'll let you out."

"It's not *our* wish, it's *your* wish," I told her more than once. But she just smiled and shrugged, as if to say, Call it what you like. Stubborn. And she knew that I was faking it.

I'd always been the one to wish for him. Every second of every day for a while, and then only when things weren't going well. I'd wished on fallen eyelashes, first stars, pennies thrown into the Copley Square fountain. None of it had ever worked, and I couldn't see how incarcerating a plastic statuette was going to be any different. Aunt Simone had always told me that the future was as unalterable as gravity, and nothing in my experience had proved her wrong.

Not long after the wish, my mother called from Mexico. She worked at the ticket counter at Logan Airport for American Airlines, and one of the benefits of her job was discounted travel. She had just finished taking a Yucatán cruise and she didn't have to be back at work right away. Wouldn't it be fun if she stopped in Oakland for a visit on her way back to Boston?

"We specifically asked for our *father* to come," Lisa said when I told her that Carolina would be staying in her guest room for a few days. She leaned her face over the Virgin's prison. "I hope you understand, Mary, this is not an acceptable substitute."

My mother arrived at my house two days after her phone call, hauling two large suitcases and dressed like the cocktail waitress at a Mexican restaurant. Her waist-length black hair was gleaming, and she was wearing a ruffly white dress with red embroidery, a pair of lipstick-red cowboy boots, and an immense purple sombrero.

"*Buenas noches!*" she sang and spun around so the dress fanned out around her. "How do I look?"

This was not an easy question to answer. She looked tan and beautiful and ridiculous, and for a brief moment she looked like my grandmother Irma, which was odd because the two of them had always gone out of their way to be unlike each other.

"You look relaxed," I said and gave her a kiss. It was a little awkward getting past the brim of the sombrero.

Lisa was still at work, but Aunt Simone had come over. Their greetings were always wary, a blend of need and suspicion, and

I could see Steven watching them intently as they kissed each other on both cheeks like the presidents of rival nations. I knew he would ask me about it later.

When the welcomes were done, Carolina flung herself onto my sofa, lit a cigarette, and began raving about Mexico. How blue the water was, how white the beaches. "One night we watched the moon rise over Chichén Itzá," she said. "I think it was the most beautiful thing I've ever seen."

I looked over at Aunt Simone, who was perched on the edge of one of my sunflower-print easy chairs, gripping its arms as if expecting it to take to the skies. I gathered she was not enjoying Carolina's travelogue.

"To think, Simone, we could have been born in Mexico," Carolina was saying. "I can't imagine why Papa didn't want to stay there."

Aunt Simone looked grim. "Maybe you should have asked him."

"I wish I could ask him now," Carolina sighed. "I bet he could have told me all about Mexican culture and history."

"Our mother could have taught you about the history, too," Aunt Simone interjected. "If you had ever wanted to listen."

Steven shot me a worried look. He hated conflict of any kind, especially between people he's close to. He was plagued by empathy, that boy. If he picked up two rocks on the beach, he had to keep them both, even if they were identical, because otherwise one might have its feelings hurt.

"Well, they're both dead, so the question is moot," Carolina said and exhaled a long stream of blue smoke. "I learned a lot from the tour guide. Did you know that the ancient Mayans just disappeared one day? They think maybe they were taken by aliens. That's why Quetzalcóatl is always pictured diving headfirst into the sea like an astronaut."

I could see we were about to be treated to one of my mother's extended flights of fancy.

"Did you meet any nice men on the cruise?" I asked, hoping to head her off at the pass.

Carolina tapped the ashes of her cigarette into the bed of a toy truck that was lying on the coffee table. "The cultural guide was very nice," she said. "He gave us a lecture about *Día de los Muertos* that I found quite interesting. You know, I'd always wondered why my mother left plates of food around her bedroom. I thought she was just messy."

"She would have been happy to explain it to you," Simone said.

"But she never did," Carolina said, and I couldn't tell if the regret in her voice was for the question she hadn't asked or the answer that was never given. She sat with her feet propped up on the coffee table, the sombrero still resting on her head. With her straight-legged posture and outsized hat, she looked like a little Mexican doll, the kind you might see for sale in a gift shop in Acapulco.

"Do you know what *Día de los Muertos* is?" I asked Steven. "In Mexico they have Day of the Dead on November second, and people leave food out for their dead ancestors."

"I know what it is," Steven said from the floor. "We learned about it in school last year."

"It's coming up," Aunt Simone said and leaned forward a little in her chair. "Now that you know all about it, Carolina, perhaps you should try leaving something out for your dead parents. The spirits get upset if they aren't fed, you know."

It was clear to me that she was saying it just to nettle, but the words had the strangest effect on Carolina. She opened her mouth as if to make a retort, and then shut it again and looked past Simone at my living room windows, hung with slightly uneven cornflower blue drapes that I'd made by hand. I thought she was going to comment on the fact that they were different lengths, or maybe note the fact that they clashed with the turquoise bedspread I'd draped over the sofa. But instead she took a long drag from the cigarette smoldering in her hand and let two small streams of smoke wisp from her nostrils like twin ghosts. "The spirits are upset because they're dead," she said at last. "And as far as I know, there is no cure for death."

Lisa called me at work the next day.

"Listen," she said. "How long did she say she was staying?"

"She didn't," I told her. "But I'm assuming she has to be back at work before long."

"Well, then why is she unpacking all her things and putting them in drawers? And putting little Mexican postcards and folk art on the walls of my guest room?"

"She's just nesting," I said. "Relax."

Lisa sighed, a gust of air that rattled inside the receiver like a pebble. "I can't relax. I wanted Mitch to move in with me and instead I've got a woman who dresses like the Frito Bandito. And was she always this morbid?"

"What do you mean?"

"Last night when I got home from the restaurant she wanted to watch this hospital show she likes. I never would have agreed if I'd known what I was in for. Every time some sick person came into the hospital, which was about every two minutes, she had to make some creepy comment about it, like 'His number's up' or 'That girl looks like worm-food to me.'"

"She's always talked to the TV," I said.

"I know, but then it got weirder. Then she started talking about how Irma and Angus were the only dead people she'd ever seen in real life. She goes, 'When my parents died, I learned that dead people stay close to the members of their families, even when their bodies are nothing but meat.' And *then,* as if that wasn't creepy enough, she grabs my hand and goes, 'You'll know what I mean when I'm dead. When you see me dead, you'll think of this conversation.'"

"What did you say?"

"I guess I should have said something reassuring like 'You won't be dying for a long time, Mama,' but I was so pissed at her for telling me what to think when she's dead that I didn't say anything." Lisa was silent for a long moment. "This is not helping me," she said at last. "This is not cheering me up at all."

The next day I took Steven and Carolina swimming after work. September is the hottest month of the year in Oakland and we were having a rare spate of warm evenings. At the public pool, sparrows came down from the trees to bathe themselves along the edge. I watched them as I swam, fluttery brown balls dipping their wings in the turquoise water.

The five-to-seven P.M. swim period was really supposed to be for lap swimmers, but Steven never had any trouble following adult rules. He swam his labored, little-boy crawl up and down the slow lane and I swam in the lane beside him, watching him from underwater. He'd recently shed the last of his baby thickness and turned lean and lanky. I couldn't believe those long legs had ever fit inside my body.

Later Carolina and I lay drying on our towels in the grass. Our bodies gave off a faint scent of chlorine.

"This reminds me of Irma," I said. "I used to love going swimming with her."

"I don't like to think about her swimming," Carolina said. She sat up and began unbraiding her hair. "Her drowning all by herself in that slummy pool. It's tragic."

She squeezed the ends of her hair and a fat stream of water spilled out of her fist. "Imagine loving something your whole life and never knowing it was going to kill you. I wonder which of the things I've loved will be the end of me."

"The pool didn't kill her—she had a stroke. She would have died anywhere." I sat up to look for Steven. I'd left him swimming in the slow lane, and I wondered if he was tired.

Carolina shrugged and began combing out her hair with her fingers. "I thought about this in Mexico. You know, half the people on the cruise were afraid to swim in the ocean because they were worried about sharks. Not me, I said. I've never loved a shark. It's what you love that kills you—my mama showed me that." She flashed me a bright, incomprehensible smile. "Speaking of which, hand me my cigarettes, will you? They're in my purse, right on top."

I did and then went back to scanning the pool. Steven definitely wasn't in the slow lane anymore. I tried to make out his figure in one of the other lanes, my stomach clenching.

"And what about you?" my mother continued. "Are you ever going to fall in love?"

"If the right man comes along," I said, although I wasn't really listening. I could picture Steven floating underwater as the other swimmers splashed around him, ignoring his still, breathless shape. I told myself not to panic. Maybe he had just gone into the locker room to pee.

"That's what I used to say," Carolina said. "After your father left."

There he was, sitting on the far edge of the pool, kicking his feet in the water. I felt my breathing rekindle. Seeing him there, drifting among his own thoughts, it occurred to me that he was probably too introspective for a boy. Every other kid I'd ever seen at a swimming pool spent the whole time yelling, "Mom, look at me!" Steven didn't seem to care who was watching him—he was too busy watching everyone else. Now, feeling my eyes on him, he looked over at me and smiled.

"He's cute," Carolina said, following my gaze.

I nodded, although cute didn't even begin to describe Steven. Sitting there splashing away, he reminded me of the little brown birds at the edge of the pool, cooling their wings. The kind of thing you're amazed to even be able to see up close.

"Your father loved the water," Carolina observed. "When we went to the beach in the summer, he used to spend the whole time floating on his back like a seal."

The words were enough to tear my attention away from Steven. In twenty-two years, I had never once heard her say a word about my father without some prompting from me.

"Must be where Stevie gets it," she went on. Then she ground her cigarette out on the cement. "What I don't understand is why you've never wanted him to have a father. You were always so hot to have yours back, I can't see why you'd want your son to grow up the same way."

"If you'd met Steven's father, you'd know why I didn't marry the guy," I said crossly. "Steven can't miss something he's never known."

"Well, I'm sure you'll do what you think is best. I always did." Then she looked at me. Carolina didn't usually look at people for the purpose of seeing them. She turned her face toward you to communicate something by her expression or to elicit some response. But not to look at you. Not to take you in. Still, she was staring at me as though she was trying to see something, and it made me uncomfortable. "I hope you aren't staying single out of spite," she said. "Because that's what I did, and I wouldn't recommend it."

I breathed in, treading carefully. "You always told us you were staying single because he was coming back."

Carolina yawned and stretched, as if the topic were one she'd long since tired of. "Maybe I thought he would. What did I know? He didn't exactly leave me a note telling me his plans."

I was nine when I realized I didn't know anything about him. He was only this absence that my mind kept returning to, the way my tongue would touch the gummy gap in my mouth after a tooth fell out. *I had a father, but he was blown away by a gust of wind.* I had long ago stopped asking where he went, or if he was coming back— the answers to those questions were always vague and contradictory. But sometimes when it was just me and Carolina together, I'd ask about him. It was always one question, stored up and considered for days beforehand. *What kind of food did he like? Did you love him? Where did you meet?*

"Is he nice?" I asked her once, sitting on the toilet while she shaved her legs on the side of the tub.

"Who? Your father?" The razor slid over her leg, scraping away the white veneer of foam to reveal a thin stripe of brown skin. I waited, knowing that her answer would be a lie, but so hungry for knowledge that it almost didn't matter. I've read how starving people will eat whatever they can put in their mouths: shoe leather, the scrapings from a horse's hoof, grass. My mother's answers were like that to me—not food, but better than nothing.

"Nice? Well, who do you think is nice that you know? Is Grandpa nice?" The razor uncurtained another stripe of my mother's leg. She rinsed the razor under the faucet.

"I guess so."

"Well, your father isn't anything like Grandpa. Grandpa is much better educated, for one thing. Did you know that he graduated from Harvard when he was only nineteen?"

She slid over toward the faucet and dangled her left calf under a stream of water. Then she ran her hands over her shins.

"Feel this, Julie, isn't it smooth? Like a baby's bottom."

She held her leg toward me and I stroked her bare shin. Cold from the water, it felt like the leg of a marble statue.

"Thank God for Irma's Indian blood—not too many hairs," she said. "That's something to be thankful for."

She drew her leg away and went to work on the other one, covering it with a creamy lather and then scraping the soap away by inches.

"Nice is hard to say about," she said. "You have to know someone really well to know if they're nice. I'm nice, for instance, but maybe some people wouldn't know it if they met me. You'd have to decide for yourself."

I waited for more, but that was all there was. And now, so many years later, she was dropping bits of information like candy wrappers, as if they meant nothing. He loved to swim. He didn't leave a note. Still, with my mother, nothing ever was completely revealed. It was just layers on top of layers.

The warm nights kept me awake, or maybe it was something else. That night I stayed up long after Steven was asleep, puttering around the apartment with a dust rag and a damp sponge.

I lived on the second floor of a brown-shingled Craftsman home that had been divided into two apartments. It was an eccentrically designed flat, with a big, sunny living room, a small, dark kitchen, and two east-facing bedrooms that overlooked the backyard of the college-student house next door. The arrangement of the rooms was awkward, and having my bedroom next to Steven's ensured that I never invited a man to stay the night, but I loved it all the same. I'd painted it bright colors and re-covered my thrift-store furniture in charismatic fabrics. The flat felt like something I'd accomplished, and since there weren't many things that fell into that category, I tried to keep it clean.

At around midnight I found myself in the kitchen, taking the cups and plates down from the shelves. I still wasn't close to being tired, and it suddenly seemed important to scrub the insides of the cabinets. Before long I had lifted all the jars of spices from the spice shelf and put them on the kitchen table along with the little boxed-up Virgin.

She irritated me, Little Miss Mother of God. I found myself following Lisa's example and hectoring her as I cleaned. "What do you know about missing fathers?" I asked her. "Your son had more fathers than he knew what to do with. One in the flesh and one in heaven. Your little Jesus didn't have to go very far to search his daddy out, did he? His father was only present in every single thing."

On the other hand, I felt a little sorry for old Mary. In a way she was the typical single mother. She raises the kid while the father's off battling Satan or whatever, nowhere to be found during the crucial, diaper-changing years. And then along comes Dad, who announces he's the Creator of the Universe, and the kid spends the rest of his life talking about how great Dad is, forgetting that Mom was the one who did all the work.

"Mary," I said to her. "Forget about it. I don't need him back. What did he ever do for me?" I stopped scrubbing and turned around to look at the still, promising shape of her little gray file box. But I didn't let her out. Instead I sat down at the kitchen table, poured myself a glass of wine, and tried to remember what he was like.

I remembered him talking to me, telling me things. It was evening and we were walking to the corner Superette to buy beer for him and grape slushes for me and Lisa. It was summer, the sky was purpling on the horizon, and the air was humid, warm. My father had sweat on his upper lip and wet half-moons darkening the armpits of his shirt. When we neared Mt. Auburn Street we could hear Kenny, the retarded man at the corner, singing to the traffic light, his forearms resting between the slats of his parents' picket fence.

Come on, red light.
Turn green.
The cars is waitin'.

"Thank God for Kenny," my father said as we passed. "Those cars would be stuck there forever if it wasn't for him."

Did he ever tell the truth? If ever he tried to tell me something serious, I don't remember it. He was more like an uncle than a father, always pulling quarters from my ear and pretending to steal Lisa's nose. It was as if he felt he had to ingratiate himself to us, charm us into liking him.

He would never tell us what he did for a living. "My job," he told us, "is to gather fur from all the fluffiest dogs and cats in the neighborhood and then sell it to the highest bidder."

"But who would want to buy it?" Lisa wanted to know. "Who wants old cat hair?"

"The people who make pillows and mattresses, of course. What do you think goes into your bed to make it so soft? Those mattress-makers and pillow-stuffers come running when they hear me out on the street, singing, 'Get your fluff here! Fluff for sale! Fluffy fluff at a good price!'"

I knew better than to believe him, but I didn't disbelieve him, either. There was never any evidence of him having any other job—no office, no regular hours, no friends from work. When the mood struck him he embellished the story a little. Once he said that his customers had been asking him to sell them the softest hair from his daughters' heads, and he chased Lisa all around the house with a pair of scissors until she locked herself in the bathroom and wouldn't come out. What did this say about the kind of man he was? Maybe he was someone who thought it was funny to see children cry. Or maybe things just got out of hand.

My reverie was interrupted by a pounding at the front door. It was too late for Lisa or Dawn, and for a brief moment I thought it might be my father, come to explain it all to me and release the Virgin from her prison. Instead it was Mitch,

Lisa's ex. He stood on my front porch, his green bicycle lean-ing against his thigh, his studious, long-lashed eyes gazing at me intently.

"Hi," he said. "I was riding by and I saw your light on and I thought I'd bring you these." He handed me a paper bag and then muffled me in an urgent and unexpected hug. "I'm really glad to see you," he said when he'd released me. "I don't want our friend-ship to end because of me and Lisa breaking up."

"Me neither," I mumbled, hoping I sounded sincere. I'd always liked Mitch, but I never knew exactly how to behave around him. He was so naturally effervescent that he made me feel brooding and ill-tempered in comparison.

I peered into the paper bag, which turned out to be full of pomegranates. "These are beautiful," I told him, although I was a bit mystified. I didn't remember ever expressing the kind of passion for pomegranates that would make someone deliver them to my door in the middle of the night.

"I bought some at the farmers' market today, and they were so big and red and juicy I wanted to share them," Mitch said. "Can I come in and share one with you now?"

"Sure."

Mitch hoisted his bicycle onto his shoulder and carried it up the stairs to my kitchen. I cleared some of the accumulation of plates and spices from the table, and Mitch sat down on one of my purple kitchen chairs and started carving a pomegranate into crescents.

"You can dry these, too, and use them as a centerpiece," he said when he was done. Mitch worked as a waiter at one of the more upscale restaurants in town, and I gathered that people in the restaurant business spent their free evenings making decorations out of dried fruit.

I took a cluster of seeds and slurped at it. "Delicious," I told him.

Mitch nodded. "We're serving a pomegranate sorbet this week at the restaurant. Everyone loves it. It's really great."

I was beginning to wonder if Mitch had come by solely to discourse on the many uses of the pomegranate. If he started talking about jams and marinades, I was going to have to ask him to leave.

"You know, I really feel good about breaking up with Lisa," he said at last. "I really think it was the right thing to do."

"She doesn't."

"I know." He sighed and his face turned sad. "And I think about her all the time. But I just couldn't handle her worrying. It wasn't healthy."

"What worrying?" I didn't want to pry, but I didn't have the faintest idea what he was talking about.

"She makes herself crazy with it. Anytime I was five minutes late she'd think I'd gotten killed. Did she tell you about our last fight?"

I shook my head.

Mitch noticed the bottle of wine on the table and poured himself a glass. "I got stuck at the restaurant," he began. "A party of five lingered over their brandies and then I ran into someone I knew outside. When Lisa called to see if I'd left, the kitchen staff told her I had, but really I was right out front. And then, on the way over to her place, I stopped at the store to pick up some ice cream. All in all I was maybe forty-five minutes later than usual. When I got there she was *crying*."

"Because you were late?"

"Because I was *dead*. And when she saw that I wasn't, she couldn't stop. She just kept crying and crying. All night, until she fell asleep. It was awful. I can't live like that."

"That's not really a fight," I said, wishing he hadn't told me. I couldn't picture Lisa crying for no reason. I couldn't picture Lisa crying at all.

Mitch was silent, picking apart a clump of pomegranate seeds with his fingers.

"I guess we never had the fight," he said after a moment. "The next morning I told her I didn't think we should see each other anymore. She didn't cry at all then. She said, 'I knew it would end this way.' As if she'd been right to worry all along."

"She'll be okay." I couldn't figure out why he had told me all this, but it seemed as if he wanted some kind of reassurance.

"I'd like to cheer her up," Mitch said. "I thought maybe you'd have an idea about that."

He swept a pile of carefully separated pomegranate seeds in my direction. Spread out on the table they looked like the bloody tears wept by saints in religious paintings. I thought of the Virgin in her metal chamber, listening to us.

"Something I could give her," Mitch prompted. "A present."

"You could find our father," I said. "She'd like that."

I'd meant it as a joke, but it came out sounding flat. Mitch was still looking at me, his face open as a picture frame.

"Don't get her anything," I said. "Leave her alone. She'll get over it by herself."

His face fell, but he nodded and then got up to leave.

As I held the door open for him, he turned back and looked at me. "Have you done something different to your hair?" he asked.

I shook my head.

"Well, you look great. I mean, really great," Mitch said. "I never noticed it before, but I think you're one of the most beautiful women I know."

Then he kissed me lightly on the cheek and went away.

$\mathcal{R}$ain (Simone)

Fate is a snake and her body is longer than forever. Her skin is cool and has the texture of tiny beads. She slithers this way, that way, with her face in the future and her tail in the past. It's easy to get caught up in her coils.

Fate's body is one long muscle. Muscle sheathing the endless spine of connections, reasons begetting reasons, cause and effect. Too often we forget about the decisions we made long ago, and the way they link up, ball and socket, to all that will come later. I consider it my duty to remember. I am, after all, an archivist by trade.

So let me tell you about the year Julia was twenty-two, when she made a choice that would change her life forever. That winter it rained and rained. The earth grew heavy with water and shed skins of mud over the roads. Each night the news showed scenes of rivers overflowing their banks, rooftops swaddled in water, towns turned to liquid, and roads traversed by boat. Julia watched it all on the television suspended over the bar where she worked, a hotel bar near campus that specialized in sweet cocktails and fried foods.

She had graduated from college the previous spring and thought that when she'd saved enough money she would travel to Europe and then Asia, Africa, and beyond. She would be a wanderer like her father, footloose and feckless. Maybe she would run into him in a hotel catering to expatriates, and they would recognize each other and swap tales of foreign parasites and unusual cuisine. She didn't know it, but they wore their kinship on their faces. She thought she looked like Carolina, round of bosom and sharp of face, but she had her father's slyness around the corners of her eyes and mouth, an ironic look that deflected the glance of strangers and made them fail to see her open heart.

In the meantime, rain seeped in through her apartment's leaky windows and coaxed mushrooms from the yellow carpets. Julia hated going home to her mildewy apartment, and in the evenings, when her shift was over, she lingered at a nearby café with her friend Dawn, drinking cheap wine and talking about men.

One night one of the other waitresses invited them to a party. Her name was Lydia, and she was pale as a salamander, with peroxide-whitened hair and purple lipstick. Julia wanted to go, and Dawn didn't, and in the end Julia won out. They arrived in the midst of a downpour that plastered their blue jeans to their bodies and flattened out their hair. They stood dripping in the living room, watching five or six black-clad figures dance to music eking from a pair of tinny speakers.

"New Wave morticians," Dawn observed. "Promise me we'll leave soon."

"Okay," Julia said. "Let's just wait until the rain stops."

Just then a boy with a tangle of brown curls squeezed past them and then turned back and cocked his head to one side.

"Are you two sisters?" he asked, looking at the two dark-haired girls. Dawn was tall and rugged, with unflinching brown eyes and a mass of dark brown hair that she pulled back into a single braid. Julia was small and elfin and kept her hair cropped short so that it jutted from her head in shaggy spikes.

"Twins," Julia said. "I'm Shawn, she's Dawn."

The boy looked at Dawn and then back at Julia. "It's cool you dress different. I guess that's so people can tell you apart."

Dawn's nostrils twitched with suppressed laughter. "I'm gonna grab us some beer," she said and left Julia alone with the New Wave boy.

He was pretty as a girl with his brown doe eyes and the neck of his sweatshirt sliding down to reveal one shoulder. He looked at Julia as if she were some rare, rain-fed orchid that had just dampened into bloom. "I'm Bobby," he said. "Want to dance?"

Embellishment is mating's first and most faulty step. We bestow our partners with the qualities we most desire, whether they are worthy of them or not. As she followed Bobby into the center of the living room, Julia thought of the religions that teach their followers to filter out the mind's reflective commentary so that they can be in the moment, like the birds and fishes. Bobby was like one of these disciples, she thought, his soul soft and white as a shorn lamb.

Through the speakers a woman was chanting: *I might like you better if we slept together, I might like you better if we slept together.* Had I been there with Julia, I would have told her to pay attention to the lyrics of the song. Look how the rain fertilized your carpets, I would have said. Look at the way raindrops merge and grow fat.

But Julia wasn't thinking about the future as the pretty curly-headed boy danced bonelessly by her side. She was thinking about the sensation that was bubbling in her chest, like the weak upwelling of a water fountain.

When the song ended, Dawn hadn't come back with the beer, so Julia went into the kitchen to find one herself. Bobby followed her doggedly.

A fat man with a Mohawk was leaning against the sink, singing "Lydia the Tattooed Lady" to their hostess. Julia tried to edge past him and open the refrigerator door, but a wraithlike girl seized her by the arm. "There's no more beer!" she screeched over the din. "We took up a collection to buy more, but no one has a car!"

"I have a car," Bobby said. He turned to Julia. "Want to go buy beer?"

Julia looked around, but Dawn was nowhere in sight. "Sure," she said.

His car was parked out front, a red Lincoln Continental.

Bobby started it up, turned on the radio, and drove into a tree. It wasn't that he skidded on the wet streets. He did it very slowly, almost deliberately, a straight line from the parking spot to the tree. Branches scraped the roof of the car.

"Don't worry about it," he said when Julia got out to inspect the damage. "It's rented. My dad doesn't let me buy cars anymore because I keep cracking them up. Want to drive?"

While Julia drove, Bobby talked about himself. His father was an investment banker; his mother lived in Europe. For the most part he had been raised by a devoted male servant named Neil, who insisted on running his bath every evening until the day he left for college. When he was fourteen he had discovered the combination to his father's safe, and since then he'd had easy access to as much money as he could spend.

As raconteurs go, Bobby could have used more punch, but his story was enough to keep Julia entranced. As he talked, she zig-zagged through the leafy campus neighborhoods, never thinking about the destination. It wasn't until they had gotten out of the car that she realized they were in front of her apartment.

Bobby found every aspect of her life bewitching. He walked through the apartment, peering at things as if he were in a museum. "You read books?" he asked, picking up the novel she had left on the arm of the sofa. "You cook?" staring at the basket of onions and potatoes hanging over the sink. He stood for a long time in front of a Degas reproduction in the living room and then stretched out in the same arabesque as the dancers in the painting.

"I love this," he said. "I'm studying to be a dancer."

When he came to the bedroom, he lay down on the bed and spread his arms out over the quilt. "Is this where you sleep?"

Julia nodded. He sat up and pulled his sweatshirt over his head. Then he leaned forward and began unbuttoning her shirt.

"Do you like painkillers at all?" he said with his face between her breasts.

"Not really." She was mystified.

"I like them pretty well. Two Demerols and you can make love all night. Total stamina."

And that was exactly what they did.

All men have their surprises, and Bobby's was that he was a sweet and inventive lover, who whispered compliments in Julia's ear the whole night. As they rocked and sweated and touched each other's skin, the rain fell like a shower of seeds. Julia shut her eyes and listened to it pour.

Around daybreak, the fun ended. Julia got up and looked out the window at the moist scrim of pink fog. When she looked back at her bed, she saw the tousle-headed boy curled in a kittenish sleep and wondered what had possessed her. Soon it would be time to get up and fetch the morning paper, and the idea of chatting with him over coffee and newsprint seemed ludicrous. "It's time to go," she whispered in his ear.

He rolled over and buried his face in her neck, begging to be allowed to stay. She was firm.

"Can I call you again?" he asked as he stood at the door.

"Of course," she said and submitted to a final kiss.

He called later that morning, but Dawn had called first.

"Thanks for ditching me last night," she said. "You didn't go home with that fashion casualty, did you?"

"Worse," Julia confessed. "I took him to my place."

"I must have dialed the wrong number. I thought I was calling my friend Julia, an intelligent woman with good taste in men."

Julia covered her eyes with one hand and tried not to remember Bobby forlornly zipping up his jacket and stepping out into the rain. "Shut up. It's your fault—you disappeared."

"I thought you could take care of yourself. Is he still there?"

"No."

"Good, I'll come over with coffee."

So Dawn was there when Bobby called. Under her cool gaze, his dreamy, vacant voice lost whatever sheen it had had the night before. Now it was irritating, laughable.

"No, I'm sorry I can't," she said in response to whatever it was he invited her to do. He may have been dense, but he got the picture.

"I had fun last night," he said wistfully and then hung up.

A few weeks later her abdomen began to itch, a persistent nettling that could not be soothed by calamine lotion or aloe vera juice. In the rest room at work, she pulled up her blouse and inspected the skin for fleabites or rash. The skin was smooth and pale, but when she covered it up again, it began to tingle and then to prickle and sting.

At last she called me, as she always did when she was in trouble.

"I need your advice," she said. "I have some sort of rash on my stomach. What can I put on it to make it go away?"

"Honeysuckle flowers are good for rashes," I told her. "But they won't cure what you have."

"Why not?"

"What's irritating you is below the surface."

She knew what I was getting at, but she refused to admit it. And who can blame her? She'd spent the night with a boy as clear and untroubled as a mountain lake, there was no sin in that. But water has a way of seeping into the most unlikely places. Now Julia had a pocket of salt water in her belly, and inside it was a tiny fish.

I wanted Julia to decide for herself what to do about the pregnancy, but she refused. Her mind turned gauzy and filled with air. At work she delivered entrees to the wrong tables, served salads twice, forgot to bring people their dinners and then served them cold. The other waiters covered for her and no one asked if there was a reason she seemed preoccupied. She couldn't have truthfully said that there was, for she was thinking of nothing at all, not about the baby, nothing.

Lisa was gentle with her, cooking for her as if she were sick, calling once a day to see how she was feeling. At the end of every phone call she asked, "Have you decided what you're going to do?" and Julia said, "No, not yet. Maybe tomorrow."

But when Dawn found out from Lisa what was going on, she marched over to Julia's apartment in a rage and sat down on the couch with her arms folded.

"What the fuck is wrong with you?" she demanded. "Did you catch a brain disease from that flashdancer?"

Julia didn't answer. She had been reading a Jane Austen novel when Dawn dropped by, and now she picked it up and started a fresh chapter.

"Hello? Julia? Shawn?"

"Shhhhh." Julia turned a page.

"Listen to me, Julia. Are you going to have this baby?"

It wasn't until Dawn asked her point-blank that Julia discovered she had made a decision. She put down the book and nodded.

"You're not thinking clearly," Dawn said. "Do you realize what you're going to be? You're going to be a *mother*. We're too young to be mothers. We *have* mothers. Mothers are the people that drive us crazy. Why on earth would you want to *be* one?"

"I'm not going to be like my mother. I'm just going to be me with a baby."

"That's what you think now. Wait until you find your mother's voice coming out of your mouth. Do you think your mother was like she is now before she had you? You made her what she is."

"Shut up. There are plenty of normal people who have babies."

"There are not. Julia, when you're pregnant, you can't smoke or drink or even have coffee. You have to be pure as the driven snow. Then you have to be fat as a cow. And afterwards your cunt gets all stretched out and it'll take King Kong to satisfy you."

"You have no idea what you're talking about."

"Yes, I do. I've watched my sister go through five pregnancies. Mark my words. You'll have to use half a cantaloupe for a diaphragm."

Julia shrugged. "Maybe I just won't have sex again."

"How are you going to support yourself? How are you going to pay for the delivery? What if the baby gets sick? You don't even have health insurance." Dawn pounded her fist into her own thigh as she enumerated each of the obstacles. "You're utterly unprepared to be a mother. You have no money and no understanding of what's involved."

"Those aren't the requirements," Julia said and grinned. "All you need to do is sleep with a nineteen-year-old ballet dancer."

"This is serious, Julia. And I can't believe you would have that guy's baby."

But it's not his baby, it's mine, Julia thought. Suddenly she knew why this had happened. No father would ever launch this baby into the air and forget to bring it down again. No father would ever break this baby's heart. She would raise the baby by herself, and it would reach adulthood still believing the world was good. That is why people have children, she told herself. To undo everything that was done before.

Dawn needn't have worried about the baby's financial future. Once Julia had made her decision, the drafty Victorian in Cambridge went on the market, and I put all my possessions in cartons and shipped them to California.

Carolina claimed to be sentimental about me selling the house we had grown up in, but I was glad to say good-bye to it. For twelve years after our mother died I had stayed there with our father, cooking his meals as our mother did before me. Now he was in the ground and my nieces were in California. I knew which destination interested me more. I offered Carolina the house, but her sentiment didn't extend to the upkeep of a large old building. She preferred her high-rise apartment, with its tiny, carpeted rooms, its view of Boston Harbor, and its easy access to the airport. We split the profits.

Real estate in Cambridge was taking off and the sale price brought us a tidy sum. When combined with my pension from the library, my portion of the proceeds was more than enough to support Julia and myself, and I invested in a few blue-chip stocks for the baby's future. Within a few weeks I had rented an apartment on the tenth floor of an art deco building near Oakland's Lake Merritt. I filled it with the books I'd salvaged from thirty years of library sales and a few choice pieces of furniture shipped from home—a plum-colored settee, a mahogany curio cabinet, two carved armchairs, and a brass bed. Once I was settled in, I went to the pound and chose two large black cats for company. I named them Swami and Svengali, and late at night, I sat with them, lit a few candles, and inquired about the baby's future.

The first thing I had to do was rid Julia's apartment of bad thoughts. Julia laughed at me as I burned clusters of sage and cedar and walked through her rooms clanging the lids of pots together, but I knew it had to be done. I didn't like how Dawn had scowled at the unformed baby and conjured up a future of poverty and dismay. Evil is a parasite and it settles in where it won't be disturbed. If you don't chase it out with smoke and loud noises, it begins to nibble at the substance of your life, like the caries between your teeth.

"You must not think bad thoughts while you are pregnant," I told Julia. "Bad thoughts affect the baby. You must not look at ugly things, either. The baby is mutable now. He will become what you imagine."

Baby Steven rocked in Julia's womb like Rambeau's drunken boat, unmoored, restless, a tiny blankness on his palm. His future was malleable, soft as the soft bones of his head. Soon enough the serpent Fate would slither across his hand and leave behind her crooked trail. But for now he was Julia's to shape.

Julia had only one thought, to teach her child everything she knew. "Don't be fooled," she whispered to him. "Keep your eyes open." Steven's tiny lidless eyes had no choice but to stay open. She sent pictures down into her belly for him to see, turned her mind inside out so he could hear her thoughts. He saw the street she lived on, cherry trees pink with blossoms, the last oily puddles evaporating in the sun. All the faces she could think of: Carolina's pretty one, her father's lost one, Lisa looking strong and blunt, even my own thin visage, peering at him through my cat-eye glasses.

He grew, stretching out his tiny arms and legs. His tail shrank into his spine and disappeared, fingers unwebbed themselves. A penis poked out between his legs. Steven swam among her body's murky salts, and even after lids formed above his eyes, he kept them open.

All through her shift at the restaurant she joked with him, made up funny names for the customers that only he could hear. When two blond sorority girls came in for lunch, only the embryo-that-would-be-Steven heard Julia predict they would both want orange sherbet to match their sweaters, and only he could chortle bubbly laughter when her prediction turned out right on the money.

Only once did anything go wrong. She was in her fourth month, riding the 51 bus to work, when a man climbed on and stood in front of her. From the back he was just an old man in a brown suit, sturdy, pale-haired, solitary. But when he turned to face her, she saw that his head was a mass of white scars that erased most of the contours of his face. Nose and ears had been melted into unfamiliar lumps, lips seared away. Only his eyes were untouched. They were shaped like boats, and she thought of his irises as passengers who had seen more than they set out to see. Those eyes looked at her gently and she looked away, remembering what I had told her. But Steven kept his eyes open. In the watery stillness of Julia's womb, he contemplated the old man's scarred face and met his weary gaze.

In the searing red-black moments just before Steven was born, an image of the old man flickered through Julia's mind, irises watching her out of a face like a pool of candle wax. When they placed Steven on her stomach, she ran her fingers over his features to make sure it was all there, his little upturned nose and shell-shaped ears, his lips suckling the air. It was only when she looked into his green eyes that she saw what she had done. She had given him eyes that were too perceptive, the old man's eyes that saw what others looked away from. Now as they rested on her face, she knew someday she would have to lie to him, and when she did, he would never forgive her.

$\mathscr{A}$ ttraction   (Julia)

"You have the most incredible eyes," the woman said as I handed her her change. "They just draw me right into them."

"Thanks." I grinned, embarrassed, but delighted, too. Suddenly this was happening all the time. In the two hours since the Psychic Fair began, I had been propositioned by two of the exhibition security guards, three customers, and the guy at the coffee cart out front. I was attractive. There was no other way to put it.

And not just to people. I was sticky-sweet, scented like honey. That morning I had discovered ants coming into my apartment from all sides. They seeped through every window and under the front door. They climbed up three flights of stairs to be near me, marching in a little devoted line. The day before, a black kitten had followed me all the way home from the BART station. What could I do? I brought it inside and gave it some milk. That night it slept on my chest and stretched its little paws out to touch my face.

I've never been anything close to charismatic. I'm not bad looking, but I'm not a head-turner, either. If I were a color, I think it would be olive green. Lovely in its own way, but not likely to inspire zealous devotion. And yet on the day of the Psychic Fair I suddenly became magnetic. Post-Its, burs, foxtails, lint—everything stuck to me. On the way to the Oakland Convention Center I somehow managed to get gum stuck to the bottom of my shoe. In the ladies' room, toilet paper fastened onto the gum. When I came out, a man noticed the toilet paper fluttering from my heel and stepped on it to stop me. Then he was stuck to me, too. "Hi there," he said, looking me up and down. "I think I knew you in a past life."

Whatever the reason for it, it was great for business. The ten-by-ten Enhancement Press booth was overflowing with women in lilac sweatsuits. They clawed their way through the stacks of books on prosperity, wellness, success, beauty, meditation, crystals, and psychic surgery that I had arranged by subject on a large table in the center. I couldn't add up their purchases fast enough. Usually it was only like this when Shantra had a new book out, and then only if she came to the booth to sign autographs. But now I was the one who drew them in. They swarmed around me as if I were an apostle, asking my advice on everything from the phrasing of affirmations to the blessing of household appliances.

The Convention Center had been outfitted with lavender carpets for the fair and a flutter of mauve curtain hung between each of the booths. I don't know what it is that spiritualists have about the violet end of the color spectrum, but every New Age fair I've ever worked has been decorated in the boudoir shades. Ralph's idea of complementing this inevitable color scheme was to have our booth displays and table skirts done up in fluorescent fuchsia. The result made me feel as if I were standing inside a Chuck E. Cheese's, but when I complained to Ralph that the signs were hideous and clashed with everything else in the fair, he told me that if I wanted to have an opinion about colors I should get a job selling eye shadow at Macy's. Just to be spiteful I always worked the booth wearing mustard yellow or burnt ocher, which, when contrasted against the fuchsia and lavender background, made me look like a large blob of phlegm.

The fair was packed. Hordes of people tromped down the aisles, clutching brochures and breathing deeply. Seekers and believers, they meandered past the booth in a kind of daze, eyes darting from one side of the aisle to the other. Crystals, blue-green algae, natal charts, firewalking, amulets for blocking out electromagnetic rays and bad energy—every booth had a different solution, and the seekers weighed them all, certain that every spiritual rip and tear could be mended if only they had the right tool for the job.

Usually when I had to chat them up in the booth I merely parroted the blurbs on the back of the book jackets, since any endorsement of my own would make me feel like a hypocrite. I'd see them nodding and smiling as I talked and I'd always feel a rush of embarrassment on their behalf. And yet on this particular day I found myself discoursing about affirmations in a way that was positively mellifluous. My usual squeamishness receded and a brand-new side of me leaped into the breach and motioned to the seekers to step right up. I was the world's greatest huckster of hope and I was warming to my audience. I understood how they could be so credulous and optimistic, how they could go soldiering on against the flow of destiny. I had, as they say, been there. I had entertained the Virgin Mary in my very own kitchen. I'd even begun to imagine—secretly, furtively—what I would do if wishing worked.

"What exactly are spirit guides?" a woman demanded, holding up a loathsome little treatise Ralph had written called *Full Potential Through Spirit Guides*. She was a stout matron with short graying hair. She gave the book an experimental squeeze as if testing it for ripeness.

"There are beings on the astral plane who can help you get on the right path and stay there," I told her. "Better sex. A better love life. A better job at a higher salary than you ever dreamed of. Their purpose in life is to help *you*, and this book will help you find them."

I was making it up as I went along, but it didn't seem to matter. She bought the book, and two others besides. People were buying everything I pointed at.

I was pitching Shantra's beauty book *Glow by Glow*, when I noticed a man browsing the prosperity section. He seemed familiar somehow, even though I could only see the back of his head. Something about the coiled way he held himself, as if he might begin leaping and pirouetting at any moment, reminded me of Steven.

"You can't be acted upon, you have to act," I was saying to a very blond woman in her mid-forties. "What Shantra teaches you is to stop thinking of yourself as a victim of the ravages of time and instead begin acting out your own beauty."

"That's exactly it!" the woman said. "I'm so mad at nasty old Father Time for making my boobs sag."

"Start the program now," I ordered. It came out sounding like "programme." Not only had I become obnoxiously bossy, I had also developed an English accent. "Go into the ladies' room and look at yourself in the mirror. Tell yourself, 'I'm a knockout. I'm a siren. Men come at the mere sight of me.'"

"I think I'd feel funny saying that," the woman said.

"Not as funny as you'll feel when salesclerks start offering you the senior citizen discount."

I was trying to see past her, to where the oddly familiar young man was contemplating the jacket blurb on *The Midas Touch,* but her frizzy yellow mane kept blocking my view. I had to wait until she paid for the book, and then I scampered over to the prosperity section.

"Can I help you find anything?" I asked.

He looked up from the book jacket and stared at me with a loose, admiring smile, the kind of smile men had been giving me all day. My heart cannonballed into the pit of my stomach. It was Steven's father, Bobby. He looked almost exactly the same, except updated for the late eighties. He was wearing gray acid-washed jeans and a teal rayon T-shirt with a blazer over it. His curls had been shorn to almost scalp length in the back, but he had left them long in front, so that they trickled over his forehead. I stared at his face, inventorying it. The nose was like Steven's. The mouth, too, those same Cupid's bow lips. The eyes were different—Steven clearly had my eyes. And my hair, too, straight as a pencil.

"I need a book that will make me rich," Bobby said. "Do these books make you rich, or what?"

"Well, they made the authors pretty rich," I said.

"So they work." He nodded and then turned back to the book jacket, examining it studiously. I had forgotten that his irony sensors were stuck on low.

"Is there any kind of method you're more attracted to?" I said. "Affirmations? Visualization? Worksheets?"

I was hoping that if I talked long enough my voice would trigger some glimmer of recognition, but it didn't seem to be working. Clearly he didn't remember me. I have to say I was disappointed. Somehow I thought that our encounter would have stuck in his mind, even if he didn't know what came out of it.

"I really need to get out of debt. I wrecked my car and it wasn't insured."

He shifted position, rocking his weight back through his hips. That was Steven all the way. Fluid, like water running over rocks.

"You know, you look kind of familiar to me," I said.

He cocked his head to one side and looked me over the way a parakeet looks at you when you approach its cage. "Do you ever take aerobics? I teach aerobics. Maybe you've taken my class."

I shook my head.

"Really? You look like you do. You're in great shape."

"I have a kid," I said. "That keeps me active."

"Wow. You don't look like it. Most women who have kids are fat."

"His name's Steven," I said. "He's seven."

"That must be cool. I'd like to have a kid someday."

"Maybe I know you from school. Did you go to Cal?" I don't know why I was pushing the issue, but I couldn't help myself.

"Yeah, but I probably wouldn't remember you. I did a lot of Demerol in college. The whole thing's one big blackout." He smiled his limp, unexpressive smile and then stretched, swinging his arms out with the money book still in hand. "I guess I'll take this," he said.

At that moment Ralph arrived. He sidled up to me and surveyed the crush of seekers with an expression of unmitigated avarice. "Looks like we're doing great," he boomed.

"I need a break," I said. "Can you cover the floor for a few minutes?" And without waiting for an answer, I bolted to the rest room.

The ladies' room was big, magenta, and miraculously empty. I planted myself in front of the mirror and stared at my own face. There I was, a five-foot-four mother of one. Short black hair, hazel eyes, oval face. As I stared at my venomous reflection, I could pick out little traces of the members of my family: my father's mischievous eyes, my mother's heavy-lipped mouth, Irma's broad cheekbones, Angus's long nose.

But Steven looked like Bobby. Moved like him. Danced like him. Had his cute little nose and his bow mouth and his long eyelashes. It was infuriating. Here I had raised him, nursed him, taught him every stupid joke I knew, and simply by virtue of genetics he had taken after his father. How had I never noticed it before?

As I stood there glowering at myself, the door to the bathroom squeaked open and the blond woman from the booth took her place next to me by the mirror.

"I am so beautiful," she said to her reflection. "I'm a vixen. I'm absolutely glowing."

I fished a lipstick out of my purse and began applying it hurriedly.

"Damn, I'm good!" She raised her eyebrows for emphasis. "I look like a million bucks. Men are falling all over me. I'm hot stuff."

"You were right, this is great," she said, turning to me. "Were you just doing it, too? I mean, don't let me interrupt you."

"That's okay," I said. "I've got to get back to the booth."

When I got home that night, the ants were everywhere. Dawn and Steven were in the kitchen killing them, and the little black kitten was sitting on one of the counters, watching.

"We're surrounded," Dawn said as I came in. "I think we're going to have to surrender."

She was holding a sponge flecked with tiny black corpses, and a few live ones were crawling on her forearms. Steven was on the floor, trying to mop up ants from around the kitten's dish. They did seem to be surrounded. A four-lane ant highway encircled the whole kitchen, and I could see more coming in through the window. I felt like turning around and leaving. After standing all day on a slab of concrete covered with a thin piece of lavender carpet, I was not in the mood for a major housekeeping project.

"Here, you take over in the killing fields for a while," Dawn said, handing me the sponge. "We've been at it for about half an hour and I'm completely grossed out."

"We've killed about ten million of them," Steven said. "I think we need an anteater instead of a kitten."

"You know what the Pink Panther said when he stepped on an ant?" I asked him.

He shook his head.

I sang the response to the tune of the Pink Panther theme song: "Dead ant. Dead ant. Dead ant, dead ant, dead ant . . ." Steven laughed uproariously even though he'd probably never heard of the Pink Panther. He had picked up this loud, fake-sounding guffaw from the other boys in his class. I hated it, but the only way I could think of to break him of the habit would be home schooling, which could probably be construed as an overreaction.

Dawn saw me cringe and winked at Steven. Despite having been utterly opposed to him in the abstract, she was probably his closet adult friend. He loved Lisa and Aunt Simone, but they tended to treat him as if he were a visiting dignitary from the land of children. Dawn knew how to josh with him in the stupid, bathroom-humor way that seven-year-old boys like, and she was better than I was about tolerating the crass fads of the classroom. She had, for example, coached him for hours until he learned how to make himself burp.

Suddenly I remembered that I hadn't told Dawn yet about seeing Bobby, so I told Steven to go get the latest Terratarantula drawings he'd done so he could show them to Dawn. Terratarantula was a planet Steven and I had invented together, populated by spider people who lived in houses made of webs. Steven was always drawing elaborate Terratarantulan scenes, filled with intricately cross-hatched web castles and web chariots.

"Guess who came to the Psychic Fair today?" I said as soon as he left the room.

"The Pope."

"No, weirder. Bobby."

Dawn looked blank.

"Steven's father," I whispered.

Dawn scowled. "I hope you didn't agree to see him again."

"No, and I didn't tell him anything about Steven, either. It was just funny to see him after all this time. Steven looks like him."

"Presumably the resemblance stops there." Dawn reached across the table to squish a wayward ant with her thumb.

I waited, hoping that she would ask me for details, but she didn't, so I went on, trying to stir her curiosity. "He's very good-looking. I think he's actually improved."

Dawn made a great show of flicking the ant corpse onto the floor. "If you've decided you want a boyfriend, I don't think he's the one you're looking for," she said.

"I didn't search him out, he just came," I snapped and turned around to attack the quivering trail of insect bodies advancing along the counter. They were so determined, it was almost admirable. You would think they'd have second thoughts about the whole campaign after having two-thirds of their army crushed with one wipe of the sponge, but there didn't seem to be any unacceptable level of casualties. They wanted what they wanted, and death by sponge was no deterrent. I mopped up another few feet of them and tried to figure out what it was they were after. Was there a bag of sugar open in the cupboard? Had I forgotten to mop up the maple syrup I'd spilled when making Steven's pancakes?

I followed the line down the counter and up across the cabinets. The two freeways seemed to be converging on a single point: the spice cabinet. I opened the cabinet door. The box that held the Virgin was covered with quivering black beads. The ants were piled on top of each other, nudging one another out of the way in their eagerness to find an entrance. Somehow she had beckoned them from the darkness and they had come to worship her or to carry her off with them. When I tried to pick up the box, I felt them snap at my fingers with their tiny jaws.

"What are you doing?" Dawn asked when I finally managed to knock the box into the sink.

I made my voice sound casual. "I found what the ants were after," I said. Then I turned on the faucet and began hosing down the Virgin's metal prison.

Dawn got up and looked over my shoulder at the writhing ant bodies in the drain catch. "Gross," she said. "Whatever's in that box, I think you should throw it out."

I waited until Dawn had left and Steven was in bed before I freaked out, but then I freaked out completely. I understood now what was going on. It wasn't me that attracted ants and ex-lovers, it was the come-hither call from the statue in my cabinet. It was the Virgin who had made me attractive, who had beckoned Mitch to my door, and Bobby to the Psychic Fair. We had ordered her to sing like a siren from the rocks, and her faint notes trailed me like perfume.

Well, that may be fine for some people, but I didn't believe in it. Not in wishes, not in magic, not in free will, not in an open-ended future, not in blasts from the past, and certainly not in a plastic Virgin Mary with the power to woo insects and seekers and who knew what else. Dawn was right, I should throw her out.

I called Lisa at work.

"I need you to come get your box," I said. I must have sounded like a lunatic.

"What box?"

"The *Virgin,*" I whispered. To tell you the truth, I was afraid the statue could hear me. "I can't have it here anymore. It's making me uncomfortable."

Lisa sighed noisily into the receiver. "Why do you have to obsess about everything?"

"I'm not obsessing," I said. "I just don't want to be part of this whole father thing, it's regressive. I need to think about the future."

Lisa stayed silent just long enough for me to gather that I was being difficult. "Fine," she said at last. "I'll pick it up on my way home."

$\mathcal{S}$ilver Stones   (Carolina)

I would never think of him at all if my girls weren't so hung up on
the whole thing. I don't believe in dwelling on the past; it doesn't
do any good. So when he left, I didn't sit around weeping like some
women would. I got on with my life. I waited two months for him
to come back, and then I got rid of every last trace of him. His
clothes, his toolbox, his cuff links, his old navy uniform—it all went
in the trash. His spy novels and record albums, the snapshots of him
and the girls, the photos of our wedding. Sure, I was disappointed,
but I wasn't going to be like my mother-in-law, spending my life
weeping over the loss of a husband. I'm an optimist. I believe in
looking to the future.

Not that everybody in sight didn't do their best to drag me
down. It was bad enough to have my husband disappear in the
middle of the night, but then to have every single person around
me harping on it constantly; it was depressing. My mother was the
worst. I guess she thought that she and I finally had something in

common, now that we'd both been abandoned. She and my father were married in name only, even if he hadn't actually left the house. But if she thought that I wanted to hang around having a pity party with her and Simone, she was dead wrong. As soon as we moved back into my parents' house and I had a built-in baby-sitter for the girls, I started going out at night, looking for a new man.

My mother used to sit at the bottom of the stairs waiting for me to come home. I'd open the front door and there she'd be, sitting on the bottom step in her nightgown. She scared the daylights out of me, lurking there in the darkness with her eyes glittering. I never knew what she wanted from me. "Tell me, daughter," she asked me once as I came in the door. "Who are you looking for?"

I didn't bother replying. At two in the morning I just wasn't in the mood for a chat, and even if I was, how do you respond to that kind of question? I didn't need that kind of grief with everything I'd been through, I really didn't.

It was around then that I went and paid my mother-in-law a farewell visit. Every cloud has a silver lining, and while I wasn't too happy about losing my husband, I wasn't shedding any tears about losing his mother.

Maureen Harris, now there's a piece of work. Our Lady of Perpetual Sorrows. She'd gone blind when she was a young woman and then her husband died, and as far as she was concerned, she was a modern-day martyr. She kept Bill tied to the old apron strings, running over there every day to help her out with this or that, tell her stories, listen to her complain. I did my part when I was married to him, but now that he was gone, I figured my obligation was over.

I took the girls with me for the final visit, thinking Mrs. Harris would want to see her granddaughters, but she didn't even acknowledge them. As soon as we got there she started sobbing. "I never thought I would end up like this," she bawled. "Completely alone. You don't know what loneliness is until you've lost both your husband and your child."

I couldn't believe what I was hearing. I felt sorry for her and all, living in that dingy little house with mildew on the walls and carpets that didn't look like they'd been cleaned since the first World War. But for God's sake, the girls had lost their father, I'd lost my husband. What made her think we didn't know what loneliness was?

"It's hard for all of us," I reminded her. "It's probably hardest for me. I have to raise two girls by myself now."

I was kidding myself if I thought she was going to be sympathetic. "I know exactly how you feel," she said. "After my husband died, I had to bring Billy up myself. It wasn't easy for me without my sight. Billy had to be my eyes. And now he's gone, too." And then she was off again, sobbing and sniffling. She was huge and pale and she cried like a child, her chest heaving and shaking, her lips curling. I hated the way those blank eyes looked as they leaked their tears. It was enough to give you nightmares.

The girls were already gloomy enough, and when they saw their gram bawling away, they looked ready to join in. Lisa was staring at the floor and Julia's lip was trembling. "Pull yourself together, Maureen," I said. "You're upsetting your grandchildren." I was about to deliver the little speech I had prepared, about how we weren't going to have as much time to see her now that we had moved in with my parents, but before I could start, she announced she had a present for us.

"Go get it out of the cabinet for me, would you, Julia?" she said. "It's on the bottom shelf, wrapped in paper."

So Julia went to the cabinet in the corner and dug around under the piles of dusty linens until she found something wrapped in brown paper. "Your father used to love it when he was a little boy," Mrs. Harris told Julia as she unwrapped it. "It was a wedding present from my husband's parents. Very pretty fabric as I recall."

And it was, I have to admit, quite beautiful. It was an antique bedspread, a turquoise brocaded silk decorated with golden birds of paradise. But when she held it up for us to see, I saw what kind of gift it really was. There was an enormous brown stain in the center. The brown that blood turns.

I didn't know where that stain had come from, and I didn't want to know. She was aching to tell me, I was certain, but I wasn't going to give her the satisfaction. I just thanked her as if I hadn't noticed a thing, and told the girls to put on their coats.

But just because the woman had a martyr complex didn't mean I had to hang on to her bloody relics. I would have put the whole thing in the trash when we got home, except that Julia insisted we keep it. She didn't care about that disgusting smear, all she remembered was that her father had supposedly loved it when he was a little boy. She took it off to her room and kept it in her closet, and at some point she must have covered the stain with a silk patch. When I walked into her house last week, I found the bedspread draped over her living room couch like a slipcover. I just about keeled over.

Maybe that's what it was that got me thinking about him. Ever since I arrived in California, he's been on my mind. I'll be lying on Lisa's fold-out bed, trying to fall asleep, and a picture will flare up behind my eyelids. Him in his boxers, shaving in front of the bathroom mirror. Him swinging the girls around by their wrists, into the stream of the sprinkler on the front lawn. I can see every detail of it. His short, taut forearms dampening with spray. The girls shrieking as he swings them. It's always the early days I remember, before he got so quiet and remote. The way he used to like to kiss me, with both hands on my ass, squeezing me up against him. I even remember the taste of his mouth. It was always musky, like meat and liquor, or fire.

I met him at the Ritz-Carlton. In the bar. Handsome like you've never seen, like something out of a movie. Green eyes and black, black hair and this smile that absolutely slayed me. It was wicked, a real bad-boy smile. I couldn't believe how gorgeous he was.

I was there because I had lost my virginity the night before and I was celebrating with my best friend at the time, a slutty girl named Amy who worked as a secretary in the anthropology department. She and I got along because we liked to have a good time and we didn't care what other people thought. The other girls in the department were skinny, studious types who couldn't imagine anything more scintillating than a gawk at some two-thousand-year-old skeleton. I was majoring in anthropology to please my father, but I never did see the appeal. To me, it was just a bunch of dull facts about people I was never going to meet. Why should I care what a bunch of ugly savages ate for dinner? I wanted to know what was on the menu at the Ritz, and whether there would be dancing afterward.

Bill was at the Ritz-Carlton because he had just sold his first life insurance policy for Prudential. He was an insurance salesman. I couldn't believe it when he told me—it seemed so tacky, it almost kept me from going out with him. But the green eyes convinced me.

So there we were in the bar of the Ritz-Carlton, just about the most elegant room on earth. Amy and I were at one table, drinking champagne cocktails. Bill and two of his insurance buddies were at the next, drinking Manhattans. We were all drunk and I was feeling naughty and excited about having slept with one of my father's graduate students the night before. Amy was being bawdy, asking how I liked it and how long it took the fellow to climax. And then Bill leans across to our table and holds out his empty glass with the maraschino cherry floating on the bottom in a little puddle of bourbon. "Would you like my cherry?" he says to me. "I hear you recently lost yours."

I guess I should have been offended but I wasn't. I burst out laughing and then I reached into his glass and took out the cherry. I tilted my head back and lowered the sticky red fruit into my mouth as if it were a peeled grape and I was Cleopatra. When I finished I looked over at Bill and he was grinning at me sideways, this sexy, uneven smile. I knew we were meant for each other and so did he. I knew we were going to have a great time.

He was a smart aleck, full of himself and his own charm, but he had this way of talking that I just couldn't get over. Up until then I had only known two kinds of men, the ones who talked all the time to impress you, and the ones who left all the talking up to you. I was a chatty girl, so I did fine with the strong silent types, but I knew eventually I was going to get tired of the sound of my own voice. Bill, he could talk like nobody else.

A few weeks after we started dating we went up to Gloucester for a weekend at the beach. We stayed at some cruddy little boardinghouse, in a tiny room with old-fashioned rose-covered wallpaper and a window that looked out onto the sea. Late the first night, after we'd made love, we were lying in the lumpy, concave bed, flat on our backs because of the heat, and Bill suddenly said, "What do you see behind your eyelids?"

I'd never thought about it before, but I shut my eyes and looked at the inside of my lids. There were stars there, comets that swirled and danced, and below them was a long strip of dark shadows like tankers pulling into the harbor at night.

"It's like a movie, isn't it?" he said. "Sometimes I just sit back and watch it. It's better than TV."

"What do you see right now?" I asked.

What he saw put my boats and stars to shame. First he saw a hail of silver stones, falling all over a city like an avalanche. "That's you," he told me. "You're the silver stones, falling all over me, so little and hard."

"I'm not so hard," I said, snuggling up against him so he could feel my soft breasts and belly. But he was lost in the world behind his eyes. He saw a woman, "a beautiful woman like you," he said, running his hand along my thigh. His voice was quiet and far away, like a pilot's voice on an airplane narrating the scenery. "Imagine her walking through the cobblestone streets, with silver stones falling around her like rain," he told me in that hushed, trancelike voice. His fingers drummed along my thigh like little pebbles.

"Ouch! That would sting," I said, laughing.

"More than just sting—one of them falls on her head and knocks her out cold. Knocks her memories out of her head and onto the pavement. She forgets her own name, where she lives, even the name of the man she loves."

"Who does she love?" I was still flirting, not really following the story.

"It's a mystery now, isn't it? There's just a residue left in her mind, like the ring on a table left by a glass. She can't remember what was in the glass, or the character of the man, only that maybe there was someone once, long ago. But I heard he was a sailor, a fisherman from right here in Gloucester. One day he went out to sea and didn't come back. She waited for him at the harbor. Every day and night she walked along the beach in case his body washed up onshore. Once she found a driftwood log that was just about the height and breadth of a man. She brought it home and put it in her bed and slept with her arms around its trunk. That's how much she missed him."

"What happened to him?" He had captured me now. I put my fingers around his arm and held on tight, waiting for the story to finish being born.

"He was shipwrecked in a storm. He floated for a long time hanging on to the mast, and then he was picked up by a slave ship on its way to the Caribbean. He spent a month on that ship, with the sound of the slaves shrieking and moaning all around him. It took a long time for him to find a boat back to Gloucester, and when he did, his lover had forgotten him."

Then he pulled me on top of him and kissed me on the mouth, tender as the lapping of the waves outside. "So the moral of the story is 'Beware of falling rocks,'" he said and grinned his bad-boy grin.

I started to giggle and then I couldn't stop. It seemed so funny to me, his wild stories out of nowhere and his movie screen eyelids. I laughed and laughed and so did he, bouncing me up and down on his chest with the convulsions of it. Afterward he was all over me again, his mouth everywhere, consuming me. I felt like candy must feel, like a flower yielding up its pollen to a bee.

He loved sex. He loved it so much it would make him laugh and tell jokes, right in the middle of it. He'd roll on top of me in the morning and start belting out this silly old song: "Nothing could be finer than to be in Carolina in the morning." If I'd tell him to be quiet, he'd start laughing and sing even louder, pumping all the while. "Nothing could be finer than to be in her vagina in the moooooorning."

"It's pronounced Caroleena," I'd correct.

"Nothing could be keener than to be in Carolina," he'd sing, in a funny voice like on old records. "Nothing can be keener than to stick my wiener een her . . ."

He was fun, he really was. In those days he was a lot of fun.

My mother was crabby on my wedding day. She was jealous of my happiness and she couldn't keep her spite to herself. She tried to ruin my mood by painting a picture of doom for me, even as she and Simone were helping me get dressed. There we were, crammed into the tiny ladies' room at the church, and my mother had to start in with her sour pronouncements. I was standing in my bare feet on the tile floor, trying to get a pair of white nylons on without falling over, and Simone was busy sticking various kinds of oddball weeds in my bridal bouquet—for good luck, she said, though she doesn't believe in luck. It was spring and everything she stuck in there was dripping pollen. I nearly tore a hole in my stockings sneezing. And my mother, instead of handing me a Kleenex or doing anything in the least bit helpful, just stood there, holding my wedding dress by the shoulders as if it were something she wanted to keep at arm's length.

"Carolina," she said to me as I stood there in my stockings with my eyes watering. "A man's heart is very small. They love too much at the beginning and they use it all up. Listen to your mother. Be small-hearted like a man."

Then she dropped the dress over my head. When I emerged, Simone was there, looking smug as she handed me my bouquet. "She already is small-hearted," she said to my mother, who was behind me now, fastening up my zipper. I kept my mouth shut. Neither of them ever really understood me, or anything about my heart. I was the tender one, even if I kept it to myself.

They thought they were right when they saw how well I did after he left. See, they probably said to each other, when I was out looking for a new husband. See how small her heart is. But he had been gone for so many months before he left, I was already used to it. He had stopped telling me stories, stopped singing me songs in the morning. He went around the house quietly, like a tenant, not telling me anything.

My girls think it's some big mystery why he left, but it was never any mystery to me. I told my father I was worried about foul play, and it's true that Bill was working with a pretty rough crowd. He'd quit the insurance business about three weeks after we met and ended up fencing stolen TVs with some friends from high school. There were always feuds going on and people accusing one another of tipping off the cops, but it wasn't anything more than posturing. That wasn't why he left.

He didn't love me anymore. Excuse me for not wanting to take out a full-page ad in the newspaper. It's not something I'm proud of. I wanted to forget it as quickly as possible and get married again, but the men I met on my nights out were all of the kind I'd already decided I didn't like. The ones who talk to impress or the ones who leave all the talking to you. I wasn't stuck on Bill so much as I wasn't about to settle for less.

Anyway, it's strange that I've been thinking of him now, because I really had put him out of my mind. I was never like the girl in his story, scanning the horizon from a widow's walk. Yet suddenly he's there, behind my eyelids like one of his own movies, green-eyed and wicked-mouthed, singing me dirty songs. I'd really almost forgotten his voice, even though I remembered the way his mouth looked when it sang. Which is why when I called home this morning to pick up the messages from my answering machine, the voice didn't sound familiar. "Uh, Carolina?" it said. "This is Bill, um, Harris. I was just in town, and I thought I'd look you up. I'm staying at the Ritz-Carlton. Could you call me there? Just ask for me at the front desk and they'll put you through to my room."

*G*hostly Delivery   (Julia)

The moment the Virgin passed from my hands into Lisa's, all the fear and tingly excitement vanished. By the next morning, my panicked phone call to Lisa the night before seemed like an overreaction. An ant invasion and a profitable day at the Psychic Fair do not a *Twilight Zone* episode make.

In the late afternoon I dropped Steven off at a friend's house and went for a walk in the cemetery with Carolina. She was leaving the next morning to go back to Boston for a few days to deal with some sort of emergency at work, but the airline had agreed to fly her back at the end of the week to finish her vacation. She seemed excited about the trip, which I attributed to her being flattered that she was so invaluable to her employers. She scampered along the cemetery's rutted paths, and every few minutes she darted off to read the inscription on a nearby gravestone, her high heels making deep punctures in the turf.

"Now, that's hubris," she said when we came to a huge crypt that had been cast in the shape of a pyramid. "Who the hell did these people think they were, anyway?"

We had reached the part of the cemetery where the city's richest and most influential citizens had built themselves ever-lasting stone mansions, each one with a pillared portico and a wrought-iron front door. It looked just like a swanky neighbor-hood for dead people. We sat down on the front stoop of a Gothic manse with a turreted roof, and Carolina leaned her head back and looked at the sky. "Can I show you something?" she said after a moment.

Carolina has two voices. You could know her for years and only hear one of them, the breezy, coquettish trill she uses every day. But there's another one, low and level, as unornamented as a Shaker table. Every time I hear it something starts in me, because it lives there inside her throat like some serious mother I've never met who might suddenly announce that she's my real mother and the other one is an imposter. It was this other voice that she used to ask if she could show me something. I said, "Sure."

Carolina began unbuttoning her white cotton blouse. "I think something's trying to kill me," she said and slid her right breast out of her bra. Cupped in her hand, it looked like a piece of pale fruit, the cinnamon-colored nipple pointing upward like a stem.

"Right here, can you see it?" She fingered the under-slope of her breast just above her rib cage.

I shook my head and Carolina took my hand and touched my finger to the spot. There was something jagged under the skin, as if a pebble were embedded there. I pulled my hand back squeamishly.

"Feel it?"

I nodded, sweat prickling my armpits. "Have you shown it to a doctor?"

Carolina shrugged and the old, girlish voice came bubbling back. "Doctors can't do anything. Radiation, chemotherapy, all it does is make you feel so sick you don't notice you're dying. No, the trick is not to let what's after me get me."

The sun had started to sink and her breast was pimpling with cold. She tucked it back inside her bra and began buttoning up her shirt. I sat beside her and tried to think of some comforting, sensible thing to say. The inside of my head felt fuzzy, as if it had been filled with thousands of fiberglass spindles.

"What's after you?" I asked at last.

"I know you were close to her," Carolina said. "I know you never wanted to hear anything bad about her. But it's Irma. I think her ghost is trying to kill me."

"That doesn't make any sense." An understatement, but I didn't know how else to put it. Carolina had always had crackpot theories, but this one was remarkable even for her.

"I know it doesn't make sense." She began fidgeting in her purse for her pack of cigarettes. "I've tried asking her why she's after me, but she never answers. She just lurks around my bed, pressing on me. I don't know what she wants."

"Maybe she's upset that you never left her any food on *Día de los Muertos*," I suggested. I was trying to lighten the mood, but Carolina didn't smile.

"I never told Simone this, but the day Irma died, I saw her spirit."

"Where?"

"In my room. She just stood there in the doorway as if her eyes were made of glass. Not saying anything, not smiling, not scolding, just watching me. And as she stood there it occurred to me that my father had wanted her dead. As if that was her message."

"Maybe she just wanted to say good-bye to you."

Carolina waved her cigarette at me, brushing the suggestion aside. "No, no, we weren't like that, we weren't close. And I knew my father well enough to know that she was right. He didn't love her."

"But even if he wanted her to die—she died of a stroke. He had nothing to do with it."

"It's the mind, Julie, the power of the mind. Listen, I've thought about this a lot. My father was a brilliant man, a sharp-minded man. He could do anything he set his mind to. He could have done it by accident, just by thinking, every day, *I wish she were dead.* And then after death, maybe she went after him. The dead have no limits; once they get out of their bodies, all they are is thought. Powerful thought. Couldn't she have thought cancer into my father? Couldn't she be thinking cancer into me?"

She stared at me intently, waiting for a response.

"I think you should go to a doctor," I said. "Why don't you see a doctor while you're in Boston?"

Carolina stood up suddenly and I knew the serious part of the conversation was over. "I'd have to find a cute one," she said coyly. "I'm not going to show my tit to just anyone."

A moment later she was frolicking down the path, threading between the crypts to get to the lower-rent headstones embedded in the lawns below. I followed, my head spinning. I felt the way I always did when I tried to talk about something important with Carolina—as if I had been trying to find the place where a rainbow touches ground. Every time I got near it, it dodged me and reappeared somewhere else, sparkling with promise.

"Look at all these dead people," Carolina said, plopping down in the grass. "Every single one of them is dead, dead, dead."

I sat down on the lawn beside her and leaned back, feeling the grass prick against my shoulders. I had a thought that seemed true to me, even though it smacked of psychology. I shaped the sentence carefully in my mind before I said it, and when it came out it sounded very wise.

"Sometimes I think the fear of dying is really a fear that you're not living the life you want."

Carolina was making herself a tiny bouquet of pink and white clover. She looked up, holding the flowers under her chin like a bridesmaid. "That's probably true. But I think a life can take a sudden turn for the better. When I get back from my trip, I'll tell you if I'm right."

Then she looked back up the hillside at the crypts standing in a row like mansions. "I have an idea," she said.

At that moment I would have done anything for her, even if it did mean walking all the way down to the cemetery gates. We found a newspaper rack a block away and took every copy of the *Oakland Tribune* that was left. Then we walked back to the top of the cemetery and placed a folded newspaper on the front steps of each of the crypts so that it looked exactly like a suburban neighborhood first thing in the morning. Carolina thought it was the funniest thing she'd ever seen. "I wish we'd had a camera," she said, giggling, as we walked back to the car.

As it turned out, we didn't need one. Two days later, the *Tribune* published a photograph of the scene on its front page under the caption "Ghostly Delivery." I cut it out and saved it to give to Carolina when she got back.

That night when I got home I noticed I'd lost an earring. I didn't think much of it at the time. But in retrospect, I realize that was when the unraveling began.

$\mathscr{T}$he Town of the Souls (Simone)

The dead, like most of us, don't like change. You have to usher them out of this world with food and praises or they end up trapped on the beltway of the city of the dead, where there are only fast-food restaurants and shopping malls, but no sidewalks, nowhere to rest.

My mother told me this because she came from Mitla, which was known in ancient times as the town of the souls. Once a man from her village wanted to visit his dead wife, so he turned to Owl, the bird who can fly between the worlds. "Follow me," Owl said and flapped his great brown wings. The man found himself in the city of the dead, and he walked along the road until he came to his wife's house. She was there tending her peppertree and the man called her name.

"Wife," he said. "I've been looking for the money you were keeping, but I cannot find where it is hidden."

The woman smiled and told him where to find the money, and then a strange man came out of the house and held out his hand to her, and she went inside. Seeing this, the husband grew furious. He wanted to rule his wife from both sides of the divide, and like most men, he never thought about consequences. He took a matchbook from his pocket and set the house on fire. The smoke turned into owl wings and flew him back to the land of the living. But when he tried to go home, his house was gone—reduced to ashes. The dead, you see, live in our houses with us, and the air we move through is really the thin membranes of their bodies.

So Carolina looked up not long ago and noticed our mother standing by her bed. Lucky girl, you'd think, to have her mama by her side, watching over her with a loving eye. But Carolina could never see the good in our mother. Her mind was a giddy Ferris wheel, always circling back to herself. "What does this mean for me?" she asked instead of wondering what unfinished business had made our mother visible.

All my life my mother wanted to go home. So her husband didn't love her anymore, that was of no consequence. The love of a man is a bouquet of flowers, pretty while it lasts, but not likely to last long. But the love of a family, of her own mother and father, of her six siblings, this was the loss that dried her throat like thirst. Later, of course, she remembered Eligio and his way of talking as if words were so bountiful he could waste them as he wanted. But at first what she remembered was the clay houses of her village with their fences made of tall, green cactus, and the river running through town where the women gathered to wash clothes and bathe and comb out their long hair. She remembered the plaza shaded by fig and ash trees, and the market. The church near the ruins where she had danced during the Festival of the Corn wearing a yellow skirt that opened up like an umbrella when she spun around and around to the sound of guitars and whistles. These were the thoughts my mother had when Carolina and I were babies. And these were the thoughts she had, every day, until she died.

Is it any wonder her soul flew out of her body? It happened when I was three. Too young, you might say, to remember, but only if you forget that time is a rope you can ascend and descend freely. My father had gone to do research in the Congo, and Irma was alone with her father-in-law, Craig, in a house so big it seemed to her like all the houses of her village stacked one on top of the other. One night she woke up gasping to find a man standing in the doorway of her bedroom, watching her. It was Craig, lurking perhaps, perhaps only sleepwalking. She locked her door after that, but it was too late. The fright sent her soul into the howling winter wind, where it spun among the snowflakes and tried to find its way home.

Soon afterward she found herself tired even at midday. Her arms and legs felt as if they were filled with sand, and her stomach, too, so that while she cooked for Craig and for me, she herself could eat nothing. Soon her breasts emptied of their milk, and when infant Carolina put her mouth to them, there was nothing for her to taste.

Craig was a doctor, but unlike most of the doctors of his time, he believed in the curing power of exercise. During his wife's cancer he had tried to get her to ride a bicycle and she, a meek mouse of a woman, had agreed until the cancer sent her to bed. Now he rolled this same bicycle out of the carriage house and tried to put my mother on it. It was a disaster. Her skirt got caught in the bicycle wheels so that she felt she was being sucked into the machine. After that he led her on brisk winter walks to the Cambridge Commons while my mother hunched over and trembled with cold. I have to laugh when I think of Craig and his curing schemes, but in the end he did find the solution. Swimming, he said. This is what would cure her.

He hired a nurse to take her to the baths. It was a cavernous place that reminded Irma of the ancient city of Mitla submerged in water. Here were the same wide, blank plazas and the same stone pillars, but all of it now was flooded and the air was full of steam like the spirits made visible. Irma looked up and the ceiling arced over her, braced and crisscrossed at the top, and the light that came down through the skylights reminded her of the high clouds pressing down into the bowl of the valley in Mitla, her home.

Water would save her, but what did she know of water? She knew mountains, dirt, corn, cactus, and the low scrubby trees of the foothills. She knew clouds, thunder, lightning, wind, and yes, she knew the rain that came all summer and turned the village into mud. She knew the river below the bridge where the women washed, and the streams with their deep pools that faded to mere glimmers in the dry season. But these were only to kneel and wade in, never to fall into as you would fall into the arms of your mother.

This is what she did now. The nurse held her head and taught her how to give way to the water. How to float. And Irma was so sick and listless that she never struggled. She gazed at the ceiling with her head in the nurse's hand, her body weightless as dust. She dreamed she was at home, lying on her back in the fields staring at the sky. The water lapped at her arms and sloshed at her legs. Kick, the nurse said.

And so little by little she learned. Each day a new gesture. She gave a little kick and glided, moved her arms and glided, and a tingle of hope flickered in her limbs and for a moment pushed back the tide of despair. Soon she could propel herself from one side of the pool to the other. Soon she would even put her face in the water and let her breath fall down to the bottom of the pool like a hand-ful of glass beads.

When she got home she was ravenous. She began eating as she cooked again, pulling beans out of the pot when they were still hard. At night she fell asleep and dreamed only of water, cool as the cold sheets draped over her body. If you ever asked my mother about her illness, she would have told you this: My soul left my body, but water brought it back. Seeing the body of my mother floating, her soul returned, curious. And the body, finding the soul nearby, snatched it up like a lizard eating a mosquito. After that, my mother resolved to swim every day so that her soul would never again try to go home without her.

The seasons of reckoning come in youth, midlife, and old age, each with its own flavor of realization, regret, or nostalgia. For my mother, reckoning came late. At sixty-one she saw that her life was an arrow, pointing only to one unfulfilled desire. She must go home to Mitla, the city of the dead. It didn't matter how. In today's world you might wonder why she didn't go before, why she didn't leave my father and return to her family with her daughters in tow. But it had always been impossible for her to contemplate making the long journey alone. Fate is the choice that we make because we think there is no other.

Now suddenly she knew she couldn't be homesick anymore. She must either go or perish, she told my father. She asked him to come with her, to escort her. And he refused.

He was afraid, although he wouldn't admit it. Late in life, after journeying around the world, he grew frightened of travel. At fifty-five he had retired from fieldwork and devoted himself to lectur-ing. He wouldn't get on a plane to save my mother's life. And he wouldn't let her go alone. She was trapped, again, always, forever. I blame him for her death, still.

She died in water, as you know. Water, in the end, couldn't weigh her soul down any longer. The day she died I told him what I thought. Concisely, as there was little point in going on about it. I said, "I hope you're satisfied with your decision, Papa."

But Carolina, oh how she carried on. You'd have thought she was her mother's darling the way she sobbed. Maybe it was the first time she noticed what he was. Most people cry for themselves and their illusions more than they ever cry for others.

I spent the days after my mother's death trying to coax her over to the dead world with prayers and food and incense. But she lingered, a fly that buzzes through the room and won't go out the open window. She circled around on the beltway of the city of the dead and couldn't see the exit.

And so, at last, she's turned to Carolina. I would rather she had come to me, but I understand her logic. Carolina always was her father's favorite. And so it's up to her to do what he never would. Like the owl in the story, she must escort our mother to the city of the dead.

$\mathscr{L}$osing It (Julia)

On Monday, Ralph came into my office, leaned into my face, and asked me how the show had gone. He had the smallest space bubble of anyone I'd ever met, which was unfortunate since his was not the kind of face you want to see in extreme close-up.

"Did you make me a lot of money?" he inquired with a squint-eyed smile. I slid my chair back a few feet.

"Lots and lots of money," I said. "I think we set a record."

"You see, the new signs work," he crowed. "Fucking fuchsia brings in the customers."

"Fuchsia had nothing to do with it. It was my amazing salesmanship." I don't know what made me say it; I should have known better. As soon as the words were out of my mouth, I knew I had just set myself up for a glimpse of Ralph's dark side.

"*You* got them to buy the books?" he said, dropping his voice to a moist whisper. Every time he pronounced a word beginning with the letter B, I was bombarded by flecks of spittle. "That's brilliant.

That's like the fucking salesgirl at B. Dalton taking credit for selling *Bleak House*. My books sell themselves, Julia. All you have to do is put them out where people can reach them. But thank you for being there to take their money, it was a great service."

He punctuated this lecture with a deep and mocking bow. As he straightened up, his elbow caught the vase of freesias I had placed on the filing cabinet next to my desk to simulate fresh air. It capsized, sending a stream of fetid plant water gushing across Shantra's manuscript.

"Brilliant, Julia," Ralph said, stalking to the door. "This is an office, not a flower garden."

I waited until he had shut the door and then I scrambled to get my keyboard out of the way of Lake Freesia. When it was safely stowed on top of my monitor, I rummaged around in my drawers until I found a pile of paper napkins I could use to wipe up the spill. Shantra's manuscript was completely drenched, and when I tried to wipe it dry, the ink from Ralph's rewrites and my corrections blurred into a hideous smear. Finally I gathered up the whole pile and dropped it into the recycling bin under my desk. I'd already entered almost all the changes anyway, and for some reason I no longer cared whether or not Shantra's book was a hymn to the English language.

What I needed at that moment was to get outside. I told the receptionist that I was going to get a cup of coffee and burst out into the sunlight, gulping air as if I'd been underwater. I hated the way Ralph made me feel like a bullied first grader. I hated the way my hands were shaking and my chest felt shredded with rage. I sat down on the curb and covered my eyes with my palms and tried to take regular breaths. I was a grown woman. I lived in an apartment with my serious, tenderhearted son and a black kitten that didn't have a name. And my mother had a stone in her breast, a sharp little stone like a piece of flint. I took my hands away from my face and looked down at the cigarette butts and candy wrappers in the gutter. Two painful knots of tension had appeared between my shoulder blades. They throbbed gently, like the blinking lamp of a lighthouse, warning that I was headed for trouble.

It wasn't until I went back to my office that I noticed that Shantra's manuscript wasn't on my computer screen anymore. The screen was gray and blank, and when I looked closely, I could see my own bulbous reflection. Apparently I had accidentally shut down the computer when I grabbed the keyboard to get it out of the spilled flower water. But when I booted up again, I couldn't find the manuscript on my hard drive. Somehow it had been deleted.

I took a deep breath and tried the backup disk I kept just in case something like this happened. *Drive not ready reading drive A,* my computer said. *Retry? Cancel?*

I hit Retry about fifty times. I pulled the disk out and looked at it and put it in again and hit Retry some more. But the truth was obvious: The disk was a dud. Shantra's brand-new book, scheduled to go to the printer next week, had vanished.

I dove under my desk to grab the wet manuscript pages out of the recycling bin so that I would at least have something to work from, some way to reconstruct the thing. My mind was clicking furiously, trying to figure out how long it would take to retype the manuscript and put in all the coding and whether I could possibly do it in time to make Ralph's deadline and get those play-off tickets for Steven. But the bin was empty. When I reached my hand in, all I touched was its smooth plastic bottom.

It was only after I'd spent ten minutes crawling around under the furniture looking for the missing manuscript that the obvious explanation came to me. It was the second Monday of the month, our office's recycling pickup day. While I was sitting outside on the curb, a green-and-white truck had come and taken Shantra's manuscript to the city dump, where it would be rinsed clean and transformed into unbleached toilet paper.

I sat back down at my desk and dialed the number for Shantra Maloney. "Hi!" a voice chirped at me. "This is Shantra! I'm on a vision quest in Nepal at the moment, but if you'd like to leave a message, I'll get back to you as soon as I return. And remember, blessings are already shining on your path."

When I heard the beep, I tried to make my voice sound urgent but not hysterical. "Hi, Shantra, this is Julia from Enhancement Press. Can you call me as soon as you get back into town? We're having some computer problems here, and I'm wondering if I could get a fresh copy of your manuscript."

Then I turned back to the computer and loaded Tetris. There was nothing to do but play a few rounds while I waited for Shantra to call me back.

Tuesday, the kitten wandered off. Steven was devastated. We walked around the neighborhood calling for it, which wasn't easy since we still hadn't named it. Steven made a heartbreaking sign with a drawing of a kitten on it and the words "Have you seen me?" in crooked letters underneath. We put copies on all the nearby telephone poles and then we moped around the house waiting for the phone to ring.

I tried to tell Steven that the kitten might have left because it had another home, but he was hung up on the idea of accidents. When he spilled something he would say, "I dropped the glass *by accident,*" as if I were planning to blame him for it. So the kitten, in his mind, had wandered off *by accident,* which meant it really wanted to be with us but had been blown off course by some random force. I think he was intuitively grasping at the idea of fate, but in his mind the force of accidentalism was something to be struggled against, not something to be accepted. "The kitten accidentally didn't come home yesterday," he told Dawn on the phone Wednesday night. "But now I think it wants to, only what if it's lost?" He went to sleep worried, with his forehead creased and his hand gripping the side of his bed for stability.

On Thursday I lost my favorite sweater. It was a blue-green Shetland that I'd bought in the basement of Emporium's for six dollars. The color reminded me of the Bay, and since it was a men's large, it was big enough to fit over anything I wore. I had it tied around my waist as I walked to work from BART, and I remember that the wool on the sweater arms scratched my stomach with every step. It wasn't until I reached the office that I noticed it was gone.

A force field seemed to have surrounded me, making me repellent. It wasn't limited to the earring and the kitten and the sweater and Shantra's accursed manuscript, it was everything. My attention would wander for a moment, and in that lapse a possession of mine would vanish. I felt as though there were gaping rents in the fabric of the air into which things were falling. I tore my place apart looking for things—the book I was reading, my toothbrush, Steven's coat. On Friday I lost my lunch, literally lost it. I put it down somewhere in my office and then I couldn't find it. I was beginning to feel distinctly unglued. I found myself meditating on the word *lost,* which means both to have become disoriented or misplaced and to have failed to win.

In the meantime, I was becoming very good at Tetris. Shantra still hadn't called, even though I had left her two more messages. But I couldn't bring myself to say anything to Ralph, mainly because

I thought that if Shantra called, I could still find a way to get those play-off tickets.

Saturday, Steven was still depressed about the kitten, so we drove down to the batting cages and took turns struggling against thirty-mile-an-hour pitches. The only other people there were a father-and-son pair in the cage next to us. The father was a desiccated white man who kept barking orders at the kid: "Keep your head down, son. Follow through with your stroke. I said keep your head down, boy." The son was a stooped, big-shouldered kid, around twelve years old, who looked like he was having the worst day of his life. Steven was so distracted by the two of them that he almost got beaned by a pitch. While I was batting he stood outside the cage watching the older boy, his green eyes shaded with empathy.

When we'd each swung at fifty pitches, we sat down on top of a wooden picnic table and shared two packages of those peanut-butter-and-cracker sandwiches they sell in vending machines. A gaggle of brown sparrows gathered below us, waiting for a handout.

"What do animals think about?" Steven asked.

Tough question. I pried the top off one of the sandwiches and licked at the peanut butter, trying to come up with a good answer. Steven followed suit, his tongue lapping at the cracker like a kitten drinking milk. I'd taught him all my bad habits. On Steven, they were always charming.

"I guess they think about whatever it is they're doing," I told him. "What do you think they think about?"

He shrugged and continued licking. "I wish I knew what the kitten is thinking about," he said. He crumbled his soggy, denuded cracker into bits and tossed it to the sparrows jittering below.

"I think maybe he's thinking about his next destination," I said. "He always seemed to me like an adventurous kitten. After a few days in a nice comfortable house, his paws start to get itchy and he knows it's time to hit the road. You know, yesterday I thought I saw him down by the railroad tracks, trying to hitch a ride on a Southern Pacific freight train."

Steven was watching me, his eyes shining equal parts skepticism and belief. "I hope he doesn't go to Boston," he said. "It's too cold there for a little kitten."

Sometimes I didn't know who was comforting whom. Did he buy my fantasy about the rambling cat, or was he just pretending to because he knew I couldn't bear to see him sad?

It was late that night when Carolina called. Steven was asleep and I was sitting on the kitchen floor with a bottle of red wine braced between my knees. Melancholy is a full-body experience for me, a great weight that sucks me down off the furniture. In my darkest moments I always end up with my butt on the ground.

I was contemplating the week day by day and concluding that giving the Virgin back to Lisa had been a spectacular mistake. It was as if she had been an elemental force, like gravity, and when I evicted her everything in my life had wafted away like a loosed balloon. What in God's name was I going to do on Monday when Ralph asked for Shantra's manuscript? I took a slug from the wine. It was a cut-rate Zinfandel and it tasted clotty and mucoid, as if I were drinking a nosebleed. I began hacking at the kitchen linoleum with the corkscrew.

That was when the phone rang. I rushed to answer it before it could wake Steven and in the process knocked over the bottle of wine. Ha-ha, the Fates seemed to be screeching. Got you again.

"Hi, babe," Carolina said when I picked it up. She giggled.

"Hi. What's so funny?" I righted the wine bottle and threw a pile of dish towels on the spill.

"Nothing. I was just thinking of something funny I saw in a movie tonight."

"What was on?"

The towels had dammed up most of the wine, but one rivulet kept migrating toward the impenetrable territory under the stove. In desperation I sat on it.

"Nothing, so I went to a theater."

"Really? By yourself?"

"No, with a friend from work."

Wine was soaking into my pants. I stood up.

"You're lying, Mama. Is there a new man in your life?"

"No, there's no new man in my life." There was a squawk and a muffled sound as if her hand had gone over the mouthpiece.

I couldn't believe that my mother was drunk, had a guy over at her place, and was calling to chat. I could feel myself blushing, as if the two of them could somehow see me standing in the kitchen with a wet red splotch on my ass.

"What are you up to, Mama? When are you coming back out?"

"Tomorrow. Can you pick me up?"

"Sure. How's your trip been?" I wanted to ask her if she'd seen a doctor, but she didn't seem in the right mood.

"Fabulous!" There was another muffled palm-in-the-receiver sound. Then the palm came away with a gasp of air and I thought I heard a man's voice saying "Exactly the same."

"Why don't you give me your flight info," I said curtly.

She did, and then signed off, all pep and merriment. After I hung up the phone I took off my sopping pants and threw them into the bathtub to soak. There was a time when my predicament would have made me laugh. But not now. On top of everything else, I seemed to have lost my sense of humor.

🇸neezes (Simone)

Carolina came back from Boston with her eyes sparkling and invited everyone over to Lisa's house for dinner on Monday night. At five-thirty when I arrived she was whirling around the apartment like a festival dancer; the same steps over and over. To the mirror and back, to the dining room to straighten the table, to the kitchen to peer over Lisa's shoulder.

Lisa stood at the counter, her fingers pinching herbs whose meanings she never thought to contemplate: rosemary for memory, salt for tears, basil for death. These she rubbed into the oiled skins of chicken breasts until they were gleaming and flecked green.

In the living room, Steven was drawing pictures of spider people dangling in their webbed houses. Lisa had picked him up from school, and now his mother was running late. At six o'clock she called to say she had to stay late at work. "I'll be over as soon as I can," she said. I didn't speak to her; perhaps I should have. She told Lisa she would be over soon and not to forget that Steven didn't like dressing on his salad.

Knock knock. Steven looked at me; he knew it wasn't Julia. Then Carolina began her whirling again, a dust devil spinning in place. She was wearing her Mexican flounces—a red tiered skirt and a white ruffled blouse, cowboy boots, the whole illusion. She spun once to set it all in motion, and again just to make herself dizzy. "Lisa," she said. "Why don't you answer the door." So Lisa dried her hands and took off her apron and went to the door with her troubled nature showing on her face.

The man on the doorstep wore gray chinos, an Izod shirt, and a pair of white running shoes. Sweat shone on his naked head, and his body radiated hot, moist waves. He smiled a slinking, half-cocked smile and blinked a pair of watery green eyes at her.

"Hi, baby," he said and opened up his arms.

Lisa took a step back and looked.

"Daddy?" she asked, and he nodded, for it was he. Her paunchy, bald, and slippery daddy, just as she had wished for. She let him fold her in his arms, and he held her long enough for her to discover that time can flip sideways like pages of a book. In his embrace she was five years old again. Too young to talk back. Too young to ask questions.

After a moment she grew shy and stood back, not knowing what to say. He didn't know either, since he wasn't sure which daughter he was addressing. Carolina was too busy preening and flirting to say the proper thing, so I came and stood next to Lisa and made the introductions—Bill to his youngest daughter, daughter to father, and then I called Steven over so he could meet his grandpa.

After a time Carolina and Lisa steered him into the living room while Steven and I tagged along behind. He sat on the couch with his wife and daughter on either side of him and threw his arms wide to squeeze them to his chest. "Oh, I missed my girls," he said. Over their shoulders his eyes met mine and I saw recognition there. He knew I'd been watching him since the night he blew away, tracing him through his switchbacks and evasions. He knew I saw right through him.

"Well, Simone, you're a picture," he said. "You look exactly the same as you did when I first met you. I bet your hair's still black as midnight under all that silver hairspray."

"She's a vampire, she doesn't age," Carolina rushed in as I patted the hair piled on my head. It was clear she was going to be doting and simpering all night long. If he had been the sun, she couldn't have done more to avoid looking at him straight on.

They all began talking at once. Carolina wanted to reveal how Bill had left a message on her answering machine in Boston and she'd flown back to see him. "We spent a few evenings together and it was like old times," she told Lisa. "We laughed and laughed, just like we used to. I even called you and Julie on the phone so he could listen in and hear your voices. And that's when he decided to come out and see you for himself. He wanted to surprise you."

Then Lisa had to say that she had been surprised. Her cheeks were flushed with the heat of his return and she blushed every time she spoke. She wanted to tell him about her wish, but she was afraid that if she spoke the words, he would disappear in a puff of smoke. So she kept quiet and the wish became one more unspoken thing between them. Later in the evening I saw her go to her bedroom and let the Virgin out of her metal box.

While the three of them were cooing and smiling, Steven crept close to me and leaned against my chair. If he had been a cat, he would have put his ears back and gone to lurk under the bed.

He could see that the man with the bald head and the creased green eyes held the present by the corners and was getting ready to shake it out. He didn't think he was going to like seeing it all go flying.

And then there was the matter of the ghosts. It seemed that Bill wasn't traveling alone. There were two men with him and they were wandering about the room looking at Lisa's knickknacks. They were young, with dark skin and hair, and they were dressed in soldier green. When they saw Steven staring at them, they scowled and stuck out their tongues. And all this time Lisa and Carolina were talking over each other about their amazement.

Finally it came time for Bill to offer some explanations. Lisa had brought him a Coke, and he took an ice cube from the glass and swirled it around his mouth.

"I found your mother in the phone book," he told Lisa. "It was pure luck."

"How did you know she would still be there?" Lisa asked.

Not, why were you looking for her after all this time? Not, what made you think she would be glad to see you?

"Didn't. It was a whim, really. I was just thumbing through the white pages in my hotel room. It had been a long time since I was in Massachusetts, and I was just sitting there with this book in my hands, thinking of all the names of people I used to know and wondering if they were in there. I've spent a lot of time in phone booths over the years, just standing there waiting for a call. And to amuse myself I sometimes look up names, you know, stupid stuff. Is there anyone whose last name is Shit? You'd be amazed what you can find in the phone book. I once found someone named Greene Booger. Anyway, Bill Harris is kind of a common name, so I usually look myself up wherever I am and see if I'm already there. And I was doing that last week when I found Carolina. She was right where I should have been, after Bert Harris and before Catherine Harris. And so I rang her up."

"And to think I could have missed him," Carolina said. "It's a good thing I have an answering machine."

And so on, until dinnertime. Lisa served her chicken breasts and baby potatoes as if they were cakes she had just cooked up in her Betty Crocker oven. I remembered eating those little white mounds of carefully presented, lightbulb-cooked dough, and so did Carolina. But where was Bill when six-year-old Lisa was first baking cakes? I didn't need to ask; I already knew. But I did anyway because someone had to.

"Aren't you going to tell us where you've been all these years?" I said when the meal was finished.

He leaned back in his chair with his hands on the bloat of his stomach. "All over," he said. "Wherever business took me. New York, Detroit, Miami, New Orleans, San Diego. I spent a lot of time in Latin America, too. Mexico, Bolivia, Nicaragua, Honduras, El Salvador, Colombia, Panama, Costa Rica, Peru. Maybe that's why me and Carolina get along so well these days. We've got more in common."

"Carolina's never been to those places," I said. What the two had in common was a habit of slipping out of the truth as if it were last year's snakeskin. I could see him warming up now, a cricket rubbing his legs together before the song begins.

"Yes, but it's in her blood! Carolina can salsa!" Bill said and stood up to grab his wife by the wrists. He twittered out a snatch of samba and shook his hips while Carolina spun and snapped her fingers. The two ghosts laughed and shook their heads, and then one stuck out his stomach and lurched around the room satirically. Steven watched them like a wolf, his green eyes steady. Lisa and Carolina should have prayed for such clear vision.

"Sheesh, it's hot in here," Bill said when he was through dancing. "How about walking off some of this dinner?"

The man was feeling confined already. He kept mopping his glossy forehead with a handkerchief until we were all out the door and striding through the foggy night. Then the pollen got to him and he began sneezing. Loud, abrasive sneezes that turned the heads of passersby. "You got too many damn plants around here," he said between blasts. "I'm going to sneeze my brains out onto the sidewalk."

The only thing that seemed to stanch the sneezes was storytelling. So he talked about his travels, recounting nights of drinking and knife fights until his wife and daughter were woozy with the romance of this man who had lived among men in a haze of liquor, slang, and blood. Then he talked about a carnival in Bolivia where the main attraction was a tiny snake charmer. He was reminded of her by Steven, he said, because she was about Steven's age, a tiny dark-eyed wisp of a thing. They kept her in a wagon painted on the outside with pictures of fire-eyed reptiles. But the inside, Bill said, was more frightening than any painting. Inside, the wagon was filled with slithering, writhing snakes piled on top of one another like old clothes. The little girl sat among them eating her dinner, the picture of insouciance, as the snakes looped around and over her body and draped themselves in her hair.

"Children aren't children over there," Bill observed. "They'll stay up all night selling crafts and chewing gum in the town square and then work all day in the markets. Once I found them living in the jungle like monkeys."

The moon was at half-light and the air was damp as a dish towel. We fluttered around him like starlings as he talked, even me, who knew better.

"It was in the jungle of a country that had been split by civil war," he went on. "The jungle was a dangerous place, especially for bystanders. The bushes hid three different armies, none of whom wore uniforms. So you can imagine how it was to walk through this wet green place; it was like swimming through a murky sea that was filled with sharks. I was so afraid just walking that my knees were trembling. And then I heard something rustle. And a human sound, a murmur.

"I stood so still my heart stopped beating, waiting for the bullets to rip me into pieces. And then I thought to look up. There was about a half dozen of them sitting in the branches of the trees overhead. They were all different ages—some teenagers, others no more than four or five. They were too scared to move and I was, too, so we stared at each other until I found my voice. I told them I wasn't a soldier, I was just a man, lost in the woods. So an older one, a girl of about fourteen who seemed to be mother of them all, told me their story. I had to climb up into the tree to talk to them, which isn't so easy for an old man, although I was younger then. I sat perched on a branch, holding on to the tree skin for dear life and praying the snakes would stay away.

"It seems that they were from a nearby village that had been attacked by one of the armies. They never knew if it was rebels or government; it didn't much matter. Raids were frequent on both sides, and when they came the women and children would run into the jungle to wait while the men fought. But this time the women didn't run fast enough, and only the children made it to the forest. The soldiers killed everyone and burned the village to the ground.

So the children stayed in the jungle and lived in the trees, eating mangoes and bananas and birds they killed with slingshots. They were like birds themselves—so afraid of the war that they wouldn't put their feet on the ground."

"What happened to them?" Steven said.

Bill shrugged. "Who knows? For all I know, they're still there."

Those weren't the first or the last children you abandoned, I wanted to say, but I held my tongue. It would all come out in its own time. Even as he thought he was clothing himself in stories, he was stripping himself naked.

Then Lisa turned and looked at him as if he had just arrived. Her expression seemed to say, Who is this bald man, this sneezing, storytelling man, this man who slunk out in the middle of the night and rode away on the wind to foreign lands? Was this the man I wished for? Her curiosity was a bit late in arriving, but it was there at last and Bill saw it.

"I suppose you're wondering why I went away," he said. "Maybe I should explain what I've been doing."

And then as a prologue he began to sneeze.

"It all happened by chance really," he said, and I thought, This is how he makes twenty-two years of injury disappear. A shrug of the shoulders, a moist-eyed confession. I'd seen him narrate his way out of trouble before. Still, I kept my mouth shut and let him talk. "I hadn't ever thought about leaving," he continued. "But every man has a weakness, and my weakness is for flying."

It's true Bill had always loved the queasy, upside-down sensation of turbulence and the bright forgiving eye of the open sky. He fell in love with the sky when he was only sixteen and started lurking around airfields, watching landings and volunteering to help the pilots wax their wings. After a time, a few of them took pity on him and let him ride along. They liked his eagerness and his bravado, and bit by bit they taught him how to fly.

In those days flying was a rugged venture, and the men who taught him thought nothing of taking off from a cow pasture and touching down on a frozen lake. They didn't need radios or runway lights, and they taught Bill to delight in rough weather and the thrill of running just below the clouds. He earned his pilot's license in two years, and when he could wrangle a little flying time he practiced daredevil tricks, taking the plane out over the ocean and swooping so low that wave-spray spattered the windshield.

"I think it has to do with the elements," he said now. "Earth, fire, water, air. We live on earth; the earth is our home element, and there isn't a man alive who doesn't love the smell of soil and the feeling of solid ground. But there's something about the other elements that pulls you to them, the way men are pulled to women and women to men. If you've ever watched a fire burning, you know what I mean. It seems that if you only knew how to walk through one of those doorways of flame, you'd find yourself in a fire-land where the trees throw off sparks instead of leaves. I've felt that way about water, too. When I lived in South America I'd go scuba diving and sometimes I'd find myself in a kind of blue cathedral, with beams of light slicing down and fish spiraling around me like angels. It felt like I'd come to a forbidden place, a place from which I could never go home.

"But the air was my element. It dissolved me into what felt like pure spirit—the most vigorous chilling-bright essence of aliveness I could ever be. Just to be up there in the sky, to *be* sky. Clouds are walls that turn into doorways when you dart through them, and in that misty alley you can lose everything that moors you to the earth, even your sense of which way is down."

When war broke out in Korea, he joined the navy. He told the recruiter he was game to fly top cover, bombing missions, reconnaissance, anything, but instead of making him a pilot, the navy sent him to sea. He spent the whole war on an aircraft carrier, certain that his flight skills were rusting in the salt breeze. Whenever a jet lifted off, he felt like a jilted lover watching his girl walk down the aisle.

After the war ended, he took his bitterness home with him. He spurned the little airports where he used to fly and bounced from one line of work to another, never finding anything that suited him. He painted houses, sold insurance for a while, and after he was married he went into business with some friends from high school fencing stolen televisions and cars. And on Tuesdays and Thursdays he made a little run around the city, picking up the protection money the bars paid the police department. He was ashamed that he couldn't tell his daughters what he did for a living, but he didn't know what he wanted to do instead. So he simply waited for something to change. All the while the sky was inside him, a deep breath waiting to get out.

One afternoon he went into a bar called Paddy's Lunch and found the devil sitting on a bar stool with a cigarette in one hand and a bottle of Rolling Rock in the other. This devil's name was Terence Haskins, and he was a gap-toothed, freckly fellow who had served with Bill on the aircraft carrier in Korea. Haskins had been a pilot before the war as well, and the two of them used to pal around during their off-hours, swapping tales of airborne bravado.

"You still flying?" Haskins said after they had slapped each other on the back and resurrected a few long-forgotten nicknames. Bill shook his head, shrugged, explained about having a family to support. "But I sure would give anything to get in a plane again," he said.

"Anything?" Haskins asked.

It seems that Haskins was a smuggler, carrying planeloads of marijuana into Miami and Galveston from South America and the Caribbean. There was plenty of work to go around, he said, and since Bill was an old buddy from the war, he was willing to help him get started in the business. "Tell you what I'm gonna do, my friend," Haskins said. "I'm gonna lend you my plane while I'm on vacation in Puerto Rico. I'll introduce you to the people you need to know, and by the time I get back, you'll have earned enough to buy yourself a plane of your own."

The two men shook on it and raised their bottles to having the last laugh on those golden-haired navy pilots who were now hauling bulky jetliners from one end of the country to the other. Even as he drank to his own sky blue future, Bill knew what kind of deal he had made. "But," he told us, "you never know how good it feels to sell your soul until you've done it. Your soul feels so heavy and worthless, like an old Chevy engine you've been hauling around for years waiting to find the right body to stick it in. Any offer you get seems like the deal of a lifetime, and here's the devil not only willing to take it off your hands, but offering you your heart's desire in exchange."

He cast an eye at Lisa, to see if she disapproved of her drug-running daddy. "This was the sixties, honey," he said. "I mean, we didn't think about drugs in the same way back then. To me it was just a new kind of opportunity, no different from what I did before.

Just a little more money and a lot more fun." He needn't have worried. Lisa had fallen headlong for this tale of his pirate antics. She listened with her lips parted, a baby bird waiting to be fed.

Bill took her hand. "I was only planning to be gone for a couple of weeks," he said. "I thought I could fly a few times, make some money, and come back with flowers and presents and a plane of my own to take my girls for rides in. I should have told you where I was going, but I thought it might be best if no one knew where I was going. I had just moved a load of hot TVs, and the store I sold them to was raided. Better to just disappear for a few weeks, I told myself. And that's what I did."

But of course it didn't work out that way. Bill wasn't as deft a pilot as he thought, or maybe he was just out of practice. He made it through the first two runs, but on his third he found himself taking off from a narrow, potholed runway in the Colombian jungle, the plane overloaded with fumy cargo. Just as he lifted the plane's nose off the ground, one of his wheels sank into the mud, pulling him hard to the right. When he tried to pull back to center, his wingtip snagged in the vines hanging over the airstrip, and the next thing he knew he was buzzing through the underbrush, tossing up a spray of foliage. By the time he came to a stop, Haskins's white Piper was missing both wings. It took him three weeks to find a way back to Miami.

Replacing Haskins's plane took nearly all the money he'd stowed away, and then he had to charm his new employers into lending him a plane he could use himself. He worked a little longer and a little harder, and after a year had passed, he had saved enough money to buy himself a Piper of his own. He named her *Demon* after his old friend Terence Haskins.

But by then he was hooked. He liked the long flights over water, and he liked coming in low, flying in the nap of the earth where the radar couldn't find him. He was caught up in the writhing currents of the air, and there seemed no reason ever to touch down. "I stayed away until I could have some profit to bring home," he told us. "And I guess it's that old story—the longer I stayed away, the easier it was to keep staying."

Listening to Bill talk, I thought of an old nursery rhyme I'd learned in school: "For want of a nail, the shoe was lost. For want of a shoe, the horse was lost. For want of a horse, the rider was lost. For want of a rider, the battle was lost." For want of a plane, the family was lost. For want of a family, the man was lost.

"It wasn't that I didn't miss you," he said to Lisa and Carolina. "You know I did; I thought about you all the time. Every little girl I saw reminded me of my girls back home. But after a few years passed I thought Carolina would have remarried and you girls would have a new life and a new daddy, and if I came back it would just mess everything up. How was I to know that a beautiful woman like Carolina wouldn't marry again? God, it's too hard sometimes having a memory for all the stupid things you've done in your life. If I could change it, I would, but the past is gone forever. I never found a thing in the air I couldn't have found with my own family. Every time I landed it was with a thud and a heartbreak."

I've heard better lines in country music. But once he'd hit this maudlin note, the story wrapped up quickly. He stopped smuggling marijuana in 1975 and lived on his savings in Mexico and Brazil. In the eighties he came out of retirement to join a new enterprise that involved flying guns and cocaine in and out of Costa Rica. When that grew too dangerous, he sold his plane and started wandering again. "I've been circling and circling, waiting to get cleared for landing," he said. "It's only now that I'm with you again that I feel I'm on the ground. Now I remember how elemental the earth is, the earth of my own family. I know that I can't ever get back the years I lost when I left you, but Carolina, I'd like to be your husband again, and Lisa, I'd like to be your daddy."

$\mathscr{F}$ light   (Julia)

I wasn't as brave as I planned to be. On Monday I cowered and scurried about all day, until Ralph came in at five-fifteen and asked if the manuscript was ready.

I steeled myself. "I lost it."

Ralph said, "Come again?"

I didn't answer him. It was painful enough once; I wasn't going to say it twice.

"You lost it?" Ralph said. Why do people always ask you to repeat things they've heard perfectly well? "What the fuck are you talking about?"

I told him. He listened, nodding his head vigorously as if the whole thing confirmed everything he had always known about me. "It wouldn't have happened if you hadn't knocked over the flowers by my desk," I finished.

"I wouldn't have knocked them over if you hadn't put them there, Julia. I want you to write down, 'I accept responsibility for my actions.' Write it down now. Write it down!"

If anyone had been taking nominations for person most likely to spontaneously combust, I would have known whom to suggest. Ralph was turning crimson. "Is there any fuck-up you're not capable of?" he shrilled. "Is there any colossal error that's beyond the grasp of your incompetence? Just tell me, in your whole pathetic, dim-witted life, is there any cretinous move you *haven't* made?"

"I don't need this," I said, surprising myself. It was a murmur I had meant to make under my breath. The knots in my shoulders were killing me.

"*You* don't need this? What about me? I have really tried to be patient with you, Julia, but I've fucking had it. Do you know how many hours it's going to take to reconstruct that manuscript? Your next job better be a high-paying one, because you owe me. You owe me, Julia!"

"Shut up!" I shouted. I was afraid he was going into cardiac arrest, and I wasn't looking forward to the ethical dilemma I would have to face if he needed mouth-to-mouth resuscitation. "You're spitting on me and you have bad breath!" I took a shaky breath, remembering that I had promised Steven those play-off tickets. "Don't yell at me. It's . . ." I floundered and trailed off. "It's negative languaging."

"Negative languaging? You don't want negative languaging? Then let me state it in the affirmative for you: *You're fired.*"

It took me a moment to grasp what it was he was saying, but when I did, my tongue loosened. "Wiping Shantra's book off the face of the planet would be doing humanity a service," I said. "It *doesn't work!* None of these books work! You know how I know? Because if affirmations and spirit guides and all that other crap worked, you wouldn't be such a complete asshole."

Ralph's heavy eyelids lowered a fraction, cloaking the tops of his irises.

"That kind of thinking will take you far, Julia," he said with a reptilian smirk. "Now pack up your desk and get the fuck out."

It was twilight when I left the office. The clouds were low and pink, and as I walked to the BART station, I imagined unfolding the crimped, painful wings beneath my shoulder blades and flapping into the sky. I was free. I cocked my head back and gazed at the flaming clouds, and in spite of everything, I had to smile. I was fucking free from Enhancement Press.

A moment later I heard someone running behind me and felt a sharp tug on the strap of my purse. I whirled and found my face in a man's chest. It smelled of hot adrenaline and beer.

I clenched my fist around my purse, and the man leaned back and pulled at the strap like a dog playing tug-of-war with a leash. To my astonishment, I began to yell and then to beat at the mugger's head with my free hand. The purse strap was wrapped around my wrist, and as he pulled, it chafed the skin. I had time to notice this and even to think that it felt like that old childhood prank: Indian Sunburn. Time had flattened into a series of squashed, slow moments.

Then, finally, I saw someone running toward us in fleet-footed cheetah strides. "Help! I'm being mugged!" I shouted and kept beating at the purse-snatcher. He dug his nails into the pulse point of my wrist, trying to pry the strap out of my hand.

Then the rescuer was standing in front of me with a gun in his hand. "Step back, you crazy bitch," he said.

I let go of the strap. Time shook itself and resumed. In an instant the two men had climbed into a car at the end of the street and driven away. I stood there with my hands empty and my wrist flaming and I began to cry.

The police gave me a ride home and used the opportunity to warn me not to sleep at my apartment that night since the muggers had both my house keys and my address. They also, it turned out, had my car, because when we pulled up in front of my building, I saw that my little blue Honda was missing from its usual spot out front. The sight of the empty parking place made me start sniffling again, and the two officers crossed their arms and affected a look of extreme world-weariness.

"These guys are professionals," one said and offered to come up to make sure no one was in my apartment. I got a spare key from my landlord and the police took big leathery strides through all the rooms, jangling keys and handcuffs with every step. Their presence was so overbearing that I was relieved when they finally left.

As soon as they were gone, I drew the safety chain across the door and lay down on my bed. I was woozy from adrenaline, and every time I turned my head, kaleidoscope fragments maundered across my vision. But when I shut my eyes, images of the struggle kept returning. The man who was supposed to help me had pointed a gun at me. I had looked at him with my face open and trusting and he had pointed a gun at me. I felt very small and miserable.

I lay there feeling sorry for myself for a while and then I remembered that I was supposed to be at Lisa's hours ago. They were probably wondering what the hell had happened to me. But when I called Lisa's apartment, all I got was the answering machine. I didn't want to sound too alarming in case Steven heard the message, so I ummed and ahhed and finally ended up saying only that my purse had been stolen, which made it sound as if it hadn't necessarily been stolen from my person. But then I asked if Steven could spend the night there since it was late and I didn't feel safe having him at home until I'd changed the locks. That, I realized, probably sounded quite alarming, but there was nothing I could do about it once I'd said it, so I merely added that I was going to go get something to eat and not to worry if I wasn't here when they called back.

Once I was on my feet, I knew I had to get out of the apartment. It was too creepy to sit there going over what had happened and waiting for the sound of my muggers tugging at the door. I needed to go out and have a drink and then see if I could spend the night at Dawn's. Outside, the wind had risen, ever so slightly. I could hear it rattling the blinds.

I found a twenty-dollar bill I had stowed in my desk for emergencies and then changed into a pair of black leggings and a rayon minidress splashed with yellow and purple pansies. Before I left, I put a note on the door that I hoped would scare away any thieves: BUTCH—HANK AND I ARE DOWNSTAIRS. WE'LL BE BACK IN FIVE MINUTES.

My bicycle was chained to the back steps, covered with cobwebs. I brushed it off and rode it to a nearby café. It was an arty little place located in a converted warehouse and decorated with enormous, abstract canvases. Lisa used to work there, so I knew both of the waitresses on duty: Melissa, a chunky, foul-mouthed art student, and Janine, who was pale and English and very serious.

"You would not believe the day I've had," I told them and proceeded to recount my tale of woe. They squealed and swore at all the dramatic parts, and then they brought me two free glasses of wine. By the time I'd drunk them both and had some dinner, I was beginning to feel a little better. I had lived to tell the tale, after all. I leaned back in my chair and looked around the room.

A young man with dark eyes and a closely kept goatee was reading and drinking tea in the corner. At first I was just trying to figure out what he was reading, but once I started looking at him, I had to admit that he was easy on the eyes. He had thick black hair and brown, almost penny-colored skin. When he caught me looking at him, he smiled. His smile lasted long enough to acknowledge that our eyes had met, and a second longer. Then he went back to reading.

Melissa brought me my third glass of wine. "Do you need a place to stay tonight?" she asked, and then noticed I was still looking at the man in the corner. "Or have you already picked out the bed you want to climb into?"

I laughed and shook my head. "My days of café conquests are long over," I told her. "I think I'm going to stay at my friend Dawn's."

Still, after she cleared my plate, I found myself imagining how it would be to lie in the arms of the man in the corner. It had been a long time since anyone had been really tender with me. As I watched him, imagining the feel of his hands stroking my forehead, he looked up and met my eyes. Then he smiled and went back to reading. Looked up quickly, saw I was still staring, and went back to reading. Now it was my turn to look away, so I pretended to be studying the green-and-burnt-orange abstraction hanging on the opposite wall. Out of the corner of my eye I could see his head lift, and when I glanced at him, he had his chin resting in his hand and was giving me a long, uncomplicated look.

Then Janine came by and sat down and asked me what I was going to do now that I was unemployed, and so I had to disengage from the game at its most interesting point and reexamine my depressing future.

"Maybe you could work here," Janine said. "I think Olaf is hiring."

"I don't want to wait tables," I said and then realized how peevish that sounded. "I really want to be home in the evenings because of Steven."

So then we had to go through all my options one by one. I would have preferred not to think about it for a while, but Janine insisted. "You've got a lot to do," she said, slapping the table with her pale little hand. Once we'd exhausted the topic of my job hunt, she marched me through all the other tasks I had ahead of me: applying for a new driver's license, changing the locks at my apartment, reporting my stolen car to the insurance company. Thanks to the wine, I had been feeling fairly numb, but by the time she was done giving me advice, I was despondent again.

I was saved by a large party of high-school kids who had come in to get high on black coffee and free refills. Janine went to take their order and a minute later I looked up to find the man from the table in the corner gripping the back of the chair I had been using as a footrest.

"Hi," he said. "Can I join you?"

"Sure." I slid my feet off the chair. "I was just getting tired of my own company."

It's embarrassing to report the things you say when you're flirting because most of them sound like they were written for soap operas. He told me his name was Gabriel and I told him my name was Julia and then, to keep the conversation going, I asked him what it was he had been reading. He sauntered back to his table and came back with a book called *Abandonment to Divine Providence*. The title gave me immediate misgivings since it sounded an awful lot like something I would have to proofread at my now ex-job.

"The writing's very beautiful," he said as I looked at the cover. "But I hate it. I don't agree with it at all."

I thumbed through it and felt my interest in Gabriel snuffed out with every page. I couldn't get much of a sense of what it was about, but the pages were heavily seasoned with the words *God* and *Christ*. Another seeker, I thought darkly. Spare me.

I handed the book back to him with a little shrug, not knowing how to get him to take his religious propaganda back to his own table. By now he was sitting down, so unseating him would take a little time.

"I'm reading it for school," he explained. "I'm at the Jesuit school, up on the hill."

"Are you going to be a priest?" My interest flickered on again. I'd heard intriguing rumors about the bedroom antics of divinity students.

"I was going to be a priest," he said, "but now I'm not so sure. I'm having a crisis of faith."

He smiled as he made this last remark and shrugged. It was a revealing, openhearted smile, and I momentarily forgave him for being a seeker. "What's your crisis?" I asked.

"I'm not sure I believe in divine providence. I think it's all up to us. This guy"—he tapped the cover of his book with one finger—"says that the events of every moment are stamped by the will of God. But that leads to some disturbing conclusions about God's will. Does He—or She—will AIDS? Or poverty?" He smiled and shrugged again, and I saw that it was a characteristic gesture, a gesture that said, Let's not take any of this too seriously. "I'm not the first person to be tripped up by this problem," he said. "In fact I think I'm coming to it pretty late in life. I bet you've already discarded religion."

"I never was religious," I said. "But I don't believe in free will, either."

"Why not?"

"It's logically impossible. Everything you do was caused by something else that was caused by something else that was caused by something else, all the way back to the beginning of time. It's a domino effect—there's no room for free will to get a word in edgewise." It was a little embarrassing to be trotting out an argument from Introduction to Philosophy while sitting in an arty café drinking white wine. But Gabriel was on the trail of something, and I was on the trail of Gabriel. As he listened to me, he had his chin raised a little, like a dog that stops midstride to catch a familiar scent.

"But if there's no free will, how do you have moral responsibility?" he asked. "If a murder was predetermined, is the murderer morally absolved? Are any of us responsible for anything we do or can we blame it on destiny and dysfunctional families?"

"We're each responsible for our fate because it's ours," I said. "The way you're responsible for people in your family even though you didn't choose them."

He smiled at that and rested his forearms on the table, with his hands clasped together. He had nice hands, with long, blunt fingers and agile wrists emerging from the cuffs of his sweater. The sweater was blue Shetland wool, with a familiar faded yellow streak on one sleeve. I reached across the table to touch it.

"I have a sweater just like that," I told him. "Or I did, until it mysteriously disappeared." I pretended to be looking at him suspiciously, although it wasn't all pretend.

"I stole it," he said. "Forgive me, it wasn't my fault. I was fated to do it. Here, I'll give it back."

He pulled the sweater over his head and handed it to me. Now he was flirting recklessly. The removal of the sweater had tousled his hair, and the tank top he was wearing underneath revealed him to have hard, well-defined shoulders and biceps and a scribbling of black hair on his upper chest.

I need to call Steven, I thought. I hadn't talked to him since dropping him off at school that morning. He was probably wondering what was going on.

"Excuse me," I said to Gabriel. "I have to make a call."

"There you are," Lisa said when she answered the phone. "Where have you been? You won't believe what's happened."

"What? Is Steven okay?"

"He's fine—it's nothing bad. But guess what?"

"What?"

"Daddy's here."

"What?"

"He came tonight. Mama brought him back from Boston. He's still here; they went to bed. *He's sleeping in Mama's room.*" Lisa sounded giddy, and a bit perplexed. "It's him, Julia. He came back, the way we wished. It worked. You won't believe it until you see him."

I put my forehead down on the pay phone's square black top and asked myself why I never seemed to be in the right place at the right time. "Did you tell him why I wasn't there?"

"Probably." Her voice was vague. "I'm not sure it came up. We were kind of tired when we got your message."

"But why didn't you call and tell me he was there?"

"There was a lot going on, Julia. I thought you were coming over."

"I got held up. I would have tried a little harder if I'd known."

I could hear her take a deep breath and decide to be magnanimous. She could afford to after all; she'd seen him and I hadn't. "He's still here. It's no big deal, you'll see him tomorrow."

Drop it, I told myself. Act your age. "What's he like?"

"He's bald," Lisa answered and chuckled. "He has hay fever. He seems kind of shy. I think he's a nice man, you'll like him."

"I can't believe this."

"It's kind of frightening," Lisa said. "Do you realize what the implications are? We could get anything we want. I want a new car, all I have to do is lock the Virgin Mary in a box and presto, one appears. I could get Mitch back."

"Maybe it's just a coincidence," I said. "Maybe he was going to come back anyway."

"He's not what I expected, but I don't know what I expected. He's magnetic. He tells stories. I can't wait to see what you think. Come over in the morning, okay? Can you take the day off?"

"That won't be any problem," I said dryly. "Can I talk to Steven?"

"He's asleep. I just went in to check on him."

"Oh." I felt wistful. I wanted to hear Steven's voice. "I'll see you tomorrow then."

"See you tomorrow."

When I came back to my table, Gabriel was still sitting there, reading his creepy religious book.

"I have to go," I told him. "I've just had some unsettling news."

"Are you okay?"

I nodded and handed him back the sweater, which I had tied around my waist.

"Keep it," he said. "Give it to me next time you see me."

"Thanks," I said. I'd forgotten to bring a jacket and I was in for a cold ride home.

I was a little unsteady as I pedaled away from the café. My whole body was blooming emotion, but the emotion didn't seem to have a name. My father! My father was sleeping in Lisa's guest room. But it was impossible. My father wasn't a man who did things like sleep and sneeze; he was an absence, a mystery. And yet Lisa was insisting that he was a man. A bald man with hay fever, she'd said, who was somehow also the man who used to sit with me on the front porch and tell me stories about the neighborhood. I shook my head to rattle it all into place and nearly toppled over.

When I'd righted myself, I cut down a side street and set my course along the yellow divider in the middle of the street. I was a little drunk and it made me brazen. I pedaled faster and bent my head down to watch my tires overtake the pavement. I knew it was dangerous not to pay attention to where I was going, but I enjoyed the danger. When I was tired of looking at the gray-violet asphalt, I tilted my head back to watch the sky. It ran above me, a blue river banked by green foliage. I could see a corner of the moon.

The more I pedaled, the madder I got. It wasn't fixed on any particular thing, I was just mad. Mad at Ralph, mad at the thugs who had mugged me, mad at the police for being too officious, and Janine for being too helpful, mad at Lisa for being smug, and at my father, my impossible father, for having a cozy dinner with the rest of my family while I was being insulted, fired, and robbed at gunpoint. I growled and gnashed my teeth and pedaled as if I were kicking something.

I still had a little while before Dawn would be home from work, so I pedaled to the top of the ridge high above campus, going as

fast and as far as my furious knees would take me. When I was pant-
ing and glazed with sweat, I perched myself at the top of the hill
and coasted down.

I swooped like a hawk, and the wings between my shoulders
shook off their carapaces and fanned the air. Houses and cars blurred
into shadows. The wind sang in my ears. I pedaled, even though
the wheels were already spinning faster than I could move them. Up
ahead, the signal turned yellow, red.

My fingers felt for the brakes, but hesitated. I remembered
walking with my father, listening to Kenny control the traffic light.

"Come on, red light," I shouted as I sped forward. "Come on,
red light, turn green. The cars are waiting." I rolled toward it,
unstoppable. The red light glowered at me like a cyclops, daring me
forward. I took my hands off the brakes, and then off the handlebars. *Come on, red light, turn green. The cars is waitin'.*

The light winked green just as I sailed into the intersection. At
the same time, a car coming from the opposite direction suddenly
decided to go left. I swerved around its hood, skidding and then
falling. As I fell I heard the squeal of brakes, the crunch of my
bicycle under the tire, and then a car motor rumbling near my head.
I rolled and felt the asphalt scrape away the skin on my shoulder
and hip. A car door slammed.

"Jesus Christ. Why weren't you wearing a light?"

A man stood over me, his hands hovering in the air in an uncom-
pleted gesture. I sat up.

"Are you okay?"

"I think so." My body was trying to say something, but I couldn't
figure out what. I felt an ache in one knee, and stinging where the
ground had scrubbed my flesh. There was a pain somewhere else.
I located it when I stood up: my ankle.

The man was already walking back to his car. "Are you sure you're okay?" He sat down in the driver's seat with his feet on the pavement and waited for me to say something.

"I think so." I leaned against the hood of his car and looked at my ankle. It still looked like my ankle and I could rotate it okay.

The man rubbed his forearm across his forehead. "Man oh man, this is some night. You know what? I'm late and I'm lost. I'm driving around I don't know where and I run over some girl's bicycle."

"Where are you trying to go?" I said. I looked down at my bicycle, pinned by his front tire. The handlebars hung away like a broken neck.

"I'm just trying to get back to the city."

"You're going in the wrong direction," I said. "You want to be heading west."

"Really? I guess I'm totally turned around. Isn't this University?"

So then I found myself giving directions to the freeway, while the man who had run over my bicycle nodded and parroted them back to me. When I was done, he swung his legs into his car and shut the door. "Thanks a lot, you're a godsend," he said as he started the ignition. "I'm glad everything turned out okay." Then he backed his car off the carcass of my bicycle and drove away.

When he was gone I leaned down and picked up my bike. The main shaft was bent and one arm of the pedals had been sheared off. I wheeled it back to the curb and stood there looking at it. I had two dollars in my pocket, my ankle hurt, and Dawn lived on the other side of town. "I am having," I said to the empty air, "a really, really terrible day."

I was still staring at my shattered bicycle when I heard a car pull up behind me and someone get out. "Julia?" a voice said. "Is that you?"

I whirled around, my hands rolling themselves into fists. "Stay right there!" I yelled.

"It's okay, it's just me. Gabriel, from the café."

He was still in his tank top and he had his palms raised in a gesture of weaponlessness. I felt my face crumpling and bit my lip so I wouldn't start to cry. "What are you doing here?" I asked after a moment.

"I live near here. I was driving home when I saw you. Are you all right?"

Something was tugging at the top of my head, stretching my body like a long sinew. My face was a flat, teetering sunflower, balanced on a thin peony stem of neck. Below, my intestines twirled around each other like ribbon candy.

"Did you get in an accident?" he prompted.

An accident, yes indeed. From the top of my elongated neck, I looked down at Gabriel: a nice man with brown arms who had let me have my sweater back. I would have told him everything, if only I could have found the words.

"I'm sorry," I said instead. "But I guess I don't remember."

$\mathcal{M}$onsters   (Simone)

They swallowed his story as if it were pudding and then they licked their lips and asked for more. When I saw them nodding their heads during his explanation, I nearly broke my own rules against interfering. You didn't need perfect pitch to hear the false notes.

I knew he was lying because I'd been watching him. I watched him when he went out the door those many years ago and I've been watching him ever since. For some reason Fate has chosen me to be his audience. It seems a funny pairing given how little we have to say to each other in the waking present. But the old girl loves nothing more than odd couples.

His story came to me in fragments—a glimpse midway through a dream, a card upturned in the tarot deck, a voice whispering when I closed my eyes. Sometimes I'd be scrying in a tin of water, and there he'd be, as pervasive as your least favorite TV advertisement. But I knew how to stitch it all together. I knew how the man operated.

If there was one note of truth to the tale he told Lisa and Carolina, it was that he loved nothing more than being out of his element. He was like a child on a merry-go-round: The dizzier he got, the happier he was. Especially when it came to women.

Did they really think he spent all those years alone, pining for his family? Carolina at least should know better. Bill Harris is a man who lives through women. And like all adventurers, he sought the strange because he was afraid to know his own strangeness. Why else would he have tracked down Carolina after all these years, looking her up in the phone book under the pretense of looking for himself? On a round planet, the farthest point from home is home.

Our lives are not so varied. We reweave the same patterns over and over with only cosmetic deviations. The universe is symmetrical; nothing happens only once. This is the key to everything: The future will follow the same laws as the past.

When he was seventeen he fell for a girl who had six toes on her right foot. He spied her at Fenway Park, waiting in line for bleacher tickets. She wore sandals and had painted all eleven toenails a color called Pink Pearl. Bill couldn't stop staring at them. That extra toe was like a canape to him, sprouting so delicious from the base of the big toe and resting on the back of the one next to it. Her toes were white and curved like the necks of Arabian horses. When he took her home he sucked each one of them in turn. When they made love he liked to wrap her ankles around his neck so he could feel the toe grazing against his ear with every stroke.

It went on like that for years. An extra nipple turned his head faster than the fullest pair of breasts. As I browsed his future and his past, I saw enough freaks to fill a dozen sideshows. The girl he took to the senior prom was double-jointed. Then he dated a woman with a birthmark on her face shaped like the state of Maine. She herself was from Yarmouth, Maine, and if you asked her about her home, she would point to the right edge of the birthmark in the hollow of her cheek.

Most men secretly find the female body monstrous, with its moundy protrusions and moist channels. Bill was no exception. It was his nature to think that way, but he had been aided and abetted by the parish priest who visited Bill's mother every Tuesday afternoon. While the boy's mother wept and complained about her troubles, the priest occupied young Bill with a book of paintings by Hieronymus Bosch. "This is hell, my lad," the priest whispered. "May the Lord grant that you never see it in person."

So Bill sat on a corner of the sofa and stared at the teeming infernos where urchin-bellied witches sautéed naked sinners, and a demon in a black helmet mounted a slit-eyed fish. He flipped the pages. Flayings. Tortures. Monsters with bird heads and lizard hands caressing smooth-skinned sinners. How illicit. How arousing. So this is what sex is, Bill thought.

What attracted him, then, to my sister Carolina? She was pretty, yes, with her black hair and red lips and plump round breasts, but it wasn't prettiness he was after. Pure loveliness would do in a pinch, but it really wasn't his cup of tea. No, it was the discovery he made soon after he met Carolina that made him think she was his one true love.

Imagine them kissing late at night on the back steps of her father's house. Bill's hand slips down between her thighs. She squirms, but it's in pleasure, not anger, so he keeps roving. The hand goes up to the belly, down under the elastic of her nylons and worms its way back up into her crotch. The fingers dip into her softness and go probing, probing like little burrowing moles. But then the pathway seems to fork. Bill draws away from Carolina's mouth and looks at her, his fingers still questioning between her legs. One finger, two finger, playing Carolina's stops as if she were a flute.

"What the . . . ?" he says. He fancies himself an expert on how a woman is supposed to be down there. Expert enough to know that something isn't quite right.

"I have two," explains Carolina matter-of-factly. "Only one of them can get me pregnant. The other one's a dead end."

Two vaginas. Bill was transported. What more mysterious strangeness could a strange man desire? And to top it off, they never had to worry about unwanted babies. If you had asked him, he would have said he had walked to paradise on two fingers. That's the way the man talked.

But anyplace you can walk into, you can walk out of again, and Bill eventually did walk out. I saw it coming from the moment those fingers clasped mine in a handshake. He had wide spaces between his fingers, an indication of both wanderlust and unusual appetites. He had the thick fingers of a sensualist and a small island in his heart line, which always foretells sadness.

You think perhaps that I'm belaboring the point, that there's no reason to dwell on his departure now that he's returned. But no fate is made up of a single strand. A life twists and doubles back on itself and ties itself into the most elegant macrame. I'm trying to tell you the whole truth, because you won't hear it from the man himself.

After he left Carolina, he began haunting the traveling carnivals. It was a trick he'd learned while stationed in Korea because the furloughs in Tokyo never did for him what they did for the other

GIs. He wasn't wowed by the dexterity of the performing women whose vaginas smoked cigarettes and expelled Ping-Pong balls. They were athletes, not monsters, and monsters were what he craved. So he went to the carnivals instead and took up with contortionists and dwarfs.

When, as a smuggler, he roamed through Latin America, he discovered that the southern continent had more than its share of carnivals and freak shows as well. These women were tough-talking sophisticates, but he learned to woo them by treating their oddities with respect and a feigned nonchalance. Bearded ladies, giantesses, fat women, and women covered with tattoos; Bill seduced them one by one. He spent a long time courting a handsome androgyne on display in Ecuador, but in the end he backed out, deciding that sleeping with half a man would still make him entirely a fairy.

About ten years after he left his family, he gave up flying and moved to a small fishing village on the west coast of Mexico. It was there that he began to hear the rumors. Some said it was a large hairless monkey. Others said it was Matlaziwa, the beautiful woman who coaxes men from their beds and leads them to their death. There was great disagreement as to what she looked like and where you could find her. Some said you could find her bathing in the ocean and she would call you by your name. Others said you were more likely to find her swinging upside down from a tree in the densest part of the jungle. The only thing that everyone agreed on was that she had a tail.

Bill first heard about her at the whorehouse in town where the men went to drink, brag, play cards, and fight. A night with her and you knew what paradise was, one man told him, but in the morning your parts would be withered like a tomato that's been left too long on the vine. Another man argued that it was *her* parts you had to worry about. They were spined like a sea urchin and would cut your thing to pieces.

"It's a monkey," the town mayor maintained. "A bald monkey, nothing else."

"She's more beautiful than any monkey. She's a spirit," said a fisherman whose uncle claimed to have seen her.

"Does she have tits?" Bill interjected. "Monkeys don't have tits."

This caused some dissension, and the card game was halted while two men drew knives over the question of whether the apparition had breasts.

"They shaved a monkey, I'm telling you," one of the men started again when order had been restored. "My wife's cousin worked in a carnival and that's how they do things. She wore a dead swan on her back and said she was an angel."

Several of the men remembered that carnival and now declared obstreperously that they'd known all along that the angel was a fake.

"Well, this one is real," said the baker's son, a young man who mainly kept quiet. "She isn't a monkey. I heard her talk."

Bill pulled up a chair next to him and tried to draw his story out, but the baker's son was more interested in talking about his new truck and the cost of gasoline. Soon the conversation had strayed from the spirit world to mercantile matters and Bill left at dawn without learning any more.

One morning Bill woke up before it was light and walked down to the beach. He plucked a mango from the tree by his hotel and opened it with his pocketknife as he walked. He was good at this life, better than he was at any life he lived before or after. He could spend a week doing nothing but fishing and talking and consider it a week well spent. It was only his own foolishness that kept leading him to a life with women, but he never bothered to figure this out.

So there he was sitting on the cold sand, watching the water change from gray-violet to blue with the rising of the sun. A solitary woman floated a little ways out and he watched her sink and lift with the swells as he dipped his knife into the quaggy mango flesh and cut himself bite after bite. When he was done with it, he buried the skin in the sand and walked down to the shore to wash his hands. The woman floated and frolicked, so leisurely he knew she must be a foreigner. Mexican women never had time to float in the ocean; even the little girls were always working.

Bill watched her, debating the pleasure of a morning swim versus the annoyance of walking back to the hotel sopping wet. The woman ducked her head underwater and one skinny leg surfaced ducklike as she dove. Then her head came up again, shaking water. He did a double take and waited for her to do it again, but she didn't, just bobbed up and down.

After a while she began swimming toward the shore. When she reached the shallows, she stood and shook out her hair. He could hear the sloshing sound of her stride as she climbed the sandbar's mild incline. As she emerged, a long pale tail emerged behind her.

When she noticed him, the tail jerked up and pressed against her spine as if she hoped to hide it. He sat absolutely still, watching how the tail transformed her from an ordinary swimmer into something otherworldly. It gave her an animal quality, revealing her instincts as if she were like the rest of the beasts and had no capacity for language. Now, as she stood frozen, the tail restlessly tapped against her left shoulder as if trying to alert her to a grave and sudden danger.

He was danger, but danger cloaked in the body of a man so smitten he couldn't speak. He was certain that if he opened his mouth she would startle like a mermaid and dive back into the sea and swim away. He wished he'd saved a bit of mango to lure her closer with or at least to offer by way of making conversation.

"How's the water?" he said at last in Spanish.

"Warm," she called back in English and began walking toward him, stopping to pick up the robe she'd left lying on the beach and wrap it around her shoulders. "But enough of a chill to be refreshing."

She sat down next to him and took a cigarette from the pocket of her robe. It was clear she was not a monkey, although her face had a certain monkeylike quality because of her wide cheekbones and the small ears that were pressed tightly to her head. She had short brown hair, a broad mouth, and large olive-flecked brown eyes.

"I don't smoke usually, but it's nice to have one after a swim," she said as she lit the cigarette. "Do you think doing something healthy before you do something unhealthy cancels the unhealthy thing out?"

"I hope so," Bill said. "Are you American?"

"Yes, although not lately. I haven't lived in the States for almost twenty years."

As they talked, Bill reversed his earlier perception of the tail. He had thought it gave her an animal quality, but now he noticed that it made elegant gestures as she spoke, making her seem more civilized and urbane than women without one. Her name was Justina, she told him. She was vacationing in Mexico with her father, a retired investment banker from Connecticut. The two of them had lived abroad, mainly in London but also in Frankfurt and Brussels, since the death of her mother when she was fifteen.

Bill explained that he, too, had been a virtual expatriate for several years.

"It's strange living in an adopted country," she said. "You might forget you're a stranger, but no one else does. It's like the cat I once had who thought he was a dog. We had lots of dogs and only one cat, and the cat ran around with all the dogs, thinking he was one of them. Then a dog chased him up a tree and it dawned on the cat that maybe he wasn't one of the boys. But that's my whole life in a nutshell. As you can see, I'm not like other people."

The tip of her tail made a circle in the air and then bent toward him as she made her point.

That night she and her father met him for dinner at his hotel. Bill had wondered how they could meet in a public place without causing a stir, but she came in wearing a full skirt that masked the tail in its many pleats. Bill caught it flicking occasionally under the table, nosing the fabric next to her thigh.

Her father was a handsome man with a thinning fringe of hair and the blotched skin of a white man well acquainted with sun and liquor. His name was Jerome, he said as he gripped Bill's hand in an ostentatiously firm handshake. But he seemed genuinely pleased to make Bill's acquaintance, as though he had found a coconspirator.

Later in the evening when they had all had a few drinks, Jerome admitted in passing that Justina had stayed with him well into her adulthood because of the strange reactions she received from the outside world.

"She's a free spirit. She doesn't like to pretend," he said. "And that makes the world a dangerous place."

"I'm really very happy with who I am," Justina interjected. "I just hate having to cover it up all the time. It's like having a diamond ring but not being able to wear it because it might be stolen. Do you think anything rare is precious?"

She liked to pose philosophical questions, but it took Bill a while to realize he was supposed to answer them. Perhaps it was her love of uncertainty that attracted him, and not just the tail. Uncertainty was dangerous, he knew, but the danger was alluring. To Bill, Justina was Eve and the serpent rolled into one.

He spent the next two weeks with Justina and Jerome. They had dinner together every night and hired local fishermen to take them fishing during the day. Some days Justina elected to stay at the hotel and it was then that Jerome confessed to Bill his worries about his daughter's future.

"Every father worries about his daughter," he said as they sat in a palapa restaurant drinking warm beer. "You'll know what I mean if you ever have children. I worried about Justina from the day she was born. As a man, I knew that men are the worst kind of animals. But I'll tell you, we're worse than I ever thought. Every man who's ever claimed to love her has only wanted to hurt her in the end. I've tried to protect her from them, but I'm only her father, I'm not God."

Bill nodded and dug his feet into the sand under his chair. He remembered his daughters asleep in their beds. In his mind they were always there, dreaming a long dream. Did he worry about these daughters walking down the path of their fates without him to warn them of the brambles and thickets? No, they were safe in bed, fast asleep.

"When she was nineteen, she had a doctor who wanted to marry her," Jerome confided. "He seemed like a nice young man, very polite, very English. Too English as it turned out; the damn Brits are always so worried about appearances. He tried to amputate her tail. She came to visit him at his office and he slipped her a mickey. He had the tools all ready; it was barbaric. It could have left her paralyzed. Lucky for us, the nurse saw what was happening and called me at home. I got there just in time. That was the end of *that* romance."

"Did you ever think of having it taken off when she was little?"

"Of course the doctors wanted us to. But my wife was just like Justina—willful through and through. She wouldn't allow it." He sighed loudly and motioned to the waiter for another round. "If I had to do it over again, I can't say what I'd do," he said after draining the last flat swallow from his glass. "It does make her special, but on the other hand it's condemned her to a life of isolation. People are terrible, Bill, terrible conformists."

"She deserves better," Bill said. "She's a rare woman."

It was the right thing to say and it made Jerome clasp his hand earnestly and say, "I'm glad we met you." But Bill meant it. Justina more than captivated him. He thought of cherishing her, protecting her, telling her stories that would make her dream before she fell asleep. Was it misplaced daughter-love, the love he kept in storage while his sleeping daughters woke, dressed themselves, and went on with their destinies? I'm no psychologist, but I know that our emotions stay lined up in our hearts like cooking ingredients. If we lack the right one, we use whatever we have on hand; milk for cream, vinegar for wine. And if the sauce tastes right, why quibble with the recipe?

Every night after dinner, Jerome retired to his hotel room and Bill and Justina wandered down to the beach to talk. As soon as they were alone, Justina hiked up her skirt to free her tail. Loosening it loosened her tongue as well and she talked expansively, her tail gesticulating.

Bill usually liked talking more than listening, and he had never been particularly curious about the inner lives of other people. But he loved to watch the tantalizing shimmer of her tail as Justina explained her thoughts. She had spent much of her life alone and so she had developed the habit of amusing herself with mental dilemmas.

"If you were condemned to death, what would you want your last meal to be?"

"Spaghetti," Bill said. This was one he had thought about himself.

"No, I don't think so. You wouldn't want to face a firing squad with a stomach full of pasta. It would be like having a cannonball in your belly. A morbid reminder of what you were about to face, don't you think?"

She sat on a cement wall that separated the hotel terrace from the beach, her skirt hiked up over one thigh, the tail draped over it. The tip flitted from side to side, like a wagging finger signaling *no*.

"What would you have?" Bill asked.

"Watermelon. Cool and sweet, a taste of heaven. Or cold plums, like in the William Carlos Williams poem. It has to be fruit, because fruit is the quintessential earthly delight."

They were sleeping together before the first week was out. It wasn't her first time, but it was the first time she had ever been willing. She knew more about cruelty than he realized. Even her stuffy

English doctor had found nothing untoward in forcing himself on her when she was unconscious in his office.

Still, she was proud in the bedroom. When they made love, the tail was all over, rubbing against him, lashing him with her ecstasy. It was flesh colored, hairless, a long undulating extension of her spine. He stroked it as she moved on top of him and she smiled broadly and wrapped it around his neck.

Afterward when she walked naked around the room, the tail arced over her back, just long enough to touch the top of her head when fully extended. She liked to show off its dexterity, opening doors with it and using it to hold a glass. Once, in the throes of passion, he made the mistake of calling her his "spider monkey." A second later he felt a painful thwack on the side of his face. The tail itself had struck him like a serpent. "How dare you demean what I am?" she spat at him. "That's like calling a mermaid a manatee!" His face was swollen for days afterward and from then on he kept his pet-names to himself.

When it was time for Jerome to return to England, Bill asked Justina to stay. He didn't expect her to say yes, but she did. Some people who have been badly hurt in life spend the rest of their lives cowering. Others notice that they've survived so far and walk forward to meet whatever fate is coming. Justina was the second type. She loved him and she'd never seen him be unkind. That was enough for the moment.

They moved to Brazil, where everything is accepted, and rented a flat in Rio de Janeiro. They spent their mornings drinking coffee on a balcony that overlooked the street and their evenings in the nightclubs. At first Justina wore stiff flared skirts that hid her tail. Bill held her by the waist as they danced, and if his hand roamed down to stroke her behind, no one guessed what it was that he was squeezing.

At Carnival he persuaded her to take her tail out in public. The streets were a mass of heaving, swiveling bodies, and no one cared about anything except for dancing. This was the time of year when nothing was forbidden. What did a single naked tail matter in this sea of naked flesh, of men dancing bare chested and women with their buttocks cleaved by a thin strap of gold fabric?

That was the start of their happiest time. Justina became a well-known if unusual beauty, and the two of them attracted the friendship of a sophisticated set of gamblers, actors, writers, and politicians. The tail acquired a host of decorations. Justina ornamented it with jewels, feathers, beads, and lace. One night a famous tattoo artist offered to tattoo its entire length with a pattern of green and purple diamonds like a snake. Justina declined, liking her tail more than ever exactly as it was.

Change always seems sudden but it rarely is. We judge the fullness of the moon by days, never noticing how she turns toward us minute by minute, revealing now her white face, now her black one. The revelry ended two years after it started. First, Jerome died of a heart attack in London. A month later Justina discovered she was pregnant.

Bill had lived the domestic life before, but being as tense-impaired as the rest of his family, he had forgotten what it led to. Now it seemed to him that Jerome's death was an augury of his own mortality. He noticed that the long nights of beef and rum and dancing had left him with a paunch around his middle and dark circles under his eyes. He missed walking and talking with Justina on the beach the way they had in Mexico. Let's raise a family, he said to her. They moved to a little house outside the city and jollied themselves with schemes for the baby's future. Justina imagined hatching a brood of tailed babies, and she made Bill promise that no surgeons would ever be consulted.

I've never met Justina in person, but I like her all the same. She's one of the rare few who can accept fate without being its victim. She loved her destiny unconditionally, the way we are supposed to love our children. Still, she had a flaw, and it turned out to be the mythic one. Pride is the scissors we use to cut off our own blossoms and put them in a vase. Justina thought her tail made her better than the ordinary human specimen. It was such a useful tool, this prehensile appendage, and it seemed to have its own intelligence. I've read that the largest dinosaur, the brontosaurus, had a brain in its tail as well as its head. Justina felt her tail was similar. She believed that she was the prototype for the next step in evolution. Once people saw how useful a tail was, she reasoned, tailed beings would be the mate of choice, and in a few hundred years those without tails would be second-class citizens. "My children won't have to hide what they are," she told Bill. "Other children will envy them."

When baby Willy was born, the nurse laid him on Justina's stomach and she stroked his sticky newborn buttocks with her hand. They were smooth and round as a stemless apple. "Normal," said the doctor and Justina scowled. A year and a half later Roger was born, and he, too, was utterly tailless. Justina kissed her babies' foreshortened coccyx bones and tried to hide her disappointment. Having babies had proved to her just how useful a tail could be. It tickled little Roger under the chin while she changed his diaper, and braced him when he tried to roll over. The baby chuckled and gummed it with his infant mouth. When Willy tried to draw on the wall with crayons, the tail gave him a warning swat even as Justina's hands were full with suckling Roger. When Willy wanted to be read a story, the tail kept Roger's cradle rocking while Justina cuddled book and boy in her human arms.

On the surface, these were happy days. Bill was uneasy but he kept it to himself. He knew too well how love can pack its suitcase and leave in the middle of the night. Justina was agile as a dancer, chasing the boys around the garden and presenting them with their first infant dilemmas. "Would you rather be a bird or a fish?" she asked them. "Would you rather eat Popsicles or ice cream?"

Bill sat in the shade watching the boys pretend to be birds and fishes in the garden. He remembered himself as a little boy and how he had worried about his parents. He remembered his daughters, who might still be worrying about their father.

As adept as he was at walling off the past, memory seeped under the door like smoke. The smell of the bandage he used to cover a cut on Roger's elbow beckoned an image of the garnet scabs on Lisa's five-year-old knees. The moist hair curling around Willy's temples as he slept conjured baby Julia at the breakfast table, her hair ringleted with sleep. The smoke clung to the fibers of his sons' bedclothes so that when he bent to give them their good-night kisses, the pungent reek of memory stung his eyes. He felt the heat of his daughters' hands as they clutched his at street corners, remembered how Julia liked to use the word *ordinary* and Lisa had a passion for root beer–flavored lollipops. At night, the smoke settled in a treacly puddle in the center of his chest. On closer inspection, it revealed itself as dread. He knew it would all go wrong. It always had. It always would. He had kept still too long, and now his destiny was catching up with him.

One day just before Willy's sixth birthday, he was wandering home from the market when he passed a low wooden building where boys came to learn *capoeira,* the Brazilian martial art. Through the open door he could see barefoot children kicking and cartwheeling and jumping through their own clasped hands. Two drummers thumped out a tricky rhythm as the boys danced and sparred. Bill leaned on the doorsill and watched. Maybe he could enroll Willy in one of these classes, he thought.

When the class was finished, the instructor came up to him and introduced himself. "I am Paulo Sant'Anna," he said. "Can I answer any questions for you?"

"How long does it take to become good at this?" Bill wanted to know. Perhaps he sensed that time was running out.

"It depends," Paulo said. He was a wiry, handsome man, with cocoa-colored skin and three gold teeth. "For some people it takes time to trust gravity. For me it was easy, it was natural. It's in my body like an animal. I think it is because I really am an animal. I even have a tail."

And here he laughed a loud expansive laugh. Bill stared and the instructor took that as disbelief.

"I do," he said and turned around to show Bill his behind. He wore the loose baggy pants of the African slaves who invented *capoeira.* When he pulled the fabric tight over his rear, a fist-sized knot showed underneath like the stubby scut of a deer.

That night Bill dreamed of the tailed *capoeira* instructor. He was smiling. Gold teeth winked like tiny fires in his mouth. He and

Justina circled each other in the garden. Their tails flickered with animal signals. Bill yelled out and they turned to look at him, but still the tails continued an erotic semaphore that he couldn't understand.

In the daytime the dream receded. Bill played with the boys and sang Justina little songs he said he had made up just for her. "Nothing could be keener than to be with my Justina in the mo-oo-rning." Sometimes when he lay in the garden shielding his eyes from the sun, he imagined that he lay in a boat drifting over a turquoise sea. In the distance he could see the ledge of the horizon, and he knew that eventually the boat would slip over the edge. But for now the sea was calm and a light breeze slid over his bare chest. He squinted his eyes and all he could see was color.

As time went on, Bill began to realize that the money he had set aside for his retirement wasn't enough to raise two boys, even in Brazil. He made some phone calls to Miami. Yes, his friends told him, of course there's work. There's more money to be made than ever before.

He told Justina he had to take care of some investments in the States, and in a few weeks he was back in business. He figured he could make four runs a month and still have two full weeks to spend with his family. He told Justina he was doing some secret work for the U.S. government. Coincidentally, it was the truth.

Flying reassured him. He was out of his element again, with the blue sky flashing past him and the tugging uncertainties of the world as tiny and distant as the earth's distant, tiny trees. He flew without thinking about anything except how smooth and square the lines separating the fields below him were, and how, when you fly over it, the surface of the ocean looks like the skin on the back of your hand. While he was in the air, Justina was as real to him as a sharp pinch. It was only when he came home and lay next to her in bed that she became imagined.

How do you define danger? Raising children is dangerous, love is dangerous, speaking your mind is the most dangerous thing of all. But cowards walk away from these primal dangers because no one will praise you if you face them. Men prefer the brief and intermittent bravery required by crime and warfare. Distractions from the real thing.

While Justina dedicated her life to raising sons who might someday be worthy of a woman's love, Bill was risking his life to raise money for the Central Intelligence Agency. It seems that the CIA was having trouble getting Congress to fund one of its Central American wars, and so the agency had come up with its own form of bake sale. Bill's job was to fly into the jungle with a cargo of weapons and return with a cargo of cocaine. The CIA sold the drugs to raise money for weapons, and so it went, as neat and pretty as a merry-go-round and as good at making a dizzy man even dizzier.

So here was Bill on an airstrip in the jungle. Wet country all year round but wettest now in the summer months. Rain that didn't have the energy to fall but leaked in sad exhaustion from the sky. Bill sat in his plane and waited. Here was the danger that made him feel brave: a jungle full of stalking armies. He was jumpy and tired from flying all night and from inhaling thin speed bumps of cocaine. And now there was no one waiting for him on the airstrip and he wasn't sure what he should do.

He waited. The rain slid down the windshield of the plane in tedious streams. In the misty light he could see the end of the runway, the camouflage bunkers, and beyond that the dreary continuum of green. He had been out of the plane once to look around, but he was afraid to walk very far because there could be land mines anywhere. So he sat and opened his fourth Pepsi and impatience sizzled in his chest because he is a man who would ask to change seats if he had to sit next to himself on a long flight. Look out the window, pretend to be reading, anything to avoid having to engage himself in conversation.

The Pepsi diluted the cocaine puddle in the back of his throat, and he thought for a while about how Coca-Cola used to contain cocaine. He drummed his fingers in time to the rain and watched two raindrops slide from the top of the windshield. He put twenty dollars on the right one and rooted in a loud whisper for it to pull ahead of the one on the left. It hesitated and wobbled for a moment. The left one collided with another drop, doubled in size, and slid all the way down to the bottom of the windshield.

He prepared himself another line of cocaine and inhaled it through his right nostril, since the left one was beginning to sting. What was bothering him was that these runs were usually so well organized. Usually there were six or seven men there waiting to unload the crates of weapons and pack up the plane with drugs. Usually there was at least someone there. There had never been no one.

He bet on another raindrop race and lost again. Then, because he was superstitious, he kept betting until he lost a third time. He didn't want the third loss to be something that mattered.

The rain was unvarying. He felt as though no time had elapsed at all; everything was exactly the same as when he had first landed. It was no darker, no lighter, no wetter, no dryer. Everything was still green, drenched, hazy, hot. He got out of the plane and stood outside, letting the rain run off his bare arms. The water was tepid, not at all cooling, but the sensation was soothing. His muscles were cramped from sitting and the cocaine and an unspecified foreboding. For a few minutes he felt calmed by the solitude and the jungle's damp odors. Then he remembered that the jungle was what he was afraid of. That he didn't know what was in it. That he was alone and it was all around him. He climbed back in the plane.

He wished he had his own plane instead of this CIA-issued one. Nothing had ever gone wrong in *Demon*. She was his faithful partner, Silver to his Lone Ranger. Why hadn't anyone shown up?

Something must have gone wrong. Maybe the army had intercepted the group that was coming to unload the plane. Maybe he should just turn around and fly back to Miami. The last thing he needed was to get caught with a planeload of guns and ammunition.

On the other hand, he didn't want to be known as the nervous type. If he landed back in Miami with the same cargo he left with, they'd probably just tell him to turn around and try it again. He would be gone twice as long as he had told Justina, and he'd be flying on even less sleep than usual.

Now he was soaked through and sticking to the airplane's vinyl seat. Nothing would dry in this air. He began to think about tropical skin rashes. He had gotten impetigo in Korea and had to spend two weeks dotted with purple medicine. He was sure he was getting something now. His armpits itched, and the back of his neck.

After a while he got out again and stood on the edge of the runway to piss. He took a gun with him, a nine-millimeter he'd found in the plane. Brave, brave man clutching the gun with one hand while the other directed his pee into the foliage. He listened to it spatter, a louder drizzle than the rain. His body was shivery from holding it in so long.

His eyes were slack and unfocused with the pleasure of releasing his pent-up urine. But they focused fast enough when two men crossed into his line of vision. The men were creeping through the underbrush just ahead of him and they were armed. In an instant he sank to his knees and rolled into the bushes. As he rolled he realized that these were probably the men who had been sent to unload the plane. Jesus, he'd say, you guys startled me. Made me piss all over myself. He rested on his elbows, the gun in front of him, his hands shaking.

The two men came toward the airstrip spraying bullets in sweeping arcs. *What a pair of bozos,* he thought as they stepped onto the runway, firing almost randomly. They had walked right past him. He shot one in the back of the head; the other spun around and Bill shot him in the chest. He stood up as they fell over and was revolted and exhilarated and perfectly confused. Somehow he had managed to kill them both.

It only took a moment for him to begin forming his excuses. *They were shooting at me. I was defending myself. Didn't they know why I was there? What did they think a white guy with a plane was doing on their airstrip? Did they think I was from Witness for Peace?*

He sat down on the tarmac next to the bodies and put his head between his knees to quell a sudden tide of nausea. Looking down he noticed that his penis was still dangling out of his fly like a pink turtle head emerging from its shell. He zipped up his pants and stood up to stare at the two men. One lay faceup, the other facedown, like figures on the tarot deck. They had each fallen modestly on their wounds so that they looked arranged, unbloodied. Faceup had his eyes open. He was young, not much older than seventeen. A few black whiskers grew in patches around his mouth. His face was pudgy, his mouth small and rounded like a suckling baby. Blood was seeping from under the bodies. The blood mixed with rain and ran off the edge of the tarmac and into the dirt.

Leaving the bodies on the runway seemed like a bad idea, so he lifted Faceup's ankles and dragged him off the pavement, blundering through thick leaves that scribbled in his face and on the back of his neck. When he let go of the ankles, he felt a cool hand on his shoulder and whirled around. There was no one there.

He trudged back up the runway and took hold of the second man's ankles. The feeling of cooling skin sickened him, but he swallowed and dragged Facedown's body into the forest and tried not to think of the dead man's eyes being open, the mud and ants going into his mouth and nostrils, leaves adhering to the sticky eyeballs. That day in the jungle he didn't see the second man's face. But in time it would become as familiar to him as his own handwriting.

This was a man who barely understood the living; how could he understand the dead, whose desires are so much more urgent and peculiar? His first mistake was in touching them. An angry soul will grasp on to the first thing that comes near it, like a scorpion stinging out of spite. His second mistake was that he didn't try to start them on their journey to the otherworld. What if he had dressed their bodies in jungle flowers and sang to them and told them what words to say to the dogs that sleep at the bank of the river the dead must cross to get to the other side? He could have tucked cigarettes and Pepsis in their hands as provisions for their journey. He could have explained to them why their lives had ended so quickly, and said he was sorry and promised to pray for them.

I was watching him, but I couldn't tell him what to do. So he started up his plane and flew away. And the two ghosts sat on the seats beside him and stared down at the landscape below as if it were the most amazing sight death had to offer them.

Two teenage boys can reduce a house to shambles in an afternoon, and two dead teenagers can do it even faster. When he came home, the ghosts trailed him doggedly and stood gaping while he made love to Justina. Needless to say, his desire flagged halfway through his first attempt and afterward he didn't try again.

They were both sullen, dull-eyed boys, but Facedown was the worse of the two. He had a thin head like a kidney bean, a lipless mouth, and narrow, hate-filled eyes. He liked to hunch over and scratch himself under the armpits like a monkey whenever Justina walked into the room, and he glared at Willy and Roger so viciously that Bill feared for their safety. The ghosts seemed powerless to do much more than make books fall from the shelves and write their names in the condensation on the mirror, but when a coffeepot fell from the stove and seared the skin on Roger's arm, Bill knew who to blame.

They never slept. He hated waking up in the middle of the night knowing that they were prowling around the house some-where and would run to him as soon as they felt him stir. They eavesdropped on every conversation and made faces whenever he opened his mouth. Bill grew self-conscious and stopped telling stories. He stopped singing and massaging the flexing muscles in Justina's tail. To Justina and the boys, it seemed that he hardly noticed they existed. When they tried to tell him things, he was always scowling at some fixed point in space. He seemed angry, but they didn't know what they had done.

Justina couldn't see the ghosts, nor could the boys. Had he told her, she might have known what to do; she was an expert at solving mental puzzles, after all. But language is a feminine invention. A woman will confess to a crime she didn't commit if that's what it takes to get a conversation started. Women believe that no demon can harm you once you speak its name.

So Justina asked him why he didn't touch her the way he used to, apologized for being disappointed in her tailless babies, promised to be more attentive to everyone if only he would go back to loving her the way he did before. He listened to her jabber, but he could not find the words to answer her questions. He loved language more than most men, but he feared it just the same. Words could be used to construct dungeons or palaces, and you never knew what you were building until it was too late.

He began to drink. It was still the rainy season and the six of them were cooped up inside the house. Roger was in a stage of throwing terrible tantrums. He screamed and pounded the walls at the slightest provocation until gentle-souled Willy began sobbing empathetically. More often than not, both boys were sent to their rooms shrieking and kicking the floor. The ghosts rolled their eyes and covered up their ears. Bill sat and drank even though his stomach rocked and churned with every glass of rum. Most nights he vomited before he went to bed and woke up with his stomach muscles aching. When he closed his eyes, he could see the boat that used to float on the turquoise sea. He had reached the edge of the world and the black chasm was below.

By now Justina had given up talking and had returned to the quiet introspective ways of her childhood. She sat in the bedroom, in the rocking chair in which she had nursed the babies, but she did not rock. She kept a stack of novels by the blades of the chair and read them one by one, scarcely pausing to consider the ending of one before she embarked on another. Her tail dangled by her feet and did not move. When she got up to check on the sobbing and quarreling boys, it dragged behind her like a line of mourners following a coffin.

At last Bill went to find the *capoeira* instructor at the studio near the market. The low-ceilinged room was hot and muggy despite a tiny fan that wheezed in one corner.

"I'd like my sons to learn *capoeira,*" Bill said. "But my wife says they're too young."

"They're never too young!" Paulo said, wiping the sweat from his forehead with a purple wristband. "I began teaching my son *capoeira* when he was two. Someday he'll be one of the best."

"Perhaps you wouldn't mind having dinner with me and my wife," said Bill. "I think she would be more convinced if you talked to her yourself. Tell her they won't be hurt."

The instructor seemed surprised but remained polite and finally accepted the invitation. "Come on Saturday," Bill said and wrote down the address. He felt flaccid and gray next to the vibrant instructor. He wondered if Paulo smelled the rum and vomit on his breath.

That night Bill woke up when it was still dark. Justina slept with her head burrowed between her arms. He felt as though giant hands were lifting him by the elbows. The time for resistance had ended, and so he let Fate raise him to his feet. He was relieved, almost buoyant. This, after all, was at least familiar. He took the rolls of bills he had hidden in his dresser drawer and placed all but one on the pillow where he had slept. The last one he put in his pocket.

In the kitchen, the ghosts were tossing lit matches at each other.

"Let's go," Bill said, and they followed him to the door.

$\mathscr{T}$he Interlude (Julia)

I woke up in Gabriel's bed with a ring of bruises around my wrist. The scratches where the mugger had dug his nails into my wrist were inflamed and sticky, and my ankle had swollen to an unfamiliar size as if I had exchanged legs with a fat woman during the night. I had a mottled, dimpled abrasion on my hip and another one on my shoulder. My dress and leggings lay in Gabriel's garbage can, too ripped and bloody for salvaging.

I lay in bed for a long time. Gabriel had opened the curtains, and a faint, bleak light spilled through the north-facing windows. I faded in and out of sleep, but mainly watched the light and shadows reflected on the wall. After a time the morning light hardened into noon and I got up and hobbled into the living room.

Gabriel was curled up in a black wicker chair, with his legs hung over the armrests and a book propped up against his knees. I had expected his house to be monastic, but it was almost overwhelmingly vibrant. Books and plants cluttered every surface and the walls blazed with turgid Latin American posters. "How do you feel?" he asked.

"Okay." I was wearing one of his T-shirts and a pair of his boxers, a costume that made us seem more intimate than we were. We hadn't even kissed the night before and had slept chastely on opposite poles of the bed. Once he saw how lost I was, his attitude had become fraternal.

"Are you hungry?" Gabriel said. "Let me make you breakfast."

I sat down at the black-and-red kitchen table and ate the omelette he set out for me. He sat across from me and watched my face, searching for signs of memory. The night before I had told him that I didn't remember who I was or where I lived. "It'll come back to you," he'd said. "Just be patient."

"Is it okay if I take a bath?" I asked when I was done eating. Soon I would have to stop this game and face my father. But first I needed to rinse the sweat and grease and fear from my skin.

The bathroom was tiled green and black, with towels folded in a wicker cabinet. I stretched out in the tub and stared at the ceiling, wondering what they were doing at Lisa's house. Were they missing me? Talking about me? I pictured Carolina nudging my father, shrugging coyly. "You know how Julia is, always late."

I'll call them when I get out of the bath, I thought and sank down until the water filled my ears and lapped against the corners of my eyes. But when I stepped out of the water into the air, I felt a weariness rush over me. He'd waited twenty-two years, he could wait a few hours longer. Just until I'd had some rest.

I spent the afternoon lying on a rattan chaise longue with my ankle propped up on pillows. I was wearing a pair of Gabriel's jeans, the cuffs rolled over three times, and the T-shirt I'd gone to sleep in. The windows were open and sun and breezes streamed in from all sides. Gabriel brought me iced tea with a sprig of mint leaves floating in it. He tended to me as if I were the potted honey locust weeping detritus in the corner of the room.

I studied him through the veil of my torpor as he went through his daily routine. He read, mostly, and took notes, and sometimes he just gazed into space, thinking. In repose, his face was serious and a little sad. His eyebrows were thick and dark, and he had the habit that all goateed men have of tugging at his chin when thinking. He drank tea as he read and brought successive cups for me. The color changed with the time of day: pale red, pale green, black.

At around four o'clock I found myself crying. It started when the puddles of sun on the floor around me began diminishing. The bravado was draining from the day; the moment of possibility when things could be made to happen. I missed Steven. I thought about his green eyes, his soft skin, the nodding cattails of unruly hair that sprouted from the top of his head.

"Don't cry," Gabriel said. "You'll get your memory back."

He put down his book and came over to sit on the floor next to me. I wiped my face on the knees of my jeans and felt Gabriel's hand stroke my head. Steven would be okay, I told myself. He had my father now. I pictured them together, in Lisa's living room. My father was telling stories that made Steven laugh his goofy second-grade laugh, and Steven was teaching my father to moonwalk, and they were wrestling, doing boy-things, shouting. Let them talk awhile together, father and son. I would join them, by and by. Tomorrow, at the very latest.

"Who are you?" Gabriel asked me the next day. I sat on the rattan chaise, breathing the hot, sweet air that poured in through his windows.

"I'm enchanted," I told him.

One night I rode my bicycle through an old lady's garden. A plum tree and an apricot tree stood in the corners of her yard. In the dark the apricots were luminous and golden, the plums dense and secretive. I shook the crabbed branches and stood in a hailstorm of fruit. I tossed a column of them in the air and juggled. Then I foraged in her vegetable garden for sustenance.

She found me with my hands full of spinach and nasturtiums, the green blood of plants under my nails. I got up to run, but she grabbed me by the wrist. See the claw marks she left? I never should have vexed her.

As punishment she reached down my throat and pulled out my soul like you would pull a stone out of shallow water. My gullet and chest are still scabby from her nails. I feel it when I breathe—little knots of blood, tender as berries. My soul struggled in her hand, a wriggling frog. She drew a circle in the ground with a lime and tossed it in the center. It sits there now like a garden ornament. I can't tell you who I am because I'm no one anymore.

Gabriel was looking at me carefully, his brown eyes unreadable. "If you don't want to tell me, you don't have to."

After that there were no more questions. I drank his tea and stared out the window at the purple bougainvillea across the street. Its leaves were violet fire. I craved the color the way you crave water or salt. When I turned my eyes back to Gabriel's rooms, the colors seemed to leap at me like a sharp perfume. The yellow-and-red throw rug on the living room floor. Gabriel's brown skin and eyes, his black hair. Gabriel's lips and nipples, red-brown like brick.

When he laid our dinner on the red-and-black table, I stared at the colors for a long time before I could begin eating. Purple eggplant in a sauce of red peppers. Black bread. Red wine. Yellow and white egg slices spread over bottle green lettuce. Black figs, their insides pink as anemones.

His bedroom windows were smothered in green velvet curtains. I slept curled up, protecting my ankle from the weight of the bedding, and thought that tomorrow I would be rested enough to go. I dreamed of being buried, clods of dirt in my mouth. They tasted sweet, like the veins of flowers.

Once when I asked Aunt Simone where my father had gone, she told me he'd chased after a winged demon. When I was a little girl, I puzzled over this. I didn't blame him for leaving us. It only seemed sad and unfair to me that he should lose himself that way, like a child who runs blindly into the street after a ball. I pictured him sleeping and the tiny demon circling his head. He wakes up—*what is it?* Something buzzes, a mosquito in his ear. The demon prods him with its pitchfork. My father jumps up, stung, and chases the faint red glimmer across the room, then down the stairs and out the door. Down the street he runs, swatting at the demon just out of reach, block after block, through unfamiliar neighborhoods, until finally, irretrievably gone.

How easy it would be to lose yourself, I thought then. And how easy, how strangely easy, it had turned out to be.

Gabriel always woke before me. He came and went, to classes I suppose, or prayer, but mostly I remember him in the chair in the living room, reading and underlining and staring off into the warm green air. Sometimes it was theology, other times it was physics, psychology, history, ethnography. There was a book about Job, and several on the Holocaust. When I asked him about these, he told me that he wanted to know how God could tolerate the sufferings of the poor and oppressed.

"This is the God who can work miracles," he said to me. "But His miracles are all muscle-flexing—self-aggrandizement. The Virgin Mary's face appearing on a tortilla—what is that? It's an advertisement. It's a goddamned billboard."

He was so annoyed at this thought that he had to get up and make himself another pot of tea. "It doesn't bother me that God doesn't act," he shouted to me from the kitchen. "What bothers me is that His actions are so pathetic."

He was searching. He grazed through books with an irritable hunger, but nothing seemed to satisfy his taste. He read Jung and Marx and Sufi poetry, and then Milton and Camus and Blake. When he was done with each book, he handed it to me. I think he thought reading would rescue me, even though it wasn't helping him. I thumbed through them, but I couldn't concentrate on words, not words that followed one after another after another after another like a vast colony of ants. I skidded off the page at the end of a line and turned back to the bougainvillea and the sweet smells of the lion-colored air. The only line that stayed with me was one that I found in the book about divine providence he'd had with him on that first night. It said, "There is nothing trivial about our passing moments, as they enclose the whole kingdom of holiness and the food on which angels feed."

"Tell me about your crisis of faith," I said one afternoon.

"I can't surrender," he said. "It's nearing the time for me to take my first vows, but I don't think I believe the right things."

"What would you vow?"

"I'm supposed to commit to three years of poverty, chastity, and obedience. The same things I would promise to do for a lifetime if I become a priest."

I thought of his lovely black- and brownness cloaked under robes, made untouchable, but he shook his head as if he knew what I was thinking.

"It's the obedience I'm struggling with. I can't put down my will. I love God, but I don't know Her well enough to give my whole life to Her."

I liked the way God seemed to change genders according to his mood. It made him seem less pedantic. "What made you have second thoughts?" I asked.

"I joined an interfaith group that was helping teens cope with violence. Kids whose friends have been killed or who had been shot themselves. Kids who had been to more funerals than most people in their sixties."

He got up from his chair and came to sit on the floor beside my chaise, the way he did on that first day when I was crying. "They were trying to make sense of what was happening in their neighborhoods, and because they were Christians, they would talk about how God wants us all to love each other. But the more I listened to them talk, the more I found myself shaking my head and thinking, None of this has anything to do with God."

"Why not?"

"A few months ago I went to Los Angeles for a meeting on urban violence. On the plane I sat next to a woman who was studying a pack of hyenas that had been brought to Berkeley. She had discovered that hyenas always gave birth to twins. It was surprising, because in the wild they'd only observed mama hyenas with single cubs. It turns out that one of the cubs usually kills the other. Moments after they emerge from the womb, the twins are at each other's throats."

"And you think these inner-city kids are like hyenas?"

"No, not at all. That's why this is so hard to explain. The woman on the plane was a scientist. To her the fighting hyenas were simply an interesting puzzle: What evolutionary purpose is served by giving baby hyenas such a murderous nature? But to me the question was, What sort of God endows creation with a murderous nature? Because under the theology I knew, all of creation is God's work and reflects both God's mystery and God's love. And I thought, The God that makes these cutthroat babies is not the single-hearted God I was raised on. But it wasn't that I despised this God. I was intrigued. God is stranger and more mysterious than I had thought. Capable of great beauty and great love and also great cruelty."

"More like a pagan God." I rested the side of my face on my knees, watching him tease out the strands of his internal argument. Is this how men's minds work? I wondered.

"Yes, exactly. An elemental God. Not the God of Christ. Not the God that these desperate kids were looking to for help with their problems of violence. And it began to seem to me that morality and justice and love were human concerns, not God's concern at all. And to believe it is God's concern is to create God in our own image, which is idolatry. And so, if I'm concerned with the human dilemma and the question of justice, then maybe I belong in the human arena and not with the church."

"And is that what you think now?"

"Sometimes. And sometimes I think that if God made both us and the hyenas, and endowed us each with our own natures, then

She must want us both to bring those natures to full flower. And then to us She *is* the God of Love."

"And to the hyenas He's the God of Battle."

"Yes." He looked up at me and met my gaze. "Except that the hyenas don't get to choose what they are; they just are. So why do we get to choose whether to be just or injust?"

"Maybe we don't. Maybe our natures are as prescripted as the hyenas'." I was circling back to the position I felt most sure of, the one that left us without any choices.

Gabriel shook his head. "I don't believe that. I don't believe we're all wind-up toys."

"Not wind-up toys, because we can think about what's happening to us. But you can't fight your destiny. If you try, you'll wind up getting hurt." I held out my wrist so he could see the scabs and bruises. Gabriel leaned over and touched them with his fingertips, then cupped my palm in his, as if reading my future.

"You have to believe in free will to live," he maintained. His thumb stroked the pad of muscle below my middle finger, the Mount of Saturn, which Aunt Simone says indicates a seeker. "You've made decisions in your life. Don't you feel that you make moral choices, that you choose to do the right thing rather than the wrong thing?"

I thought about Steven then, but brushed the thought away as if he were a child I'd imagined having but hadn't. *Tomorrow. Certainly tomorrow.* Gabriel stroked my palm, his thumb carelessly rubbing out the future that had been inscribed there since my birth.

One night I realized that Gabriel had invented me. He had a blue notebook that he took out after dinner and scribbled in while

I washed the dishes. I had never been curious about the notebook, assuming it was just notes on the books he was reading and musings about the nature of God. Nothing to do with me. But that evening when I came over to clear his tea mug he covered the page with his forearm. I pretended to be uninterested and reached across him to take the crumpled paper napkin by his elbow. That's when I caught sight of the phrase peeking out from under his wrist. It said, "she lay with him."

I wouldn't have thought much about it, except that I awoke that night to find his hand on my stomach. I rolled toward him and felt his lips and the soft scrape of his beard on my face blindly brushing my eyes and cheeks until they found my mouth. He wriggled inside me and I reached up and slipped my fingers into the bristly plush of hair at the back of his neck. It was so black in the room that I couldn't even see his outline. I only felt his hands reading me like Braille.

After that I tried harder to read what he was writing. I knew that every gesture I made, even prying, was written first by Gabriel. I was a mere collection of his words and punctuation, which explained why I felt so filmy and insubstantial. What puzzled me was that he wrote for so long, yet I did so little. Was he writing far into the future, or did he write every detail: *she picks up a fork, she breathes, she scratches her leg?* He hid the notebook somewhere during the day. I never saw where he took it out from; it was just there suddenly on the table after dinner.

He never touched me during the day. It was only at night, in the impenetrable black of his room, that I would wake to find his fingers questioning me. I turned to him, found his mouth, opened myself to him, but I was never sure if it was Gabriel I made love with, or the pen that wrote me, or just the darkness.

"How's your ankle?" he asked me one afternoon. He was curled up with Boehme's *Way to Christ,* the Cabala, and the I Ching. I looked down at my foot. It was hardly tender at all now and not at all swollen.

"It's better," I said, and my stomach clenched. I was afraid he wanted to launch me into the world like Frankenstein's monster. "Do you want me to go?"

"No." He looked rueful. "I just wondered if you can walk."

"Oh. Yes."

I studied his long dark eyes and the jagged angle of his jaw. His face was still unfamiliar to me despite all the time we had spent together. I looked at him, I guess, but I didn't know enough about him to make sense of what I saw. The times I stared at him the hardest were in the dark.

"What are you?" I said.

He looked so puzzled that I started laughing. "What ethnicity?" I explained.

"Oh," he said. "I'm Mexican."

And then he added, "It's nice to see you laugh."

Gabriel thought that swimming would be a good way to strengthen my ankle. At first I was reluctant to leave his flat, but he was so persistent that I gave in. Early one morning we drove up to Lake Anza, a pond in Tilden Park with a sandy, man-made beach on one shore. It was October and the lake was officially closed for the winter, but we climbed over the fence and dropped down onto the sand. We'd set out at six to avoid the ranger, and as we stood on the beach, the sky was still densely curtained with fog and the lake looked menacing and opaque. I was freezing. I wrapped a towel around my head and shoulders and huddled underneath it, waiting for Gabriel to say forget it, it's too cold, let's go home. He didn't. Instead he began peeling off his clothes and dropping them onto the sand. As soon as he stepped clear of his boxers, he took off running and dove straight in.

There was nothing to do but follow him, so I shed my clothes and found myself running stark naked down the beach with the air pimpling my skin. It was ten strides to the water and three more until I was deep enough to dive under. The lake was bracing—so cold I almost lost my breath. I came up shrieking and then thrashed forward as fast as I could, my arms and legs digging through the water in a furious struggle to get the blood circulating. When I stopped to look for Gabriel, I was floating in the green and bronze foliage reflection near the far shore.

Behind me, Gabriel was frolicking. He dove under and surfaced like a dolphin, his head and butt making alternate appearances in the air. When he saw me watching him, he disappeared into a black ripple: head, back, butt, thighs, and finally his brown feet slipping down below the surface. I waited for him to come up again, but he didn't, and I stayed treading water uncertainly until he bobbed up next to me, his hair slicked back into a thick pelt and his face merry as an otter.

"You're a strong swimmer," he said and suddenly pounced on me, wrapping his arms and legs around my body and clinging there until his weight pulled us down. His body was smooth and slippery and dense with muscle. I struggled against it in the murky underwater lake-light while he grinned and exhaled a few quick bursts of bubbles next to my ear. I thrashed and then gave him a hard pinch in the thigh and he slid off me and kicked up for the surface. I burst up coughing, my mouth full of muddy water. "What the hell is wrong with you? You could have drowned us both!" I shouted.

Gabriel was floating on his back. "I wouldn't have let you drown," he said with his eyes closed. "I was just playing."

"Fuck you, you don't get to play with my mortality," I said. "It's not yours to play with."

When he heard the fury in my voice, he opened his eyes and sat up, his face contrite. "I'm sorry, I didn't think you'd be scared," he said. "You seemed like a strong swimmer."

"I am a strong swimmer. Stronger than you, probably."

In a second he was smirking again. The lake had turned him into some sort of mischievous sprite. A water devil.

"Let's find out. I'll race you to that floating stick," he said.

"Okay. On three."

"Be careful of the snakes. One-two-three, go."

"What snakes?" I said, but he was off. I plunged after him and pulled ahead easily. My stroke felt strong and easy, and I was within a length of the stick when I felt something grab my ankle and pull me under. I kicked him off, but when I came up, he was treading water with the stick in his mouth like a dog.

"Cheater," I said.

"I told you to be careful of the snakes," said Gabriel.

We swam back to the shore slowly, stopping on the way to float on our backs and stare up at the sky. When we finally emerged from the water and walked up the beach to our clothes, I felt as amazed as the first breathless fish must have felt when she set her weary fins on land and began a new chapter of planetary life.

I was awake. My muscles were unkinked and shiny and my breathing went all the way into my chest. Cold trilled on my back and cheeks and ears. Gabriel stood next to me, toweling himself dry. "I feel reborn," I told him, and he paused mid-pat to grin at me.

When we were dry and dressed in jeans and sweatshirts, Gabriel spread out a blanket on the cold sand and we sat down to a shivery, open-air breakfast of jam-filled croissants and coffee from a thermos.

"You have crumbs all over your lips," I said when we were done eating, and I began brushing the croissant flakes from his beard. He held still, almost purring while I tended to him. When he was clean, I kissed him.

His mouth tasted of coffee and smelled of lake, and I felt a desire for him that was completely different from my murky acquiescence in his room. When the kiss ended, we looked at each other with our faces very close. Then we kissed some more and finished our coffee and decided to go for a walk in the woods before we went home. I slung the tote bag with the blanket and our wet towels over my shoulder, and we walked along the creek bed that led away from the pond. Gabriel took my hand as we walked.

"Tell me about yourself," I said. "Where did you grow up? What's your family like?"

He told me that he came from the farm country near Fresno, from a large, middle-class family that had been in California for five generations. His father was a rancher, his mother was a schoolteacher, and he had been told that he would be a priest from the time he was a toddler. He'd studied history and philosophy at Fresno State before starting divinity school and liked the contemplative life enough to never question whether this was what he should be doing.

"Did you have girlfriends?" I asked.

Gabriel thought this was a funny question.

"Of course I did," he said. "Why is everyone so hung up on the celibacy thing?"

"Because it's unnatural. And because you don't seem like the celibate type."

"Well, I'm not. Maybe I'm better suited to being a druid and making love with the high priestess in the woods on Beltane Eve."

Then he backed me up against the trunk of a redwood and kissed me until my skin turned hot and prickly.

Looking back, I can see that the first part of my stay with Gabriel was some kind of dementia. Being temporarily insane is a defense against even the worst crime, at least in California. But I don't have a defense for what happened when I emerged from my delirium that day in Tilden Park. As soon as I got the water out of my ears, I stopped thinking I was a character Gabriel had invented and I even remembered that I had a past and a future as well as a present. And this is why I cannot find a way to forgive myself for what came next. I was lucid. Yet I stayed with Gabriel.

We swam in the evenings at a pool on campus; Gabriel knew how to sneak me in even though I wasn't a student. We worked out hard together, racing and swimming timed relays, and then at night when we should have been exhausted we stayed up talking and making love. During the day we cooked complicated meals and went for walks by the marina and read, but mainly we did what lovers do—we anted up pieces of our histories chip by chip. I told him all about my father's disappearance and Lisa's wish and everything that came later. I just scumbled the edges of my narrative to obscure the one fact that would reveal what kind of person I really was.

I thought about Steven all the time. I worried about him and wondered whether anyone was drawing pictures of Terratarantula with him and tried to remember the way we used to live together before everything fell apart. But when I thought of returning, fear deadened my limbs. Everything I had made for us was ruined. I didn't know how to be his mother anymore. The mother I had been would never leave him.

As I came back to myself, it began to bother me that Gabriel had even tolerated me in my previous somnolent state.

"Didn't it irk you that I was so out of it?" I asked him as we sat out on the Lake Anza beach after another early-morning swim.

"You were troubled," he said. "I didn't hold it against you."

I tried to accept the idea of him liking some essence of me from the beginning, but it was impossible. I tried a new line of attack.

"Why did you only touch me in the middle of the night? Was it because you were repulsed by the fact that I was a zombie?"

This made him strike his forehead as if despairing that he could ever reason with me.

"I was *trying* not to touch you at all," he said. "It was just when you were lying next to me in bed without any clothes on that I found it hard to stick to my principles."

"What principles? Celibacy?"

"Jesus, leave the celibacy thing alone. I just didn't think it was principled to take advantage of someone who wasn't doing very well."

"Well, that was a very gallant sentiment, even if you couldn't carry it out."

He didn't look at me and I realized I was being provoking. Having principles was something he took seriously.

"Did you really think I'd lost my memory?" I said, trying to steer us onto less volatile ground.

"Maybe for the first day or two. And then I just thought you'd been through something that you didn't want to talk about."

"Why did you let me stay? Why didn't you bring me to the loony bin?"

"I *liked* you. You weren't any trouble and I thought I could help you. And I guess I thought you'd come to me for a reason."

"Sent by God?" I teased. "Or the devil?"

"Both," he said. "I've given up duality. It's all the same."

ℱive Will Get You Ten   (Simone)

It was a bad sign when I opened up a book for my morning fortune and landed on a blank page. I was looking for Julia, but she was hidden in whiteness like fog or snow or rushing water.

I like to find my fortune in a book, but I know plenty of other methods. So I ran some tap water into an old pie tin, set it on the table, and looked inside.

There were rust stains on the bottom of the pan and I watched them mutate into landscapes and sunsets and then back into rust. Finally I caught a glimpse of Julia swimming along the surface. Her white arm breaking the water, her kicking legs scuffing up a trail of foam behind. I squinted close to see where she was going, but she dived under and disappeared. A second later my cat Swami jumped up on the table and knocked the pan onto the floor. I knew then I wasn't fated to find my Julia, but that didn't stop me from trying.

I tried every trick I knew: tea leaves, tarot cards, and a few other methods of my own invention. I scryed in a candle flame, and in a black-backed mirror. I wasn't used to navigating the present without a map, and yet there was no denying that I had reached an uncharted stretch. The only thing I could see with any clarity was the little nuclear family that had set up housekeeping over at Lisa's house, and much of that I saw firsthand. I wasn't exactly invited over; Carolina and Lisa wanted the man all to themselves. But I was worried about Steven, so I hung around.

They were playing house, just like little children. Carolina was the mommy, Bill was the daddy, and Lisa was the little girl. Every one of them was miscast. Bill had already shown twice that he wasn't any good at playing Daddy, and Carolina had always preferred the little girl's role. But Lisa's transformation was the hardest one to swallow. This heavy and thick one, the one who used to wear a pantsuit when dressing up, what was she doing in jumpers and Mary Janes? But there she was, and with a headband in her hair. She even went to work that way.

Steven was the odd man out. Did he get to play the role of little boy? Sometimes yes, sometimes no. Bill liked to take him outside before dinner and toss him a football on the street as the sun sank low and the evening fog leaped over the Bay.

"Go long, son," Bill said as Steven ran after the spiraling ball. "Soft hands, there you go, like catching a baby."

"What baby?" I asked Svengali, who lay purring on my lap while I watched the classic scene unfolding. What baby did Bill think he was playing with? His own baby Julia, wherever she was? Or maybe it was baby Roger, who would be almost exactly Steven's age by now?

Steven was clear-eyed as usual; he saw right off that these football tosses with the man he was supposed to address as Grandpa were a poor substitute for his own mother. For one thing Julia never would chase a bad throw. She'd just laugh as the ball bounced off the roof of a parked car and wait until it stopped rolling before she went after it. But when Steven's pass wobbled and then veered toward the neighboring houses, Bill tailed it, leaped after it, and speared himself in the ribs with the door handle of a parked Toyota. He doubled over, muttering a stream of curses: "Goddamn son of a bitch rat's ass fucking cocksucking hanging piece of shit." It made Steven's insides cower, but the two ghosts sitting on the curb laughed until they had to hold their sides.

All in all, it was hardly fun and games. Steven grew silent, hawkish. "Where's my mother?" he asked me every time he saw me. He even sent his dreaming self to pester me in the middle of the night, a shadow figure in my bedroom that made my cats arch their backs in fear and wonderment.

This is how a life binds you up tight in its own spidery weave. Once I knew all about a missing parent but thought it wise to keep my knowledge to myself. Now I was lying once again, but this time it was out of ignorance. "She's sick, but she's getting better," I told him. "She said to tell you that she loves you and she'll be back soon."

As for Bill, I told him she didn't want to see him. That was on Day Two, when they all sat waiting around the breakfast table for her to show. Ten o'clock and Lisa was dialing Julia's apartment for the fifth time. No answer. "She isn't coming," I said. I knew because I had read a line from Shelley that morning that spoke of a "departure from their father's door."

Bill looked stricken. "Why not?" he said. "Where is she?" You would have thought she was the one who left him, not vice versa. "She says you missed your chance; she doesn't need a father anymore," I said.

"Well, that's Julia for you," Carolina chirped. "So dramatic."

Lisa only said, "What are we supposed to do about Steven?"

"Just take care of him for now," I told them. "Let him get to know his grandfather."

I took Steven home to pick up clothes and toys to bring to Lisa's. That was the worst day. The apartment was dank and disordered. There was a note on the door for someone named Butch, who neither of us knew. It said she was downstairs with someone called Hank and would be back in five minutes. Steven read the note before I could tear it down and ran down the stairs to the door of the neighboring flat.

"It says she's just downstairs," he called up when he saw I wasn't following.

"She's not there anymore," I had to tell him. "She's gone away for a while. I told you that."

He stood suspended on the front porch not knowing what to believe. Then his eyes filled with tears like a pair of green leaves pooling with rainwater and he trudged back up the stairs. His mouth tugged downward, twitchy with sobs. The look he gave me as he passed me and went into his room said what I already knew. That I was no help at all.

Since I couldn't scry, I fell back on more conventional detective work. I called Julia's friends, and when I found they knew nothing, I called her job and learned she no longer worked there. Then I returned to Julia's apartment and sniffed around for an aroma of danger. All I smelled was dust, which was a comfort anyway. Her car was gone, as was her purse, and from the disarray, I gathered she'd packed in a hurry. It seemed a strange time to quit her job and skip town, but in a way I understood it. Still, I strained to see just where she'd gone.

Carolina and Lisa were so addled by Bill they didn't bother to think much about the vanished Julia. It was Bill who kept circling back to her the way a clean-shaven man will touch his face during the day, testing the slickness and the whiskers' ritual return. He had returned thinking he could slip back into the past and set things right, and Julia's absence was a troublesome reminder that time only moves in one direction. He liked reminiscing about the time he spent with her when she was a little girl, as if all these instances put together would make up for the years he missed.

"I used to take Julia to the dog races when she was about three," Bill recalled one afternoon as he drove his family to the racetrack. "I'd let her pick out one to bet on, and then I'd sit her on my shoulders so she could root for her pick. She'd be shrieking, 'Go, doggy! Go, doggy!' at the top of her lungs. It was a panic."

"Did I ever go with you to races?" asked Lisa, jealous as an unfed pet. She barely remembered the father of her childhood, and it was distressing to learn that he barely remembered her as well.

"I don't think so, Precious, this was when you were just a baby."

"I remember going to the movies with you," Lisa said.

"Remember how we all used to go to the movies every night during the summer because it was the only place that was air-conditioned?" interjected Carolina from the backseat. "I think we saw the same movie about fifteen times."

"I would have watched a cat being run over by a car if I could watch it in an air-conditioned theater," Bill said.

Steven remembered going to the movies with Dawn and Julia. Just a few weeks before they had gone to see *The Little Mermaid.* He remembered how they talked over his head as they left the theater, arguing amiably about whether the movie was sexist. It was their smells he recalled now. The scent of laundry and flower-scented hand lotion as they draped their arms across his shoulders and thoughtlessly caressed him while they talked.

"Christ, those Boston summers were brutal," Bill was saying. "I used to spend the afternoon lying in the girls' little swimming pool with my feet hanging over the edge and Julia splashing around beside me. I didn't let you in the pool with me, Lisa, because you always peed."

Lisa folded her arms across her chest, pouting. If she was still mining for memories, her daddy was an unpromising quarry. Every vein she tapped was full of Julia and only Julia. But Lisa was resourceful, used to alchemizing gold from whatever minerals she had on hand. She could mint herself a set of childhood memories from the lodestuff of the present. She'd use this very excursion if she had to. "Remember how we went to the races?" she could say. "Remember how I rooted for my horse?"

Those freshly minted memories may be distinct for Lisa, but in my mind the excursions all blend together. Every time I looked into a cup of tea or a glass of soda, even when I was scrubbing out the toilet bowl, the four of them floated past on their way to some new outing. Bill was campaigning, like a do-nothing politician kissing babies before the election. He knew he had to make up for his first term. So off they went to the water slide, the aquarium, and the Japanese tea gardens. The railroad museum with its trains to nowhere. The smoky bowling alley where Steven threw five consecutive gutter balls and then gave up in frustration. Steven was the excuse for all these children's games, but he was the only one of them who was tired of being a child.

As I did the dishes in my apartment one afternoon, I parted the suds and found them flying a kite in North Waterfront Park. The wind was whipping over the Bay so fast, it skidded when it hit dry land. In a moment the kite had pulled away like a lure that some wind-borne fish had snapped up and was carrying out to sea. The family stood and watched the struggle, the invisible fish bucking and swimming while Bill tried to tame it and reel it in. Somehow they never noticed that the fight between air and man was a reenactment of the man's whole life. But I noticed and dumped out the dirty suds. I was sick of the whole affair.

About a week after Bill's arrival, Mitch came by carrying a package for Lisa. He stood smiling at the door like a bashful prom date until Lisa drew him in.

"How have you been?" he said as he stood in the apartment foyer. Lisa was all smiles in her blue-and-gray drop-waisted dress and patent-leather Mary Janes.

"Great, really great. Hey, my dad's here. You want to meet my dad?"

Mitch looked around, puzzled. The poor man must have thought Lisa was imagining things. But there was Bill, tearing himself away from the national beach volleyball championships and striding into the hallway with his hand extended.

"Hello there, I'm Lisa's father," he said to Mitch. "Pleased to meet you, son."

"Let's all sit down," Lisa said when the handshaking was done.

So they all sat down in the living room and Carolina brought them glasses of lemonade before disappearing into the kitchen. Then Mitch brought out his gift, which was wrapped in brown paper and tied with a raffia bow.

"I brought you a present," he said. "You seemed a little sad last time we talked, and I wanted to cheer you up."

"A present!" Lisa said. "Well, that's nice."

The two men watched while she undid the wrapping. Inside was a little terra-cotta pot.

"It's a garlic roaster," Mitch said. "You put the garlic in it and put it in the oven."

"It's delicious," Lisa explained to Bill. "You take the roasted garlic and you spread it on bread like butter."

"That'll keep the vampires away," Bill said and tugged his left ear nervously.

"My dad doesn't like spicy food," Lisa explained to Mitch. She seemed to think that nothing either man said to the other would be intelligible without her translation. Between her interjections Bill and Mitch surveyed each other warily.

"Roasted garlic is really very mild," Mitch said. "We serve it at the restaurant. Everyone loves it."

"Mitch works at the same restaurant I used to work at, before I started at Tiger Soup," Lisa told Bill.

"The problem isn't that I don't like garlic, it's that garlic doesn't like me," Bill said. "I used to have a devil of a time in Mexico. They dip everything in garlic; they even make soup out of it. And Brazil is worse."

"Daddy's lived all over South America," Lisa said to Mitch.

"That's great," Mitch said. "I've been to the Yucatán. It was incredible. I loved it there."

They both paused to let Lisa insert her footnote, but she seemed to think this statement was clear enough on its own.

"Where in the Yucatán were you?" Bill said. "Cancún?"

Pretty soon the two men were swapping stories about their favorite Mexican beaches. Actually it was Bill who was telling the stories while Mitch applauded and called for encores. "That's incredible," he'd say as Bill wound up an anecdote. "Say, have you ever been to Isla Mujeres?" And so Bill would be able to segue into another story, this time about a woman he knew on Isla Mujeres who got a good deal on a pig but didn't know how to slaughter it. Lisa folded her hands in her lap and watched as Bill acted out the parts of the pig and the reluctant butcher and Mitch laughed until his eyes leaked tears.

"Mitch," she said when the story was over. "What are you doing tonight? Would you like to stay for dinner?"

After that, Mitch came to visit every other day or so and usually stayed for the evening meal. Then, after Steven went to bed, the grown-ups sat around the dining room table and played cards. Mostly they played Hearts, although the message of the game was lost on them. Cards will tell your fortune whether you want them to or not, and the game of Hearts always predicts who will be most done in by love. Bill was the best liar and thus the best cardplayer, and Carolina naturally came in second. Mitch couldn't lie but he was born lucky, so in the end it was Lisa who lost most often. Hearts were drawn to her, no matter what strategy she used. But when she tried to shoot the moon, the dour Queen of Spades always wound up with Mitch.

He was courting her. He brought her a new kitchen gadget every time he came to visit, never noticing that Lisa hardly cooked at home anymore. The kitchen was Carolina's domain now, and her meat loaves and pot roasts made little use of Lisa's shiny poultry shears and copper tart molds.

If you had asked Mitch what he was doing, he would only have said that he liked getting to know Lisa's father. "Your father seems like such a happy man," he confided to Lisa when they were alone. "And you seem so happy when you're around him." He was missing the point, but that was nothing new. The truth was that Lisa and her father shared a melancholy nature, and it was that bitter flavor that drew Mitch to them. The human tongue craves contrasts: sour after sweet, food after sex, bitter coffee after bloody meat. Mitch had come back to Lisa the way a deer finds the salt lick in a forest, knowing that underneath the pinafores an exquisite crankiness awaited him.

Meanwhile I was at the occult store, trying to find out what had happened to my extra senses. The deaf have hearing aides, the near-sighted wear glasses, but what is an elderly woman to do when her second sight begins to fade? I didn't know, which was why I was poking among the zodiac coloring books and crystal pendants.

The woman behind the counter was just a little younger than me. She wore her gray hair in two wispy braids and had a sharp, angular face. Her eyes were so blue they were alarming. I tend to think colored eyes are hiding something, since brown is the color of the earth and earth is what we're made of. But at times Fate requires reliance on strangers, so I said, "I need some help with divination."

"What sort of help do you need?"

That stumped me. Occult stores are filled with paraphernalia: goddess statues and colored candles, wands, altars, incense, and chalices. Frippery, to my mind. Window dressing. I used them when I was young and then I got tired of them. Now magical accessories put me in mind of how I used to dress when I was in my twenties: girdle, bra, slip, stockings, garters, dress, shoes, handbag, hat, scarf, jacket, choker, rings, bracelet, broach, and so on. Meanwhile a man just puts on a pair of pants and a shirt and is done with it.

Still, my stripped-down ways weren't working. If they were, I wouldn't have been standing in a badly lit occult store breathing in cheap sandlewood incense. So I sized up the pointy-faced woman across from me and said, "I'm having trouble scrying."

"Scryer's burnout," she said with a nod. "It's very common. You're overtaxed."

I didn't like her instant diagnosis, but I kept my tongue in check and explained that I could see some things perfectly well. It was just that I couldn't see the one thing I was looking for.

"And what's that?"

"My niece. She's disappeared and I need to find her."

The woman shrugged and I noticed that her shoulders were thin and wiry as a teenager's. "Maybe your niece doesn't want to be found," she said. "Or maybe you don't really want to find her."

I didn't say anything to that, and after a moment she seemed to recognize that I was still waiting for a better answer.

"All right," she said. "This is what I'd try. First, clean your house. Dust can gum up the works, and so can piles of things cluttering up your surfaces. Like books, for instance."

She was taking some jars down from the shelves behind the counter, but she stopped to grin at me then. She had me pegged and she knew it. I began to glimpse her true nature: impish as well as brusque.

"Too much crap around your house causes interference," she went on. "So do some housecleaning. Then go back to basics. Light silver candles before you scry. Burn saffron incense. Also, chew these."

She spooned a handful of flat gray-green leaves into a plastic Baggie and followed it with a crumbly mixture. "Laurel," I said. "And that's mugwort."

"Make the mugwort into tea. And do whatever else you're used to doing before you do magical work. Don't skip any of the steps."

"Hocus-pocus," I said as I wrote her out a check for the herbs and the candles and the incense. The word *magic* rubs me the wrong way. Divination is about as mystical as turning on the TV. The airwaves are already out there. If your antenna's working, it's easy enough to pick them up.

The woman behind the counter didn't respond to my comment. She was too busy looking at my check. "That's interesting," she said as she read over my address. "We live on the same street. I'm about three doors down from you."

"What are the chances of that?" I said crisply and gathered up my things.

Steven's misery was palpable enough that finally even Bill noticed it. "How about we go to the ball game?" he said to Steven. "It'll just be us boys." And Steven couldn't help but look over his shoulder at the greenish faces of the ghostly boys who always tagged along.

Baseball. I'm not a fan, but it was clear enough to me that Steven loved it the way I love books, for instance, or Lisa loves food. He loved it down to the details. The slow shadow spreading over the infield dirt as the groundskeepers sprayed it down. The players in their white home uniforms stretching out on the cropped outfield grass. The smell of hot concrete and peanuts and suntan oil.

When they got to the ballpark, Steven leaned over the second-deck railing and an elation as white as the white sun shimmered through him. "I bet the A's are gonna win today," he said. A safe bet, since the A's had just clinched the division title. Too safe for Bill, who thought it was time to impart some sort of manly lesson.

"So you're a wagering man, eh?"

"Sure," Steven said, although he wasn't sure what *wager* meant.

"All right, I'll make a bet with you. I'll give you twenty dollars if your A's lose."

"They're not going to lose, they're going to win," Steven said. He jumped down from the railing and swung an imaginary bat through the air, head down, shoulders square, just the way Julia had taught him. He still didn't understand what the proposition was. And why should he have? He was just a little boy. He'd never been disloyal in his life.

"You better hope they don't win if you want this twenty. No, I'll tell you what, I'll make it forty."

Bill took two twenty-dollar bills from his wallet and held them out to Steven the way you might tease a dog with a biscuit. When the boy reached for them, he yanked them out of reach.

"Oh, you want them, do you? Then you're ready to bet?"

The A's were running out onto the field, taking their positions like a flock of white birds landing on different branches of a wide-limbed tree.

"Bet's on?" Bill prompted. "If your A's win, I keep the forty. If they don't, you're a rich man."

Steven stared. His stomach tightened.

"Shake?" Bill said, and he grasped Steven's small sweaty hand in his own and pumped it up and down. "Quit frowning," he said. "Worst thing can happen is you make forty dollars."

They took their seats just as the game began. The ghosts sat next to Bill and stretched their black boots onto the seats in front of them. For once they seemed occupied, interested. They kept their eyes on the field and didn't bother pulling faces at Steven. As always, Bill acted as if they weren't there.

He was relaxed, or pretending to be. He wore a white T-shirt and a pair of dark green shorts, and he sat with his arms folded, watching the game as if it were trying to put one over on him. When the souvenir vendor came by, Bill flagged him down and bought a white A's cap.

"My damn head's going to burn in this sun," he said to Steven as he put it on.

Steven was staring down at the field, where the Kansas City Royals were batting. He knew this was the team he was supposed to be rooting for, but he couldn't bring himself to cheer when one of their players got a hit. So he just watched the batters go through their paces.

Bill had taken the fun out of the game, just like that. You know my opinion of hope as an emotion, but there's a time and a place for everything. As far as I can tell, wishing and hoping is what spectator sports are all about. Of course, the outcome of the game was determined long ago, but the fans believe that if they cheer, pray, cross or uncross their fingers, turn their baseball hats around or upside down, it will make a difference. It's why they come.

But Steven didn't know which way to pray. It wasn't just the money; he wasn't even sure what forty dollars could buy. It was the fact that Bill had made him shake on it. The Athletics weren't his now. The two twenty-dollar bills flapped in his mind like two hinged gates, keeping him out.

Steven's favorite player was Jose Canseco, the A's right fielder. He was a big, thick-necked man, so muscled he seemed to have been put together wrong. Now he stood just outside the batter's box wagging his head from side to side.

"There's your man Canseco," Bill said. "What the hell's wrong with his neck?"

"He always does that. He's stretching."

The pitcher released the ball. Canseco swung, missed it, and stepped out of the batter's box, shrugging his shoulders. Steven was mesmerized.

"I think you're going to get your money," Bill said. "The guy does more stretching than hitting."

Usually that was Steven's favorite part. The slow building of suspense as the batters stepped out of and then into the batter's box and the pitcher slowly came set and then threw and the batter stood and watched or turned and swung. Bill had forgotten, or maybe he never knew, how a true heart loves whatever it is it's settled on. It loves utterly, unguardedly, without reservation. And so the boy sat watching Canseco and imagined the ball blazing like a firecracker, up and out. And then, remembering the wager, he pictured Canseco striking out. Which Canseco obligingly did.

And whose fault was that? You might say Canseco's, as did the fan sitting next to Steven. "What's he swinging at?" the fan said to no one in particular. He was a stocky man with a flat face like a Persian cat's. "Those pitches were in his eyes. Guy thinks he's eight feet tall."

Steven blamed himself. His thoughts had made Canseco swing haplessly, blindly. And knowing that, he didn't know what to think. He couldn't root against his favorite players, but forty dollars said he couldn't root for them, either. So when Mark McGwire came up to bat, he sat inert and kept his thoughts in check.

McGwire was a blonder, pinker version of Canseco. In Steven's mind the two men were two halves of one brawny notion, the dark one and the fair one, like night and day, shade and sun. He watched McGwire crouch, holding the bat upright, and tried not to care what happened. The crowd was cheering. McGwire swung and hit a long fly ball that vanished behind the right foul pole. The crowd rose to its feet as the ball climbed and sank down again as it went foul.

"Almost lost your money on that one," Bill said and went off to buy himself a beer. McGwire popped out on the next pitch. The inning was over. Steven sat quietly by himself and wondered why his stomach hurt.

"That was some foul ball," the flat-faced man next to him said. "One inch to the left and that's a home run. What a shame."

Steven must have looked forlorn, because the man kept chatting. Adults always think they can drown out a child's mood if they talk long enough.

"You like the A's?" the man said. "You like the Giants? Could be a Bay Bridge World Series this year—you know what that means? The Giants and the A's play each other. That would be exciting. Ever been to a World Series game? You should get your dad to take you."

"He's my grandfather," Steven said.

"Well, get Gramps to take you, then. It's something you'll never forget."

Bill came back with a hot dog for each of them. They ate in silence as the game progressed. "What are you going to do with all that money?" Bill said at last. "Buy a car?" He guffawed, and when Steven didn't join in, he shifted position. "No, really, what do kids buy these days? Comic books? Baseball cards?"

"Sure," Steven said. "I'd like to get a skateboard." By this time the A's were winning, but it didn't seem to matter. Steven felt as if the team had moved on and left him in an empty stadium. He turned and looked at Bill, flanked by the flimsy sour-faced soldiers on either side of him. "Who are those guys?" he asked. "Why do they follow you around all the time?"

He hadn't meant to ask, but the wager had made him peevish. He kicked the seat in front of him, waiting for Bill to answer. It was better to talk than to watch the game and have to worry about which side he was on.

"I guess they're ghosts," Bill said when he'd recovered from his surprise enough to talk. "Spirits."

This was such a stupid reply that Steven didn't even bother nodding. "I know that," he said. "But why are they here?"

Bill shrugged and his normal embarrassed expression turned a shade more rueful. "I made a mistake and it caught up with me, that's all."

Steven wondered if every mistake you made followed you around and made faces at the people in your family. His own mistakes were mainly spills and wrong answers on tests. He glanced over his shoulder to see if a puddle of orange juice or a paper with red marks on it was hovering behind him.

"What kind of mistake?"

Bill took the A's cap off his head and rubbed the shine from his scalp. His mouth pursed and then relaxed as if he were going to tell a tale and then thought better of it.

"Same mistake I always make. Wrong place at the wrong time. Some people just aren't very forgiving." He winked at the two ghosts, but they ignored him, their eyes glued to the game.

"Can they talk?"

"Dunno. They don't have anything to say to me, anyway. Ugly sons of bitches, aren't they? And stuck on me like a case of crabs." He chuckled and looked at his hands as if hoping to find a toy there that he could use to distract Steven from this line of questioning.

"Let me ask you something, since we're getting personal," Bill said.

"What?"

"Where's your mother?"

The question was like a brushback pitch, that hard throw a pitcher sends whizzing under a batter's nose to make him step back from the plate.

"She went away for a while," Steven said, his voice dry.

"How come you didn't go with her?"

"I don't know."

Just then Rickey Henderson hit a home run. Everyone around them stood up to watch the ball sail over the left-field fence. Bill stood up, too, and exchanged vigorous high fives with a man in front of him. It wasn't that he had become such an avid fan. He was just fleeing the look he'd left on Steven's face.

In the end the A's won the game. Bill gave Steven ten dollars as a consolation prize and bought him a frozen yogurt served in a tiny plastic batting helmet. He couldn't understand why the boy seemed so morose as they walked down the long ramp that led from the stadium to the BART station.

I could have explained it to him. The truth was that Steven was afraid. For the first time in his life he knew what it was like to choose poorly. Now he was certain that if he looked over his shoulder, he would see two twenty-dollar bills slinking behind him like his grandfather's ghosts.

It only took a few weeks for Carolina and Bill to run out of things to say to each other. At first Bill kept her amused by telling stories from his travels. Once these ran out, they reminisced about the times they'd had before he left. But eventually they ran out of reminiscences, too. So they turned to arguing.

Carolina started it. It began to irk her that Bill had just moved back into her life like a stray dog. She had quit her job at the airline so she could spend more time with him, but he didn't even have the sense to be grateful. He didn't ask what she had done with herself during the past twenty-two years, either. He just planted himself on the sofa and took over the remote control. Pretty soon his heavy masculine presence began to grate. He made himself felt in every corner of Lisa's apartment, from the seat left up on the toilet to the perpetual sound of roaring fans leaking from the TV. At night he stretched out like Christ on the cross, leaving her to scrunch herself into a far corner of the mattress.

Even when she took refuge in the kitchen, he followed and rooted around the refrigerator for a snack while she made dinner. Constant contact always makes for chafing, ask any fat man's thighs. So Carolina started needling him.

"I didn't have it so easy while you were gone," she told him one afternoon as he sat at the kitchen table with a bag of potato chips and a dish of sour cream and onion dip.

"I know you didn't, baby."

"Raising two girls by yourself is no picnic. And I couldn't get married again, either, since you didn't bother to divorce me before you wandered off."

She was coming at him crabwise, pinching him from behind. She wanted him to say that he regretted leaving her. Or she wanted him to go away. It was hard to say which.

Either way, Bill didn't give the answer she wanted. "The past is past, 'Lina," he said. "Let's think about the future."

But it was the future that was bothering her. At night, while Bill lay sleeping, she fingered the lump inside her breast. If she lay awake long enough, Irma would come into the room and stand by the window, watching her with a little smile. A smile of love, I could have told her. But Carolina didn't see it that way. So she woke Bill up and dug in ever so delicately with her little pincers.

"Bill," she said. "I'm glad you came back to me before it was too late."

"Me, too, baby," He lay on his back with his hands behind his head, his mind already spinning off into sleep again.

"It'll be easier for me to die, knowing that we had this last time together," she went on, pinch-pinching.

"I feel like I did die, 'Lina, and ended up in heaven."

Carolina was curled up next to him, plucking at his chest hairs with her fingers. "I just hope the time isn't too short," she said.

That woke him up. He tried to see her face, but it was hidden by a veil of hair. "What are you getting at, baby? Are you asking if I'm planning to leave again?"

That wasn't at all what Carolina had been leading up to, but now that he brought it up, it seemed like a good question. She paused for a moment, trying to decide which way the conversation ought to go.

"I'm not going anywhere," Bill said to fill the silence. "I'm tired of traveling. I've been everywhere in this world I ever want to go. Now I just want to stay with you." He stroked her head and ran his fingers through her hair until they caught a tangle.

"Ow." Carolina sat up, pulling his fingers out of her hair as she did. "Bill, listen to me. This is serious. I don't know how much longer I'm going to be around. I have cancer."

Bill didn't move. From the corner of his eye he could see his ghosts stalking into the room. He watched them lean up against the windowsill next to the bed and wondered why they always wanted to be near him just when he most wanted to be alone.

"Bill?" Carolina said. "Did you hear what I said?"

He was still looking at the corner of the window to his left, where a small, stooped old woman had joined the two soldiers. She looked familiar to him, but for a moment he couldn't place her. She smiled at him absently and then squatted down on the floor as if resting.

"I said I have cancer," Carolina said. "Doesn't that mean anything to you? Why don't you say anything?"

"I can't. My heart is breaking."

It was true. His body shook and rattled with sobs. Carolina scooted close to him and he leaned his head against her shoulder. When she looked down, she saw that his eyes were closed and his face was stretched into a trembling grimace, as if something very large were trying to escape his body through his mouth.

After a while the sobs quieted. Bill sat up and put his arms around Carolina and rocked her softly and kissed her hair with wet salty lips. Then she took his hand and showed him how to feel the piece of gravel on the underslope of her breast. He stroked it with the tip of his finger until she had almost forgotten that it was a part of her she loathed. Then he leaned down and kissed it and then kissed around it in slow narrowing circles until he reached her nipple. He made love to her so soberly that she was embarrassed and wished for his usual bedroom boisterousness, his dirty songs and laughter.

Afterward he surprised her by staying awake instead of rolling over into slumber a second after he was satisfied. Carolina had never seen him so sad and serious, and she didn't know what to make of it. So she began to chat.

"I know why I got sick," she said. "I saw it coming from the moment my mother died. She always hated me. It was Simone she liked. She was jealous of me because I was so close to my father. You remember what she was like, don't you? She seemed so quiet and humble, but the more I think about it, the more I think she was mean. A mean, spiteful woman."

"I don't know that she was mean," Bill said and looked over at the old woman squatting on the floor next to him. From his vantage point on the bed he could just see her head, framed by wisps of gray and black hair like the spiky rays of a black sun. She was listening with the same small smile she had worn when she first came into the room, as if she were hearing a song she liked but had forgotten the words to. Bill wasn't sure whether or not she even noticed he was there.

"That's because you don't know her like I do. I'm telling you, Bill, I know you probably won't believe me because it sounds impossible, but she's haunting me. She's trying to kill me. That's why I have this lump."

Bill looked over at his own ghosts, who were playing rock, paper, scissors. He kissed Carolina's forehead. "Ghosts can't hurt you, baby. They're just air."

"That's easy for you to say. You don't have one breathing down your neck all the time."

"I know it's frightening when you see one, but they don't have any power. Think of her ghost as a reminder, like a Post-It. That's all she is, just a sticky little Post-It."

Carolina sat up, bristling. "Don't patronize me."

"I'm not patronizing you, I'm just telling you. This is something I know a little bit about. In my travels—"

"Your travels!" Carolina shrieked. The three ghosts turned to look at them. "You think your travels turned you into Albert Einstein, don't you? You think I don't know anything because I didn't do anything but sit around in the USA raising your children by myself while you were off *traveling.*"

"That's not what I said."

"You didn't have to say it, it's perfectly clear. You think I'm an ignoramus. You think I'm exactly the same as when you left twenty-two years ago. Don't you? Don't you!"

"Stop it, Carolina, you're being ridiculous."

"See? That's my point exactly. Why can't you just believe that I know what I'm talking about?"

Bill sighed and put his head in his hands: the pained look of a rational man faced with an irrational woman. The gesture only egged Carolina on.

"What did you come back for, Bill?" she said. "Just to show me how smart you'd gotten?"

"I don't know why I came back," Bill said and leaped out of bed. "Maybe it was a mistake." He stood in the midst of the triangle of ghosts and rummaged around the floor for the pair of boxers he had left near his shoes. The ghosts parted like underwater grasses as his hands moved through them.

Once he had stepped into his shorts, he turned around to look at Carolina. She was kneeling on the bed, weeping into her hands. Irma sat next to her, her hands folded in her lap, in the moist indentation where he had been lying a moment before.

"Maybe it was a mistake," Bill said again. "Maybe you'd be happier being alone with your mother's ghost."

He went off to sleep on the couch.

The next day Bill came into the kitchen and spread a map of the Americas out on the table. Carolina was making guacamole. She scooped the green avocado flesh into a bowl and squeezed half a lemon over it. Bill sat back and watched. "Can I help?" he asked. "I used to make guacamole every day when I lived in Mexico."

"Did you?" Carolina said without a flicker of interest. She sliced cilantro, tomato. The blade of the knife beat against the cutting board like a tiny drum.

"I was thinking that you and I could go on a trip," Bill said. He leaned back in his chair, his face aglow. Carolina's knife went *chip-chop,* and a stream of tomato juice trickled from the edge of the cutting board onto the floor. Bill took a dish towel that was threaded through the handle on the refrigerator door and bent down to mop up the drippings.

"Use a paper towel," Carolina said. "We dry dishes with that."

"I'd like to show you South America. There's so much to see," Bill said. His voice had turned pleading. He blotted at the spill with a paper towel handed to him by the silent Carolina. The color seeped through the towel's white, matching him blush for blush.

Silence was Carolina's best weapon, and she used it like a pro. She remembered long ago, when Bill stopped talking to her and left her hankering for words. Now it was Bill clinging, pestering. And Carolina kept her mouth shut tight.

"Peru, Chile, Costa Rica, Ecuador—name the place and we'll go. I can show you the best of any country in South America. Mountains? Beaches? Rain forest? Ruins? What do you want to see, my sweet?"

Carolina flayed a red jalapeño with the tip of her knife.

"I'll make love to you in the upper altitudes of the Andes and leave you gasping for breath," Bill said. He was on his knees, coincidentally. The spill was mopped up, so he licked the inside of Carolina's thigh. "What do you say, 'Lina?"

'Lina wasn't saying anything. She reached for an onion and sliced it open, eyes watering.

"You cut me to the quick, your highness," Bill said and stood up. "If you want me, I'll be watching the game."

And he stalked into the living room, startling Mitch and Lisa, who had been necking on the couch.

In the kitchen, Carolina sighed and wiped tears away with the back of her hand. She scraped a few of the onions from the cutting board with the knife blade and mixed them into the guacamole. The mixture looked strange—lumpy and unappealing. She'd done it wrong perhaps; neither of us ever learned to cook with any flourish. Still, she knew Bill wouldn't complain. She put the bowl on the kitchen table, on a corner of the map, and set about preparing salmon steaks for dinner.

Watching her, I turned the day's fortune over in my mind. I'd gone to Virgil, the patron saint of bibliomancy, and found this line: "He saw our double lineage, twin parentage, how he had been mistaken through new confusion over ancient places." I understood the double lineage part well enough. Carolina and I were both born of two competing traditions, and they yanked us every which way. My little sister, standing in the kitchen in her high heels, was positively stretched.

I saw her stare at the kitchen table, rubbing her hands over her forehead. Her mouth fluttered and then hung open in astonishment.

A chip-sized dollop of guacamole had fallen on the map, obliterating the ancient state of Oaxaca, Mexico. In the light of that morning's fortune, I saw the meaning clear enough. *New confusion over ancient places.* Oaxaca was an ancient place, and Carolina was certainly confused. She fingered the dollop of guacamole and concluded that it was the hasty spillings of a ravenous spirit caught filching from the bowl.

And so, eager to make amends with the lurking mother she suspected of planting a pebble in her breast, Carolina cooked. When the salmon steaks came out of the oven, she took two of them into her bedroom and locked the door, leaving Bill, Mitch, Steven, and Lisa to squabble over the three remaining.

The next day she baked four kinds of bread and prepared a roast, two kinds of salad, and a pot of mashed potatoes. But when the family sat down to eat, the lion's share had disappeared. Afterward, when Bill went into the guest room to take his after-dinner nap, he found the bed strewn with dishes and Carolina in the center, reigning over them like the Queen of Plates.

"Carolina," he said cautiously. He was cowering, the dog with the slashed nose approaching the clawing cat.

"Yes, dearheart," Carolina said, licking her fingers. Mashed potatoes and pale beef blood had spilled onto the sheets, and a parchment-colored fragment of salmon skin rested on a pillow. Carolina was eating a piece of cheese and jalapeño bread. "You won't like this," she said to her husband, although he hadn't asked. "Too spicy." Crumbs gathered in the white hammock of her nightgown-covered lap.

Bill cleared his throat. He thought about the proximity of the door, and the door beyond it that led to the front steps, and out, away. He said, "Explain to me why you are eating in here, instead of in the dining room with the family."

"It's private," Carolina said.

"Why do you need to eat privately? We've all known each other for years."

"No, the reason is private. Here, have a piece of zucchini bread. Don't take it all. Leave some for the hungry."

The hungry. Carolina, fanciful as she was, had a deadly literalness. She never could see beyond the text, poor thing. That yen she felt wasn't hunger. It was history, calling her.

Bill looked across the room to where his own ghosts were arm-wrestling by the window. They had left their hunger behind on that airstrip, long ago.

"Who are you feeding?" he asked, though he knew.

"No one ever cooked for her, do you know that?" Carolina burrowed around under the sheets until she found a slice of beef that had fallen beneath the covers. "Every day she cooked for us: breakfast, lunch, and dinner. But she never got to sit down to a meal she hadn't prepared."

"There are worse miseries." Bill lifted his shirt and rubbed his own complaining belly until the hairs under his palm crackled. "What about never sitting down to a meal at all? What about sitting down to a meal and finding that your wife has put the majority of it to bed?"

"If you're hungry, I suggest you go to 7-Eleven and buy yourself a burrito," Carolina said, still chewing.

Late converts are always the most zealous. Carolina cooked for our mother faithfully, making up for lost time. She seemed to have forgotten that our mother had always been a light eater, her sustenance coming mainly from tastes and nibbles at the stove. Now it was stews and casseroles, three-bean salads, turnovers and cakes.

Each steaming pot disappeared into the guest room and the door was locked behind. Bill looked disappointed every time; Lisa fumed. She tried to cook again for the first time in weeks, but now she and Carolina bumped against each other, battled. Pans were missing, buried in the bed. Lisa complained that she couldn't very well cook if every utensil was dirty or had disappeared. She took to eating at work or at Mitch's apartment, leaving Bill and Steven to fend for themselves.

Those two were brothers now, orphaned. They slept in the living room together, sharing the sofa bed. Bill bought them take-out dinners, which they ate out of the wrappers, sans utensils. It was hell for Lisa, who liked things neat. Her apartment was eroding, shrinking. First the guest room, gone to Carolina. Then the living room, gone to Steven. Now she had lost the kitchen, and the dining room was diminishing in a pile of cardboard cartons, Styrofoam, and greasy wrappings. She complained to Mitch, who felt strangely pleased. "My house has been invaded by savages," she said. And he said, "Well, why don't you come stay with me for a while?"

Carolina gained weight, Bill lost some. The house reeked of food, the fried scent of pizza and moo shu pork blended with the perfume of Carolina's more extravagant creations: Chicken Cordon Bleu, Coquille Saint Jacques, Boeuf Bourguignonne. Nightly, she sat in the center of the bed and laid out two dinners like a child's tea party.

"Do you like this food?" Carolina said to the air. Irma was toying with the shadows of her meal, more than sated but hungry still. She arranged the mashed potatoes into the shape of the state of Oaxaca, but Carolina didn't notice.

"What is it that you want from me?" she hissed. "I feed you, but you don't eat. You lurk, but I can't see you. Why do you hate me?"

And Irma hung her head, her ghostly love as invisible as the rest of her.

I wept for Carolina. I really did. I wept for them all, trapped in their fates like flies in a spiderweb. Sometimes second sight is like a song you can't get out of your head, a sad, plaintive song in this case, with a chorus that keeps repeating and repeating. I would rather have done something else, but I kept watching, in case Julia wandered through. Where *was* she?

One night in mid-October I sat in my evening bath gazing up at the blue tiles on the ceiling. I'd taken to filling my tub with bubbles to blur the images that kept bobbing up around me. But move my knee through the suds and a swath of clear water would open up and fill with pictures: Carolina and Bill arguing, Lisa and Mitch flirting, Steven sulking. So I stared at the opaque ceiling and breathed the fumes from the laurel leaves I'd dropped into the water and tried to keep my mind clear of everything but Julia.

I was just drifting into a sort of trance when I heard the door-bell peal. It was late for visitors—not that I have many—and I could think of only one possibility. I put on my chenille robe without even drying off and scurried into the hallway to hit the buzzer that would let Julia into the building.

While I was waiting for her to climb the two flights to my apartment, I wrapped my dripping hair in a towel and set water on for tea. I don't usually let anyone, not even Julia, see me without my hair done up in its usual gray beehive, but I was presentable, barely, when I opened the door. Which was fortunate, because it wasn't Julia.

It was a woman, slight of build, in jeans and a flannel shirt and a pair of sneakers.

"Hi," she said. "Do you remember me? Martha, from the occult store."

I did remember her of course—her wispy gray hair and startling blue eyes. But I didn't remember inviting her to drop by.

"I've gotten you out of the shower," she said. "I'm sorry, I suppose I could have called. Your phone number was on your check."

"My address as well," I said. I was baffled, frankly, but I could feel Fate's fingers at my back. So I invited her in.

"I was thinking about your situation and I decided I should help," she said as I made us tea. She had a strangely straightforward way of talking. No preambles. A dry, not terribly musical voice. I could see she had been exactly the same since she was a child. Reckless and odd. A tomboy with a taste for pretty things.

"Help in what way?" I said. I brought the tea over from the stove and sat down across from her at the kitchen table. My towel turban was beginning to come undone, so I took it off and hung it on the back of my chair. This distracted her.

"Look at your hair!" she exclaimed. "It's all black! It's beautiful." She reached across the table to feel one wet lock. Then she leaned back and stared at me appraisingly. "You look completely different than when I first met you. Without your glasses and that silver hairdo, you really look quite normal."

I admit I wanted her to say pretty. Or something along those lines. "Normal?" I said and stirred my tea a little.

"I have to say, you were the strangest-looking witch I'd ever seen come into the store, and I see some strange ones. I don't mean strange in a bad way, just not the usual kind."

"I'm not a witch," I said. "I only do divination."

I must have sounded a bit huffy, because she reached across the table and grabbed my hands. "I think we can work together. That's why I came by. I had a sense about it when I first met you, but you weren't what I expected, so I ignored it. But then I thought of you tonight and I realized I could help you, so I came over." After that she didn't let go of my hands. She stayed holding on to them and looked into my eyes with a mischievous smile on her pointy face. Her hands were soft and a little oily. She stroked the back of my own hands with her thumbs.

"I could teach you to do spells," she said.

I shook my head. "Not my cup of tea."

"Well, then, I'll do the spell and you do the divining. Let's just try it and see if we can find your niece."

I took my hands away and put them around my teacup. I could feel Fate behind me, pushing with knees and elbows now, not just with fingers. I said, "Now?"

We went into the living room. That was Martha's choice. I don't mind where I do my work, but she was particular. She wanted a little space, too, so we had to drag the coffee table off to one side and move a few stacks of books into a corner. "You didn't listen to me about clearing clutter," she said. "Where do you keep your candles?"

The candles were still in the bathroom actually. I always bathe by candlelight. At my age I prefer not to see my naked self exposed to the full glare of electric lighting. I fetched them and Martha placed them in the center of the floor and lit a few sticks of the saffron incense. I brought in my pan of water and placed it next to the candles. Then I sat down on the couch and waited.

Swami and Svengali had come in and were sniffing at the water and the candles on the floor. Traditionalists, like most cats. They disapproved of any deviation from the norm.

"Come sit here," Martha said. "Across from me."

I did, although it wasn't comfortable. It had been a long time since I'd sat on anything that didn't have a back to it. I sat Indian-style, like Martha, and adjusted my bathrobe so I would be covered up.

"Do you want to cast the circle?" she asked.

"I think not."

"Fine. I'll cast the circle and summon the Goddess."

And she did. I watched her moving lightly across my living room carpet, waving a crystal wand in the air. The candles flickered as she flapped around and my cats snaked in and out of her circle, curious. And then my mother came in and sat down.

She didn't greet me, just squatted on her haunches and looked down into the tin of water. Her hair was loose and black and she wore the crimson skirt and white blouse of her youth. I leaned forward so that my head was almost touching hers, but she never turned to meet my eye. Martha leaned forward, too, and the three of us looked down into the shallow pan until the water sheathed itself in roiling clouds. Then the clouds uncoiled themselves and faded.

There was Julia, in the arms of a man. The room was hot and velvety, smothered in heavy curtains. I could see the outline of noon light blazing around their edges. She crouched over him, her hands on his chest and her knees pressed against his ribs. Their lips tangled and her cheeks flamed with woozy blood.

"It looks like your niece isn't quite ready to be found," said Martha. Her eyes were burning blue and her thin face gleamed with mischief. What did it matter to her? I shook my head and let my eyes fall down to the water again. But now the lovers had changed their faces. The crouching one had wispy gray braids. And the one on her back had wet black hair.

I watched them kiss, amazed that old women could seem so soft. Then I swam upward, the weight of the trance on me like heavy water. When I surfaced, my mother was gone and Martha had closed her eyes.

If there's one thing I've learned in life, it's the gift of surrendering myself to Fate. When Martha's eyes opened, I leaned across the water and kissed her on the lips. It was a new experience for me, the moist fleshiness of another person's mouth, but she kissed just the way I expected her to. Impulsively, guilelessly, as if kissing were something that had just occurred to her. When she drew away and looked at me with her bold eyes, it was easy to complete the picture. I fell back onto the carpet and let her spread herself over me, like some very tart, thick jam.

*A*n Ear That Hears (Julia)

Irma was in my dream, accusing me. "Why are you walking in the wind?" she said. "Why do you drown your baby?" I was walking a foot above the sidewalk in some nether neighborhood that was neither mine nor Gabriel's. Tears came out of my hands and hair but not my eyes. "Was I swimming?" I said to Irma, but she wasn't answering any questions. "Shoo! Shoo!" she said and waved her broom at me. "Go away, weeping woman. We don't want you here!"

I woke up clutching at the blankets. For a moment I was disoriented, until I recognized Gabriel's shape drowsing next to me. It was late afternoon, but the curtained room was hot and dark. I ran my hands down my body to make sure I was still there. My chest felt like it was caving in.

"Gabe?" I said.

Silence. Then the house began trembling. The room shuddered, shifted, and then quieted. I bolted for the doorway and stood with my arms braced against the frame.

"Gabriel!" I hissed.

He sat up on his elbows and gave me a lazy, inquiring look. A second later the shaking started again, a swiveling wave that sent books and lamps sliding from the nightstands. California born as he was, it wasn't until the second tremor that Gabriel shot out of bed. He squeezed into the doorway with me, and we hung on to the doorsill as the house squirmed around us like a dog scratching a persistent flea.

At last the dog that was the house seemed to flop back down onto the floor and settle itchily into sleep. "That was a big one." Gabriel grinned. "Let's turn on the radio, see what they say."

I wasn't listening. I was squatting by the phone, frantically dialing Lisa's number. I heard a clicking noise, and then a tinny whistle screeched in my ear. I hung up and tried again. Now there was nothing but dead air.

"The power's out," Gabriel shouted from the living room. "And they're saying on the radio that the Bay Bridge fell down."

I put down the phone and began throwing on my clothes. "Gabriel," I said, going into the living room. "I need your car keys."

The room looked oddly rummaged. Gabriel's books were in a pile below the bookcase as if they had made a collective leap for freedom, and two ferns lay among the shards of their pots in the middle of the floor. Gabriel was naked on the chaise longue, the headphones of his Walkman pressed to his ear. "They say there are cars floating in the Bay," he said when he saw me. "I'm listening to the baseball announcers. The World Series game was just about to start, and they're saying that all the players are standing around, not sure what to do."

"Oh *shit*, the World Series!" My fingers scrabbled to tie my shoelaces, but they were so sweaty that they kept slipping. "The *World Series!* How could I have forgotten?"

Gabriel looked over at me in alarm. "Julia?" He took the head-phones off. "Are you okay?"

"I need your car keys," I said. "It's an emergency. I promise I'll come back."

The whole time I was driving I was praying. It was a murmur that burbled out of my mouth like a scream that can't get organized enough to come out all at once. "Let him be okay, make him be okay, let him be okay," I said as I drove. "He didn't go to the game, he's at home watching the game, he's at Lisa's watching the game, he's on the sofa watching the game, he's not on the bridge, he's at Lisa's watching the game, he's watching the game."

When I got to Lisa's house, I pushed on the buzzer without letting up, then pounded on the door itself, kicked it until the frame shook. Nothing stirred. I pressed my face against the glass and tried to peek into the apartment. There, by the door, was Steven's little sweatshirt, hanging on a hook. I hammered at the door with my fist and screamed his name as loud as I could. "Steven? Lisa? Is any-one home?"

He must be at Dawn's house. Of course he was. Lisa and Carolina didn't care about baseball, but Dawn did, and she and Steven had been watching games together since he was a baby. In a moment I was back in the car. I tried to calm myself by picturing Steven in his A's T-shirt and his green A's cap, kneeling on Dawn's floor with his nose almost brushing the screen. But who had brought him there? Who had been taking him to school every morning and put-ting him to bed at night? How long had it been? Four weeks? Was that possible? What had I been thinking?

And then the realization began to gush into my chest, cold and mossy like water trickling and pooling. I had done the thing that nobody was ever supposed to do to him. I had done it of my own free will. I had abandoned Steven, just as my father had abandoned me. I was indeed my father's daughter.

Dawn was standing in front of her house talking with some neighbors and pointing to the collapsed chimneys up and down the street. When she saw me running toward her, she broke away from the clump and stalked toward me with her arms folded across her chest.

"Where the hell have you been?" she demanded.

I ignored the question. "Is Steven here?"

Dawn shook her head. "No, he went to the game with your father." Then her face fell. "Oh, God. What if he was on the bridge?"

"I have to find him," I said. "How can I find him?"

Dawn gave me a pointed look, as if she was about to say something but thought better of it. "I'm sure he's okay. Just go home and wait for them to call."

"But he doesn't know that I'm back. He doesn't know where I've been. He must be scared," I wailed. "Maybe I should go to the police."

Dawn's eyes narrowed. "And say what? I lost track of my son a few weeks ago and now I'm wondering if he fell off the Bay Bridge?" She folded her arms over her chest. "Go home. I'll call you if I hear anything."

She turned around to walk away and then stopped and stamped her foot. "I'm so mad at you," she said. "I can't even talk to you I'm so mad. I just *knew* you'd be a terrible mother. Steven's been *miserable,* you fucking irresponsible bitch. He's been calling me every day, and he's so *sad* and he doesn't know where you are and I haven't known what to tell him."

"Please help me find him," I said. "Please? I don't know where to look."

Dawn shook her head and started walking back to the clump of neighbors in front of her house. "You're on your own," she said over her shoulder. "Call me when you find him and let me know he's okay."

I called Aunt Simone from a phone booth at a nearby liquor store. It took a dozen tries before the call would go through, and when it did there was no answer. I pressed the receiver to my ear and listened to it ring. There was a distant whirring in the background, the sound of my own rushing blood. It reminded me of the blood pounding in my ears at the moment Steven was born, and I pictured Aunt Simone standing over him on his first day of life, searching his oversized eyes with her own. What did she know about his future then that she never told me? Did she foresee an early death?

"Aunt Simone!" I whispered into the phone. "I need to talk to you."

But the rings kept coming, one after another, like the cars of an endless train. Dawn was right. I was on my own.

Back in the car, I put my head in my hands and tried to figure out what to do next. The world had split open like a bag of groceries, sending everything spinning and tumbling onto the sidewalk. Steven was out there in it, misplaced, crushed. But I was his mother. I was the one who cleaned up spills and put things back in their place. The crackers in the cupboard, the juice in the fridge, the mother with the son. If I could find him, I could fix everything.

And so I set out for the Bay Bridge. I knew he could be anywhere, but I had to make sure he wasn't in one of the cars the radio announcers had said were floating in the Bay. "Why do you drown your baby?" Irma had asked in my dream. But he wouldn't drown, if I could find him.

I don't think it took me more than ten minutes to get from Dawn's house to downtown Oakland, but everything seemed so quiet and disarranged that I felt as if time had halted completely. The sun had slid down to a low orbit near the horizon, and the trees were casting pillar-shaped shadows across the road. All day it had been hot and still, with a bright veil of haze whitening the sky. Now the air smelled faintly of dust and plaster. I caught glimpses of destruction as I flew through the streets trying to find an unobstructed route to the bridge. Collapsed chimneys and dropped cornices, buildings drooping or slightly askew. The toppled mannequins in the windows of Emporium Capwell's department store, arms flailing elegantly. An office building whose roof had landed in a parking lot, bareheaded and disheveled as a woman whose hat has been carried off by the wind. And everywhere people were standing on the sidewalks, talking over what had happened.

As I drove along the road that should have taken me to the freeway and the bridge, I noticed a cloud hovering ahead of me, a dark, reddish haze that smelled distantly of fuel. There were clumps of stretchers at nearly every corner, and people carrying ladders and sections of rope were running down the street. Downtown had been eerily silent, as if everyone had been afraid to talk above a whisper, but now I was driving toward noise, and the noise had this urgency to it that was building like a chant.

And then it was there in front of me: the two elevated decks of Interstate 880 lying on each other's backs like a fallen house of cards. There were people running toward it and away from it and ladders propped against the side of it and cars hanging over the edge of it, suspended at the point just before falling. The noise was machines trying to cut people free, or the sound of people screaming, or the thing itself still vibrating. It was beyond comprehension.

What was so hard to take in was that there were cars trapped between the two layers. The pillars that hold up the freeway had buckled and the upper deck had clapped down onto the bottom deck. The broken pillars dangled over the sidewalk, trailing hairy clumps of rebar. When I realized that this was the freeway that led to the Bay Bridge, I parked the car and began to run. Steven could be pressed between the layers of the freeway like a flower in a dictionary, and no one but me would know to look for him.

When I reached the base of the structure, the scale of the destruction was so immense that I simply stopped and stared. A steel-gray Honda had fallen from the top deck on to the street and was lying on its back like a turtle, its chassis covered with a white dust of concrete. An overturned semi was flopped over the upper guardrail, and a man had propped a ladder against the structure's crinkled edge and was inching tentatively toward it. In the narrow gap between the two decks, I could see people crawling around, dragging bodies out of the wreckage.

And so I went up to one of the ladders and started climbing. It was the most brazen thing I've ever done in my life, and I kept expecting someone to say "Turn back." But the only word of protest came from a young man bracing the base of the ladder, and all he said was, "It's dangerous up there, ma'am. The whole thing could come down in an aftershock."

"It's okay, I know what I'm doing," I said, and miraculously he let me pass.

To get inside I had to go up to the top deck and then lower myself down, swinging my legs into the dark gap between the levels. As I pulled myself to my knees, the underside of the freeway's second deck grazed my shoulders. I inched forward, my hands pressing glass, metal, buckled pavement, and in the petrol-fumed dusk, I whispered, "I will find you."

Sound echoed oddly. I could hear the terrible sound of people moaning and crying, and the buzz of open car doors, and the jangle of a clear, certain voice who I thought must be instructing the rescuers how to proceed. But when I tried to follow the voice to its source, I found that it came from the radio of a car that had been abandoned, its occupants rescued or able to crawl free. "We understand that a freeway in Oakland has collapsed," the voice declared. "We do not know the extent of the damage."

"I need tools!" someone was shouting. There was a terrible roar of a machine, and the high-pitched jar of metal being cut. Somewhere glass shattered. As my eyes adjusted, I could see the spindly silhouettes of people searching the cars ahead of me. In the shadows, they looked like gangly praying mantises.

Still I crept forward, one thought cupped in my mind like an egg. No one spoke to me as I stumbled through the havoc, except a man leaning into the window of a crushed pickup truck who shouted, "There's more ahead! Keep going."

I looked through the window of a white Buick a few yards behind the truck and saw a man inside. He looked to be about sixty, and he was leaning back in his seat with his eyes closed and his mouth open, as if he had fallen asleep in front of the TV.

I wrenched open the car door and it dinged musically. "Sir, are you okay? Can you hear me?" I touched his wrist and neck, looking for a pulse, but he didn't stir, not even when I put my lips over his and breathed into his lungs.

His lips hardly had any moisture to them, and as I went to draw my face away between breaths, my own lips clung to them for an instant, the way something dry sticks to something wet. His mouth smelled mildewy, like an old shower stall. I didn't want to be there, I wanted to be looking for Steven, but the man's chest sank like a day-old balloon each time I pulled away. I hovered over him, my breath emptying into him, my fingers digging into his face as I tried to pinch his nostrils closed. It had been a long time since I'd taken CPR and I wasn't sure if I was doing any of it right, but the man wasn't breathing, and the door kept chiming, *ding ding ding ding,* as if someone wanted to be let in.

I blew air into his lungs again and then tilted his head back and swept my fingers over the damp cushion of his tongue, feeling for obstructions. The man could be my father. He was about the right age, although nothing in his face looked familiar. The next time I turned away to get a breath of air, I looked around for some sign that Steven had been in the car. His baseball glove, for instance, or maybe a candy wrapper on the floor. Perhaps he had been there and had opened the door and walked away, into this shadow place of fumes and noises. If only the man would breathe on his own, I could go back outside and find him.

But he couldn't do that for me because he was dead. When I finally understood it, I sat up and yanked the keys out of the ignition so that the door would stop its mechanical tolling. Then I drew his wallet out of his breast pocket and checked the name on the driver's license. He wasn't my father. Someone else's father perhaps, but not mine.

I began moving again. I could see the beams of flashlights as rescue workers gathered around a car ahead, and I crawled into the corona of light. I heard voices shouting at me to be careful and then the stridulous wail of a baby crying.

I froze, the sound like something clawing at me. "Good, I'm glad you're here," a voice at my elbow said. I looked down to see a man kneeling by a VW bug with a baby in his hands. It bleated furiously, its mouth a dark O of despair, its face and fists purpling. I saw blood in its hair, and caked in the grooves of its fat little arms. "It's going to take us a while to get the mom out," he said. "Go ahead and take the baby down."

A moment later the baby was in my arms. Its eyes bulged at me through a lens of tears, and one of its hands flailed out and wiped my arm with a streak of water and blood. "Okay now, it's okay," I murmured and clenched it to my chest. It struggled and pounded its bleeding head into my shoulder.

"I'm not sure how to carry it," I said. I couldn't quite imagine getting down the rickety ladder with the infant squirming and howling in my ear. "Maybe someone—"

"It's just got a few cuts, that's all," the man said, and then his head disappeared into the car. "Hurry, we don't have much time."

I hurried forward, clutching the baby. But when I came to the edge of the deck, the ladder seemed to be swaying. A mob of tree branches poked their fingers underneath its rungs, preventing it from lying flush against the edge of the freeway. Far below us, fire engines were pulling up, and I could see people milling about, carrying things back and forth. If only I could toss the baby down into a fireman's net, it would be out of danger and I could keep hunting for Steven. But there was no net, and no one seemed to notice my head peeking over the edge, or to hear the baby's unremitting squall.

"Okay, baby, we just have to find another way down," I said and began edging around the empty carcasses of cars. But now the roof above us was sinking and I found I had to get down on my stomach to move forward. "Sorry," I said as I tucked the baby under my arm. It dug its heel into my ribs and wailed.

It was no use. The roof was dipping lower and lower, and after crawling a few feet I panicked and backed out the way I came. When I was able to raise myself onto my haunches, I could see someone with an enormous crowbar leaning over the door of a Volvo not far away. "Hello?" I shouted.

The figure turned around. He was a very small man in a pair of denim overalls, with a halo of red-tipped black hair around his face. "You all right there, ma'am?" he said.

I sat down and pulled the baby close to my body. It writhed against me, battering me with its forehead and huffing miserably. "Do you know how to get out of here?" I asked. "I have to get this baby to the hospital."

"Well, I'd get going—they say one more aftershock and we're standing in a pile of rubble."

He had the face of an old man but the expression of a young one. I scooted forward, hoping he was pointing to a way out. As I did, he put the crowbar down by his feet and stuck his head into the car. When he emerged, he was gripping the shoulders of a tiny white-haired woman, his leprechaun twin. "See that board there?"

he said, nodding his head at a narrow plank of plywood by his feet. "Could you just slide that across my knees?"

I did, resting the baby on the ground for a moment so I could use both hands. It kicked the air and wailed irritably. The man by the car slid the woman onto the board across his lap and then reached into the bib of his overalls. "Duct tape," he said, holding up the silver wheel. "Always comes in handy." Then he began binding the woman to the board with coils of tape, until she began to resemble a spider-caught fly. He did it all so quickly that I didn't have time to determine whether the woman attached to the seesaw on his lap was even conscious.

"Is she okay?" I asked.

"Okay?" the man said. "She was made in God's image."

He slid the plank onto the ground, rolled onto his knees, and then somehow managed to reach behind him and pull the board onto his back.

"Let me help you," I said, darting forward to guide the woman onto the flat of his spine. When I was done, the two figures lay back to back, her head at the nape of his neck, her feet jutting over his bent legs, so that he looked like an off-kilter Janus, one face looking forward, the other looking back.

"But you can't carry her like that," I said. "She'll slip."

"Duct tape," the man said. "Tie her to me."

I took the duct tape from the bib of his overalls. "Don't be frugal," he instructed as I looped silver strips around their two bellies and chests, knitting them together. "Make sure it holds." I felt someone's eyes on me and looked down to see that the woman on his back had opened her eyes and was staring at me intently, as if I were a strange insect that had landed on her arm and she was trying to determine if I stung. "Are you in pain?" I asked her, but she didn't answer.

"Now we're ready," the man said when I was done. I bent down to pick up the baby. At the touch of my hand it shrieked and rubbed its fists into its eyes.

"That baby sure is happy," the man called out as we crawled in single file toward the crumpled guardrail. Somehow he had managed to drag the crowbar along with him. It clattered against the pavement with every step.

"Happy?" I shouted over the baby's sobs. "I don't think so."

"He's happy, all right. And just singing the song of life as loud as he can."

He paused to consider the best route to take, and then continued. "I know he's singing 'cause I've got an ear that hears. I heard people calling to me from my house not long ago, and I had to come and get 'em free."

"Someone's calling me as well," I said. "A little boy." Tell me you hear him, too, I wanted to say. Tell me you know where he is.

But the man only laughed, and seemed to jangle the crowbar against the pavement. "Looks like you found him. And he's singing your praises."

I tensed my grip on the wailing baby. "No," I said. "I mean my own boy is calling . . ."

"Nothing's your own unless you have it in your hand, lady," the man said and eased himself over a roll of buckled pavement. "And if you can hold it in your hand, it ain't worth keeping."

This was a fine time for someone to be quoting bumper stickers, I thought. Just then we came to a ladder.

"Here we go," the man said. "Nice to have met you."

And he rolled himself over the edge, the woman still bound to his back like an oversized papoose. When he was out of sight, I tightened my grip on the baby and edged myself through the gap.

When I came through the orifice and stepped onto the ladder, voices began shouting up to me from down below: "Okay now, we're ready for you, watch your step." I backed down the ladder until a hand came up and steadied me by the waist, and I found myself face-to-face with a police officer. "Are you okay? Do you need to see a doctor?" she asked.

"No, I'm a rescuer," I started to explain, but just then another officer yanked the baby out of my hands.

"Let's get him to an ambulance," he said and strode off toward a pocket of stretchers. I watched them disappear and felt myself sinking, as if I were back inside the tunnel of the freeway and could only move forward on my knees. I could still hear the baby's wavering cry.

"Do you think you can step a bit to the side?" the remaining police officer said. "We've got more people coming down the ladder."

"But I need to go back up," I said.

The cop folded her arms over her chest. "Sorry," she said. "Uniformed personnel only."

"But I was just there. Rescuing people."

"Could you just move a few feet to your left?" the officer said and gave me an irrefutable smile. "There you go. Just a few feet more."

I let her push me aside and then kept walking, through the throng of spectators and rescuers, back to Gabriel's car. It was still warm out, and the air hung heavy with the chemical sweetness of oil and dust. There were sirens going, and flares casting an orange light across the road, and as I came into the neighborhood streets, I could hear an impenetrable wash of human voices, ordering and recounting and mourning and joking. I sat in the car for a moment and listened to the way they rose and fell, but I did not have an ear that hears, and not one of them could tell me where I might find Steven.

$\mathcal{A}$ Sleeping Man (Simone)

On the way to the World Series game, Steven decided he wanted to bring his glove from home.

"Ever caught a foul ball?" Bill asked him as they drove over to Julia's apartment to get it.

Steven rolled his eyes. "Lots of times," he said. "I have about ten balls. I'll show you when we get there."

Bill nodded, foiled again. He was trailing the boy like a bird-hunter, on tiptoes, but when he felt himself getting close, the child hopped to another branch and looked at him, head cocked in beady-eyed puzzlement. Bill felt lead-footed, ungainly.

"You must have some sort of luck to catch that many balls," he said.

He was too big for Lisa's little Toyota, or maybe it was just that he was feeling ill-suited to the spaces women lived in. His round, sweaty head grazed the roof, and the steering wheel pressed against his chest like bars. He rolled the window down as he drove and draped his forearm over the edge.

Steven was looking for music on the radio. The stations rolled over one another as he spun the tuner, submerging the notes in a wash of static. He didn't care about the songs, not really. It was just a way of letting the urgency out of his fingers. Maybe Julia would be there at the apartment and the two of them could go to the game together after all. He let the hope build up from the floor of his chest, drop by drop like a stalagmite. On his birthday she had promised him they could go to the World Series together, but the first two games had gone by and still she hadn't come. It was only reluctantly that he'd allowed Bill to buy him tickets for game three, and he still expected Julia to arrive and send her father home.

The apartment smelled locked and stale, lifeless, and Steven felt the hope crumble in his chest the moment he crossed the threshold. His room still appeared ransacked from the time he and I had gone over there to get his things. Then Steven had been dying to get in and out as quickly as he could. Now he lingered among all the tiny shrines that had grown up in his room over the years— the shell collection, the toy trucks, the crayons.

"This your mom?" Bill said, catching sight of a picture of Julia and baby Steven that was on the dresser.

"And that's me," Steven said, looking over his shoulder. Bill held the photo in his hands and scanned it for resemblances. Looking at her smiling into the camera, he thought she took after him, right down to her absence.

Steven found his glove behind the door. Then, because he didn't want to leave the room, he showed Bill the baseballs lined up on the dresser, and his Hot Wheels and his Oakland A's posters, and even some of the drawings of Terratarantula. He pulled out every possession he could think of and sat on the floor with them tucked around him, a little bird feathering its nest.

"We gotta get going, Sport," Bill said. "There's going to be traffic. You don't want to miss the first pitch."

"Want to see my baseball cards? I've got a Catfish Hunter and a Vida Blue."

Bill sat down on the low trundle bed with its Superman sheets. It came to him that this house would be a good place for him to settle. He and Steven could live there, out of the way of Carolina's temper and Lisa's courtship. The questing, misplaced daughter-love was rising in him again, and he needed a place to channel it.

Relationships are a flea market. The ones with love to give stand with their meager offerings laid out, and the ones wanting love saunter past, scanning for the best bargain. Steven was too young to know never to buy anything at the end of the day, no matter how good the price. He put his shoebox of baseball cards on his grandfather's lap and sat beside him on his knees, narrating.

"That's Rickey Henderson's rookie card. That's Doc Gooden's rookie card. And that's Kirby Puckett's rookie card. Do you know who they are?"

"You sure you want to go to this game today?" Bill said.

"I don't know. We could watch it on TV. I don't like Candlestick Park, anyway. I wish we were going to the Coliseum."

"Well, if it ends up going to six games, we can try to get tickets at the Coliseum. But I don't think it's going to. If you want to see a World Series game, we better go now."

Steven rifled through the shoebox. "Let me just show you Vida Blue."

He lifted the cards out one by one and read over the names and statistics in a low voice.

"Call me when you find it," Bill said at last. He went snooping down the hallway, peering into the bathroom and Julia's bedroom, curious about the disappeared daughter whose apartment he'd never seen. Then he wandered back into the living room and looked at the books on the bookshelves. Finally he sank down onto the sofa and shut his eyes and felt sorrowful.

The image that came into his mind was bloody and familiar and he shook it off. Enough of that. Still, once it came, it was hard to tip it off the surface of his mind. A picture of the dark afternoon kept slinking around the edges of his thoughts. The sawdust smell of his father's woodshop. His mother's glutinous sobs.

What had made him think of it? The stale air in the room maybe, or Steven's tangible sadness. He opened his eyes and looked around until they settled on the brocade bedspread covering the sofa. So that was it.

"Hey," he called to Steven. "Where'd you get this?"

There was no answer. Bill stood up and looked at the cloth from a distance before bending down to run his fingers across the soft skid of the silk. As a boy, he had done this same thing. He shut his eyes as he had then, and heard the sticky sound of his mother's breathing next to him, felt her fleshy hands stroke the textured pattern of gold-winged birds of paradise.

Doesn't that feel nice, Billy? Like cool water.

The game was just to feel it, the way his ma did, without seeing. She sat beside him on the bed, and the only sound was the scrape and rustle of their fingers. He wondered sometimes if the fabric's brilliant blue-green traveled through the pads of her fingertips and reached behind the blindness of her eyes. Nothing else in their brown-and-mustard house had color like that bedspread, so saturated that Bill felt he could stare and stare at it and never get enough. Still, he kept his eyes clamped shut.

Billy honey, do me a favor. Go check on your father, will you?

He opened his eyes. His fingers had snagged an unfamiliar circle with roughened edges. When he looked down, he saw it was a patch, sewn with tiny stitches onto the bedspread. If not for the detection of his fingertips, he might have missed it altogether.

Just then Steven came out, looking furtive. He'd been crying, and his eyes were red and shadowy. "We can go," he said.

He'd called Dawn from Julia's room, as he often did when he missed his mother. Go to the game, for Christ's sake, she had said to him. It was the A's in the World Series after all.

"Now you want to go?" Bill got to his feet. "Well, let's do it, it's almost five o'clock. We're gonna be late."

As they drove onto the upper deck of the Bay Bridge, Bill looked over at Steven, silent in the passenger seat. "You know, that bed-spread you have on your couch reminds me of one my parents used to have," he said. "I used to lie there with my ma and tell her stories. She was blind, so she couldn't read. She loved to listen, though."

He trailed off, since Steven wasn't responding. The boy was pink-eyed, swollen. He looked out the window at the Bay as they ascended the sheeny incline of the bridge. The edges of the water were pricked by pickleweed. Steven could see the tide draining out, the ripples like the strain of muscles, and their circle shapes made him think about the circles of the infield dirt and the outfield grass.

"You know what I hate about the Giants?" he said to Bill. "I hate their uniforms. Orange and black is for Halloween. It's dumb."

"Well, if they're trying to scare somebody, they should try play-ing better baseball," Bill said companionably.

"That's right. They're not very scary."

"No sir, not like the A's."

All at once the car lurched and swerved toward the bridge's metal railings. Bill felt as if someone inside the car were trying to wrest the steering wheel out of his hands. He tried to pull it back toward him, thinking that this was the moment his ghosts had finally chosen to make their viciousness palpable. Then as the car jolted back into its own lane and seemed to roll into the next, he felt himself yielding. Ahead of him and behind he could see cars careening, and he realized the great bridge beneath them was swinging back and forth and they were all caught up in its sway.

If you're expecting a metaphor here, I suggest you look elsewhere. Does the quake represent the hand of Fate? Of course it does, but what doesn't? If you're looking on the large scale, you'll miss the message completely. Fate is what makes you spill your coffee and wipe your nose and what makes dust settle in the creases of your curtains. If you focus on the earthquake, you miss the push and grind of tectonic plates, the aeons of cramp and pressure that lead inexorably to strike-slip or dip-slip. This gives way to that, that keeps moving, pushing and straining, one event giving way to another. What makes you think an earthquake is more eloquent than a tree branch bending in the wind, or sand rearranged by the tide? Fate never raises her voice or lowers it. She is always speaking, and we may listen any time we like.

Two cars ahead of them nicked each other, their sides scraping together in a long moan. Then their own vehicle was grappling with the bumper of a car ahead, locking and unlocking, until the other car's bumper came away and clattered along the roadway beneath them. But now everyone was slowing, and then stopping. A moment or two after it all began, the cars were halted in cockeyed confusion.

"What the fuck?" Bill turned to look at Steven with an expression that was almost an accusation. "What the fuck is going on?"

Steven shrugged, his lily-pad eyes rounder and greener than ever. Bill began laughing.

"Don't look so scared. We got through it okay, didn't we?" This was bravado on his part, but Steven appreciated the gesture. He smiled a little and shrugged, and Bill started up the car again.

"We've got a game to go to," he said. The cars ahead were moving now, slowly realigning themselves with the lanes. They drove in silence for a moment, Bill rubbing the place where his hair used to be, not knowing what comment to make. "Turn on the radio," he said. "Let's see if the game's started."

But now the cars ahead were slowing again, and then it all came to a standstill. "What now?" Bill said. He rolled down the window and tried to see what was going on up ahead. After a while, people began to straggle through the lanes of cars, walking back toward Oakland carrying their purses and briefcases. "You gotta be kidding me," he said and leaned his head out the window. "Hey? What's going on up there?"

"Part of the bridge fell down," someone yelled back. "You can't cross it anymore. They're saying just to leave your car here."

"Oh, Christ," Bill said. "Well, Sport, it looks like we're going to be missing the game. I'm sorry, we'll get the next one."

"That's okay," Steven said and carefully stowed his mitt in the backseat of the car.

Once they were out of the car, they walked to the railing and looked over the side.

"I guess this is something you don't get to do too often," Bill said as the blue-gray water lapped below them.

Steven shrugged. "Is this whole bridge going to fall down?"

"Do I look like an engineer?" Bill said and chuckled. But for once he felt sorrier for the boy than he did for himself. "I don't think so," he added. "We're perfectly safe."

They began walking again, the ghosts flaunting their postcorporeal grace by balancing on the railing. Bill and Steven ignored these high-wire theatrics, cloistered in their own thoughts.

"Go check on your father, will you?" his ma said.

Bill opened his eyes. His senses were keyed up, inflamed by his momentary sightlessness. He listened for the sound of his father's step. It was one of his father's dark days, the fourth or fifth in a row. On the dark days his father, a thin man with deep-set, hooded eyes and a hooked nose, grew stooped and unshaven.

"Don't look at me," he said when he came up from his basement shop and saw Bill staring. "Don't look at your pa, Billy-boy. I'll turn you blind like I did your mother."

The dark days were sudden in their onset, and they departed just as suddenly. When they were over, Bill's father was elfin, a man with nimble hands who could make toy trucks out of tin cans, and polished wood creatures with movable mouths and legs out of the scraps left over from his cabinets. Then he would ask Bill to help him in his workshop, and didn't seem to mind that his wife had gone from being a plump nearsighted girl to a blind obese one within five years of their wedding day.

Her blindness was due to a congenital disease that had dimmed her sight slowly from childhood on. Bill's father knew this, but on the dark days he blamed himself, thinking that his jet despair had somehow inked over her sight. For her part, Bill's mother blamed her husband's sadness on her own helplessness. The two of them moped in their separate rooms, leaving Bill to fend for himself.

He flitted down the back stairs to the workroom, where his father lay on his cot. The cot was against the wall, behind the saw-horses and the stacks of fine-grained wood and the chest of tiny drawers where the screws and hinges and different kinds of drawer pulls were kept. It was only used on the dark days, and it was so walled in with things that when his father lay on it, it seemed as if he was in a cave. "Go on, boy," his father said when he noticed Bill checking on him. "I'm sorry. Tell your ma I'm sorry." He stared at nothing, barely breathing.

Flit, flit, quick as a needle trying to sew the family up and the darkness out, Bill darted back to his ma, who needed him now to take her mind off the disappeared man downstairs. As she lay on the bed, her mouth curled up, trembled. "It's my fault, Billy, I'm too much for your pa, I'm just too much trouble. He didn't know he was marrying a blind girl, did he? He thought he was getting a normal girl, a normal girl." Bill cringed. He didn't like to watch her cry, so he put his head down on the bedspread and filled his eyes with the blue that was like the entrance to the sky, and imagined riding on the back of one of its golden birds.

"Look at all these shoes," Steven said. Tapped out and tired as he was, the boy couldn't help observing everything. And there were shoes on the bridge, not strewn but simply set aside neatly in pairs along the way. He noticed then that one of the women up ahead was in her stocking feet. She was in a suit with a straight narrow skirt that made her walk mincingly, and her feet were red and visible through her stockings. "Look," he said to Bill, pointing.

"Sore tootsies," Bill said and winked. He reached over and put his arm around Steven. "Hey, this is quite an adventure, when you think about it."

Look out for flea market love, I said to myself as I watched them. Bargain prices, but the merchandise may break down as soon as you get it home. But what did Steven know of that? He grinned, glad to be noticed, and let his grandfather draw him close. They walked like that for a while, body to body. Bill was thinking that Steven reminded him of himself when he was a boy. Abandoned, no one to take care of him. They were the same, he thought, mirror images, and it was only right that he should have shown up now, when the boy needed him. He liked the idea of this doubleness, this rescue of the abandoned son of the daughter he'd abandoned. It closed the circle.

"I have an idea," he said.

"Beginner's luck." A second-grade joke. Steven guffawed.

"No, really, I do. What do you say we take a trip, just you and me? We could go to Mexico. Would you like that?"

"I don't know." Steven's stomach cramped at the thought of more departures. He shook his head, his teeth clenched so he wouldn't cry. "What about my mom?" Despite the teeth, his chin trembled.

Bill backpedaled. "Well, we could wait. But you'd like Mexico. It's a great place for a kid." A lie really, but what did Bill know about kids? He meant it was a great place for himself, for the boy he still was.

Steven kept quiet, sullen again. But now the idea took shape in Bill's mind. If he took Steven with him, he could leave without leaving. He could say farewell to cranky Carolina and confusing Lisa, farewell to anyone who could thwart him with memory, and at the same time he could be reconciled with the past. Another story started up before the old ones were finished.

They kept walking, past the pairs of shoes and the abandoned cars, lagging a bit in contrast to the other walkers, who seemed inconvenienced and hurried. Steven spun around sometimes to look at the span behind them: the steel girders marching toward the island in the middle of the Bay, and the swooping undulation of the suspension bridge between the island and San Francisco. His green eyes loved patterns, loved detecting the regular repetition of man-made things. The parallel lines of the bridge's railings, for instance, or the clunky repeating crosses that made up its gaping roof.

"I heard there's a spider who lives on the other side of the bridge, in that web of metal," Bill remarked. "A giant spider who waits for airplanes to get caught in the cables. Sometimes when it's foggy out, a plane will get lost and fly too low, and before the pilot even knows what happened, his plane's jammed in between the bars of the bridge tower, and he can't get out."

He looked over at Steven, to see if the boy was listening. Steven looked over his shoulder at the lattice of metal sparkling in the late-afternoon sun. A shape that could have been a spider shadowed the silver rafters.

"I knew a man that happened to once," Bill went on. "He was a pilot I met in a bar in Ecuador. He'd come flying to San Francisco in the fog one night. He thought he could get to the airport by instruments, but he must have made a mistake when he was setting his course because all at once—*ping*—it was as if a giant hand had snatched his plane out of the air. He was caught in something, and the force of his impact had started all these cables jangling and humming. For a minute he thought it was angels singing, or the wind, but then he felt something moving toward him, one leg at a time, creeping ever so slowly. And every time a leg grabbed hold of one of these cables, the cable stopped vibrating and was steadied into silence. Just when it was all still, my friend saw something sitting right in front of the windshield of the plane. It was the biggest spider you've ever seen, big as a man, and it was milk-white and covered with tiny little hairs. And the spider was crawling over and around his plane, wrapping it in silver metal threads just like the threads that make up the suspension part of this bridge, except thin as needles. Just as the spider was about to bind the plane door shut, my friend pushed it open and jumped."

"Did he have a parachute on?"

"Luckily he did. But as he floated down, the spider came after him, lowering herself on a thin strand of wire and snatching at him with her arms and legs. She almost caught him, too, but he managed to land on the back of a pickup truck that carried him all the way to San Francisco airport. He hopped on the first plane out of town, and he told me he hoped he'd never have to come here again."

"Did that really happen?"

"Of course it did. Would I lie to you?"

After a time their path inclined more acutely downhill, and the bridge touched down on the shores of Oakland. "We made it," Bill said to Steven, and Steven nodded wearily, sensing that they hadn't in fact made it anywhere. As they walked down the avenue that led from the bridge into the heart of the city, they noticed a great commotion up ahead.

"Look at that," Bill said. "The thing's flat like a pancake."

Steven stared. The freeway up ahead of them had sunk down into itself and now looked crumpled and absurd, all too evidently human-built.

"Are there people in there?" he said, and his voice quavered.

"No, I'm sure not," Bill lied and steered them away down another street. It was hard to avoid the structure, though. It seemed to extend for blocks and blocks. Worst of all, Faceup and Facedown were fascinated by it. They hung back, craning their insubstantial necks for a better view. Bill tried to ignore them, the way a dog owner will ignore his pet when the creature starts nibbling at garbage and excrement. A yank on the leash, a look of studied indifference, and keep walking. He had the ghosts leashed, too, or so it seemed, because they refused to wander far from him. They strained, trying to saunter casually toward the smell and the bodies, but they always turned back after a point and hurried to catch up with him.

It was dusk now, and the evening air was warm. On the street, people were standing outside with their radios on, talking and drinking. Lights began to come on in the streets where the power was working, and the open windows spilled the anxious murmur of television broadcasters. When the damaged freeway was no longer in the way, Bill led his party east again, toward the fading brown shapes of the hills in the distance. Steven trudged beside him, and the ghosts hung behind, their noses lifted to the scent of death.

"Are we almost there?" Steven asked at last.

Bill looked around. He'd spent enough of his life wandering that he tended to forget about simple concepts like destinations. And he'd forgotten, too, about Steven's short legs and tired feet. "I'm sorry," he said to Steven. "You've got to be exhausted."

Steven drooped, too tired to dissemble. His insides felt achy, bruised with the sense of being unconsidered.

"Here's a package store," Bill said, pointing to a cramped-looking corner store with a sign out front advertising malt liquor. "How about we go in and get some directions?"

Bill bought them potato chips and candy bars at the corner store, and they ate them as they waited for a bus that the man at the register said would take them close to Julia's apartment. Steven revived a little after he finished eating. He climbed up on the bus stop bench and kept a lookout while Bill sat back and drank from the tiny bottle of whiskey he'd purchased along with the candy bars. "Here it comes," Steven yelled at last. "Next stop, home sweet home."

The bus was empty and the driver seemed relieved to have company. "What a night," he said. "I don't even know if my house is still standing. I just got on shift when the thing hit. Big old cinder block nearly hit the bus."

Bill felt a pressure on his shoulder and noticed that Steven's head was sinking into him. He put his arms around the boy's trusting weight and eased him across his lap. "Here, lie down," he whispered, and the dozing body pressed close to him.

"Long day?" the bus driver said. "He looks pretty tuckered out."

"We got stuck on the bridge and had to walk back to Oakland."

"Is that right? You were on the bridge?"

And so the two men chitchatted about the disaster, spilling the kind of words that didn't interfere with private thoughts. Bill stroked Steven's wiry back and breathed the sweet smell of little-boy sleep. His mind filled with balancing schemes. Steven was a good boy, a bit shy, but all he needed was a father figure. Tonight the two of them would move into Julia's apartment and begin their life together.

Up ahead, someone was waiting at a bus stop. In the twilight the figure looked misshapen—wider than it was tall and with a curiously peaked head.

"Don't tell me," the bus driver said.

He stopped the bus at the corner and opened the doors. Slowly, the figure mounted the steps and emerged by the fare box reeking of piss and liquor. It was an old man, his silver hair roiled into clots on his bent head. He was wrapped in an enormous wool poncho with a pointed hood.

"Show me your money," the driver said as the passenger collapsed on the seat across from Bill and Steven. "You can't ride the bus without money."

"I got money," the old man said, and his face split into a wizened grin. "T'may not be a lotta money, t'may not be big money, but iss 'nuf to ride the bus."

Bill watched as the old man fumbled through his pockets, the poncho flapping wildly. The man reminded him of something or someone, and he felt a little angry at him for spoiling the shadowy contentment he'd felt before, when it was just him and the bus driver and the sleeping child.

"I knew I shouldn't have let you on," the bus driver said. "You're already drunk." He turned to Bill and rolled his eyes. "I'm a sucker. Fool me once, shame on you; fool me twice, shame on me."

Just then the old man's hands came flying out from under the poncho, spraying coins. A clatter of pennies and quarters went rolling down the aisle.

"See, I got money! Jes' can't keep ahold of it," the old man said and collapsed into wheezing giggles.

The bus moved along in silence for a while, as the old man set about putting the scattered coins back in his pocket. Then the driver spoke.

"Don't you be sleeping now," he said. "I catch you sleeping, I'm going to get someone to carry you off this bus."

"I ain't sleepin'."

"You better not be. You're too damn much trouble when you sleep."

The old man had been sinking further into the woolly stink of his poncho, but this last remark roused him enough to lift his head.

"How can a sleeping man cause trouble?" he said indignantly and then shut his eyes. The bus driver looked over at Bill and shrugged. A minute went by and then the old man shook himself and spoke as if from the depths of a trance.

"What I want to know is, how can a man asleep . . . cause trouble?"

"'Cause you're too damn hard to wake up."

But the old man was impervious to outside contributions, having already sunk into a deep and unreachable sleep.

They got off the bus a few blocks from Julia's house. Bill shook Steven awake just as the bus pulled over to the curb.

"Does this look familiar?" Bill said when they were standing on the sidewalk. He knew Julia's street was somewhere close by, but he couldn't remember which way he was supposed to walk.

He thought of changing directions again and heading back to Lisa's apartment, but the thought of the two women awaiting him made him stick to his original plan. They would be worried, he realized now. They'd want to know what had happened. Just the thought of their questions made his arms feel tied up, as if the women were right now clawing and clutching at him. Or maybe that was just the sensation of groggy Steven wrapping his arms around his waist. Bill lifted the boy up and carried him.

He walked in the wrong direction. Sleepwalking, carrying the sleeping child, he set off to answer the old man's riddle. How can a sleeping man cause trouble? To ask it is to answer it.

He ambled along, the boy draped across his chest and over his shoulder. The weight was pleasant. Bill hugged Steven with both arms as he walked, embraced him, nuzzled his face into the boy's warm neck. He thought about his own children. His sons Willy and Roger in Brazil, his daughters. With his senses full of the sweetness of the moment, he forgot that his daughters had ever grown up and remembered the weight of their soft bodies as he carried them to bed in their old house in Watertown.

After a block or two, he came across an unlit neon sign that said COCKTAILS. Below it, a door was propped open and he could see candles flickering within. Just a quick drink, he promised himself, to lift his spirits. Thinking about his children made him melancholy. He took his arm away from Steven's back and used it to open the tavern door. The child in the man winning out over the child in the man's arms.

It was a dark room with black walls that were papered with yellowed business cards. An immense piano dominated the space at the back of the room, topped by a makeshift candelabra made up of empty beer and whiskey bottles. A big-chested woman was seated at its curve, warbling a lachrymose version of "Walking After Midnight." A half dozen other inebriated crooners sat swaying on either side of her.

"You can't bring kids in here."

The cocktail waitress who appeared at his elbow was a skinny, overdone redhead. She was smiling at him, but her arms were folded.

"I know that, ma'am," Bill said and flashed her his most charming grin. "But I was hoping you'd make an exception for a survivor of the earthquake."

He snared her soon enough, baiting the trap with a tale about the jostling, cracking bridge and his miraculous escape and rescue of his grandson. Soon he had deposited snoozing Steven in a booth and taken his place by the piano with a double shot of Jameson.

His voice was better suited to talking than to singing, but it had its own appeal. He sang "Danny Boy" in a low, tuneless rumble, but the pressure he put on the words made the woman next to him dissolve into tears, and the reeling Texan on his left buy him another drink.

He was drunk soon enough. It was in his nature to lose himself in liquor, because he loved being lost. He sang "Wild Irish Rose" and "Ev'ry Time You Say Good-bye." He sang "My Bonny Lies Over the Ocean" and thought of Justina and her tail lashing him to her.

"I left the most beautiful woman in the world," he confided to Tex. "I think of her every moment."

"I bet she's dreaming of you coming back to her right this minute," the Texan said, his red face shiny with encouragement.

"And my two sons, I left my sons."

"I bet they miss their daddy." The Texan was the empathetic type of drunk; his eyes misted as he looked at Bill. But Bill had changed gears.

"You know, my little girls used to think that song was 'My Body Lies Over the Ocean.' They thought it was about a guy whose head was cut off," he said. He was zigzagging now, jokes to jagged edges. He sang a bit for Tex.

> My body lies over the ocean
> My body lies over the sea
> My body lies over the ocean.
> Bring back my body to me . . .

"That's what these guys sing," he said, gesturing at Faceup and Facedown, who were leaning against the wall by the men's room. "That's what they sing, because they haven't got a body." He laughed sputteringly into his drink, perversely pleased by Tex's befuddled grin.

"Who do you mean?" Tex craned his neck, looking for the joke.

"You can't see them." Bill chuckled as he got up from his seat. "Like I said, they haven't got a body."

The ghosts went with him to the men's room, which was illuminated by a candle on the sink.

"Three *amigos!*" Bill said as they crowded in beside him at the urinal and unzipped their filmy flies. "Pissing *juntos.*"

They stayed impassive, although Faceup seemed to wink at him.

"I love you guys, I really do," Bill said when he finished urinating. "You're faithful as dogs. You'll never leave me, will you? Promise me you'll never leave?"

He had meant it as irony, but irony is squirmy stuff. This time it slipped fishlike out of his hands and he was left with the baldness of his request. Suddenly he felt he meant it.

"Don't leave me," he said again. "A man needs a through-line. A little consistency. Someone who knows me."

His eyes filmed over, and when he blinked them free of tears, he found that Facedown had covered his face with his hands.

"Don't cry, *amigo,*" Bill said. "Look at me, I'm your friend."

The hands came away. Bill saw shadowed eyes, the wisps of a five-day beard, the hooked nose he remembered grazing his cheek during bedtime kisses. This ghost was stooped, distracted. When he saw Bill staring at him, he raised his long, nimble hands to ward him off. *"Don't look at me,"* he said.

"What's your father doing?"

Bill's mother had been dozing. One of her large hands was resting on his back, blanketing him. He kept his eyes shut, pretending he hadn't heard her.

"Are you sleeping, Billy? Wake up, honey, and see if your father wants dinner."

With his eyes closed he could feel her shifting onto her side and drawing herself up slowly, like a bridge. He cracked his lids enough to see that the blue bedspread beneath him was sapped of color. It was already dark out. Five o'clock, maybe six.

"You know I can't make it down there, there's too many obstacles. I think he does it on purpose to keep me out."

Now her heavy footsteps were moving across the floor to the door. "I'll be in the bathroom. Start dinner, would you?"

She was gone, so there was no use pretending anymore. Bill sat up. He could make out her sounds in the bathroom: the thunderous stream of her pee splashing into the toilet bowl, her slippers scraping against the tile floor. From downstairs there was nothing.

He checked the upstairs rooms first. He didn't usually, but somehow he didn't feel like going down to the basement yet. Anyway, the house was dark and it seemed to him it badly needed to be roused with light. He started in the living room and flipped on the lamp on the bookcase by the door. Even with the lamp bleeding light from under its crinkled paper shade, the room seemed dreary, so Bill turned on the twin table lamps on each side of the sofa and the two-headed floor lamp behind the chocolate-brown easy chair.

Next he turned on the kitchen light and put a pot of water on the stove for cooking potatoes. As he lit the burner, he could hear his mother in the bathroom, running water for her bath. "It'll be about an hour until dinner," he called to her.

Last, he checked his own room, even looking in the closet and under the bed. He had found his father in his bed once when he came home from school, wide awake but with the covers pulled up to his chin. "How nice to be a little boy," his father had said when Bill came in. "No sorrows, no sorrows at all."

This time his father wasn't in his bed. That meant he was still in the cot downstairs, asleep maybe, or maybe staring. As he walked back through the kitchen to the cellar door, Bill found himself imagining that when he flicked the light switch at the top of the stairs, he would transform the dark day into a light one and his father would be down there fitting the legs of a table into the top. "Come here, look what your smart father is making," his father said on those days, when Bill came down the basement steps. Then he would say, "As long as you're down here, can you give me a hand?" And Bill would get to sand the seat of a chair with fine sandpaper, or hold each table leg while his father fastened it into place.

He kept listening for work sounds as he descended. The rasp of sandpaper, the scrape of the saw, the jangle of a drawer pull being screwed into a drawer. It happened sometimes, that his father just got up from his cot and started working.

"Pa?" Bill said as he came into the workroom. The unshaded overhead bulb threw everything into stark relief, with shadows gathering under every surface. Picture young Bill playing Marco Polo in his father's workroom. Marco? Marco? Silence. Silence.

He came bursting out of the men's room and went directly to the pay phone sandwiched between the rest-room doors. *Don't look,* the ghost of his father had said, and Bill wasn't about to be a modern-day Lot's Wife, turning into a cake of urinal deodorant in the men's room of a piano bar. He reached for his wallet at the same time as he reached for the phone. When the airline reservations clerk answered, he booked two seats on the morning flight to Miami. Time to make a new life: again, again. But this time, he was taking Steven.

Steven had woken up and was sitting up in the booth when Bill returned. The roundness of his face seemed diminished and his eyes were swimming.

"Where did you go? Where are we?" he demanded.

"I just had to go to the bathroom. Do you need to pee or anything?"

To Bill's dismay, Steven nodded tearfully.

"You can't wait till we get home?"

"No, I have to go."

And now the sobs began. They started soft, but like cattle loosed from the corral, they couldn't help stampeding.

"Hush, I'll take you. Stop crying," Bill whispered, trying to quiet by example.

He led Steven back to the men's room and stood with his arms crossed while the boy unzipped his jeans. He tapped his foot and

cast his eye around the candlelit room to see if his past was lurking
in the corners. Was that his father in the shadow of the bathroom
stall? He pushed the door open, slow enough to seem casual. No one.

He looked over at Steven, who was still poised in front of the
urinal, staring straight ahead in fierce concentration.

"Do you have to go or not?"

Pure malice, and he regretted it as soon as he said it. The boy's
shoulders shook as the sobs rolled over one another, nearly chok-
ing him. "I'm trying," he said.

Remorseful, Bill leaned down and put his arms around Steven.

"I'm sorry," he said. "I'm sorry. I didn't mean it. I know you're trying. But you can't pee and cry at the same time, it just doesn't work."

Steven kept crying. Bill sat down on the men's room floor and
pulled the boy into his lap and rocked him back and forth. "Take
your time, son, take your time," he murmured. "You tell me when
you're ready."

As he rocked, he looked over Steven's shoulder and waited for
the ghosts to come. They didn't.

After a time, the sobs dwindled. Bill lifted Steven up and ran a
little water in the sink.

"You want to see if we can go at the same time?"

A nod. So Bill and Steven stood side by side, little-boy hip
pressed against his grandfather's thick thigh. Pushed together in
front of the urinal, they pulled out their appendages.

"Ready, aim, fire," Bill said.

His thick stream led the way and Steven's followed, meek at
first, then gathering force. The two jets of urine arced downward,
golden as candlelight. Water, seeking its own level.

Then, as sometimes happens with overtired children, Steven
had a burst of high spirits. On the way back up the street, he

galloped ahead, feeling light as the wind. Sobs are heavy; urine, too. Now that he was unburdened of both, he was air itself.

"That was a bar we were in, right? I've never been in a bar. Do people always sing like that in bars? My friend Trey goes to church and he says they always sing in church. Are bars and churches the same that way?"

"The songs are different," Bill said. "But a lot of the rest of it is the same." The thought of churches made him wistful. He pictured the cool silence of the church in Rio where his sons were baptized, and the musky smell of frankincense and lilies came into his mouth like the flavor of a kiss. To kneel right now in that silence, to surrender. Like all Catholics, he felt most pious after sinning.

Just now Steven was impervious to moods. He darted up ahead and circled back. He danced his favorite hip-hop steps. And then they turned a corner and found themselves on an illuminated street. The street lamps shed bowls of light onto the sidewalk, and up ahead Steven saw something so shimmery and green, it could have been one of his own eyes made large and lit from within. The swimming pool was tucked in the center of an apartment complex courtyard, but he could see it through the wrought-iron gate that opened onto the street. Underwater lights sent white ripples drifting across its bottom. Steven stopped, his whole body racked with a sudden thirst.

"Can we go swimming?" he said when Bill caught up.

"I think that's private property."

"We can just climb the fence, no one will know. Come on, I've done it before with my mom."

Bill yielded. He didn't want the boy to start crying again, and he liked the way the stolen swim would sound when recounted later, a story of two wild boys adventuring on a topsy-turvy night. He gave Steven a boost and then hoisted himself over the fence.

"You sure you don't want to go home?" he said as they stood looking at the pool. Kidney shaped, it seemed to smirk at him like his own lopsided smile.

"We'll go home afterwards. We're almost there," Steven said and pulled off his T-shirt. He spun, wound up, and the shirt flew out of his hand and landed somewhere in the darkness. Next came the shoes, hurled as far as his strength would send them, and then his jeans and underpants. When he had released the last item of clothing, he ran to the pool and jumped in, feet first.

"Help, help, I'm drowning!" he said to Bill, pretending to flounder. "Glub, glub, glub." He rolled onto his stomach and lay in a dead man's float.

Bill took off his own clothes and set them on a lawn chair by the pool. His body felt thick and inflexible in the night air. As he climbed down the three steps and dunked himself underwater, he was washed by a terrible loneliness, and he realized that he had left his ghosts behind when he fled the bar. Not even the dead stuck with him, he thought, forgetting that it was he who kept coming unstuck. And so he swam underwater and grabbed Steven's foot with his teeth like a shark, and hung on until the boy shrieked and wriggled free.

Steven was euphoric, laughing and gulping water as he gnashed his teeth and chased after Bill. When they grew tired of playing shark, Bill let Steven ride on his back. They swam up and down the length of the pool with the boy murmuring "giddyup" in his ear.

"That does it for me," Bill panted when he reached the shallow end. "I'm not as strong as I used to be."

"Come on, horsey," Steven said, kicking Bill's ribs with his feet. "Giddyup."

"This old horsey's about ready to be put out to pasture, I'm afraid."

"Bad horsey. Giddyup."

"Have pity on an old man, Steven. I'm about to pass out."

"One more time. Come on. Please?"

"Here, let me rest a few minutes. Then we can go for another gallop."

Steven pouted, but when he saw Bill was adamant, he launched himself back into the water and swam along the floor of the pool like an eel. Bill threw himself onto one of the lawn chairs, his stomach heaving. He shut his eyes.

An image came to him, of standing by the edge of a dark pond. How deep was it? He stared down, worried. It seemed to him there was someone in the pond, someone he'd forgotten about. If only he could see through the black murk and the stillness. He peered, scanning for movement. Then he noticed that he was standing at the top of a staircase, looking down at the cellar in his childhood home. He felt along the wall for the light switch. If only he could turn on the light, then he would be able to see who was in the pond.

"Ma!" he yelled. "Turn on the light. Turn on the light!"

While Bill slept, Steven swam underwater. He followed the slanting incline of the pool's bottom, his stomach brushing the rough concrete. His breath pushed against his ribs. Still, he refused to surface. He let a bit of air seep from his mouth and sank further down into the water's deepest pocket.

$\mathscr{D}$eep Water (Julia)

I called Lisa after I left the freeway, but it didn't do me any good. She and Carolina had been at the supermarket when the earthquake hit, and they hadn't heard from Steven or my father since they'd been back.

"They're probably just stuck in traffic," Lisa said. "Don't you think?"

"I'm too worried to think."

"Mama's worried, too." Lisa's voice was curtained, unrevealing. "Do you want to talk to her?"

"I knew he would wander off again," Carolina said when she got on the phone. "It was stupid of me to let him back in my life."

"He hasn't wandered off," I protested. "He has Steven with him."

My mother didn't say anything for a moment. Then she said, "Simone said you went away because you didn't want to meet him."

"Is that what you told Steven?"

"No, we said you were sick."

"Sick? With what?"

"I don't know, just sick. He didn't ask with what."

I could only imagine Steven's reaction to the news that I'd disappeared because of an unspecified illness. "Oh God, he must have been frantic. You all must have been."

"Don't be so dramatic," Carolina said. "We hardly even noticed you were gone."

Before hanging up, I told them I would call every half hour to see if there was any word from Steven. They wanted me to join them at Lisa's apartment, but I knew I wouldn't be able to sit still. Mitch was there, and since they didn't have any electricity, they were playing gin rummy by candlelight. I couldn't imagine doing anything so tranquil.

Instead I drove over to Aunt Simone's and let myself into her apartment. There was no one there besides Swami and Svengali, and they were both under her bed. Some of her little glass knickknacks had fallen to the floor and shattered, so I swept them up, hoping she'd come home. When she didn't, I got back into the car and drove.

My quest was unraveling, losing direction. I had thought I could navigate by mother instinct, but I had failed. When he was a baby, I sometimes woke up moments before he started crying, my breasts already leaking. Why was it that I couldn't get a single image now, not a sensation, not an inkling of where he was?

In the end, I drove back to my own neighborhood and parked the car in front of my wood-shingled duplex. My block was one of the ones that had power, and my windows were the only ones on the street still dark. I leaned against Gabriel's car and stared up at them, trying to remember what it was like to wake up in my own bed and hear the low murmur of Steven's voice as he acted out baseball games and spider battles in the room next door. I wanted to go upstairs and sit on his bed and play with his toys. Make the action figures wrestle one another and fill the bed of the dump truck with pennies and shells. But no, that was a sure path to misery and helpless weeping. Instead I pulled a sweatshirt from the backseat of the car, wrapped it around my waist, and started walking. I needed to clear my head.

The night was hot and muggy, and I thought that if this were any normal evening, Steven and I would be sneaking into the pool at the apartment complex down the street for a late-night swim. And then my dream came back to me: my dripping hair, Irma shaking her broom. *Go away, weeping woman! Why do you drown your baby?* It was as if Simone had suddenly come up behind me, placed her cat-eye spectacles over my eyes, and allowed me to peer through the porthole of time. Without realizing that I had begun, I found that I was running through the stippled shadows of my neighborhood, until I came to the wrought-iron gate that led to the apartment complex.

I vaulted over the gate in one motion—none of the usual looking for a foothold or trying to avoid getting my clothes snagged on the iron scrolls. The courtyard was silent and shadowy, and I squinted at the lawn chairs and metal tables, trying to make them take a human shape. And then I looked at the water and began to run again, because he was there on the bottom of the pool, pale and gangly in the green half-light.

I pried the sweatshirt from around my waist as I ran and dropped it on the ground. A moment later I was breaking the surface with my arms and the water was foaming and then clearing and I could see him coming closer to me, his white limbs, the bubbles on his skin. I touched him and he looked up and reached toward me with his arms the way he did when he was a baby and wanted to be held. I put my arms around him and held him against me as I kicked and kicked, dragging us both against gravity until the water yielded us and we breathed.

When we reached the surface, Steven broke free of my hold. "I wasn't drowning," he said. "I was just seeing how long I could stay underwater." He began swimming away from me, back to the shallow end. I followed, wanting to shout that I was back and would never leave again, but his anger was kicking up a rough little trail behind him as he swam and I kept silent.

"Were you underwater for a long time?" I said when we were both standing. How formal I sounded, as if I were interviewing him. Steven looked at his hands, at his puckered fingertips, and then at the wall. Not at me.

"A really long time. Maybe ten minutes."

"I don't think anyone can go ten minutes without breathing. Maybe it was five minutes."

"How do you know it wasn't ten minutes? You weren't there."

Touché. I edged closer to him, seeing that he was shivering. "Come here, Goosepimple Boy, let me warm you up."

I reached for the sweatshirt I'd left by the side of the pool and then sat down on the steps, my wet clothes drizzling streams of water. Steven came over slowly and let me drop the sweatshirt over his head and put my arms around him. He put his head on my shoulder, but I could feel the taut muscles in his body that wanted to keep me at arm's length.

"I'm sorry," I murmured into his ear. "I don't blame you for being mad at me."

He didn't answer.

"I missed you a lot," I said.

"Then why did you stay away?"

"I was sick. I had to rest. Didn't they tell you I was sick?"

It was a cheap explanation, but it seemed more comprehensible than the truth. After a moment Steven settled into my lap and let me rub his icy feet and shoulders with my hands. He was beautiful, damp and human, with long legs that draped down from my lap and a heart full of tenderness and trust. I had to restrain myself from squeezing him with every remorseful muscle in my body. Instead I stroked his soft, clammy skin, breathed his atmosphere of chlorine and trembling, and thought that in spite of everything I hadn't done with my life, I had managed to accomplish this one good thing. When I looked down at his face, he was watching me closely through half-closed lids.

"What are you looking at?" I said.

He smiled and reached up to touch my cheek. "Your face," he said. "I missed your face."

It was a long time before I noticed that a man was lying on his back a few feet away. He was stretched out on a lawn chair on the far side of the pool, with his eyes closed and his hands folded across his bare belly. My father.

"He fell asleep," Steven said when he saw me looking over.

"He fell asleep and left you out here by yourself?" I was in no position to take the moral high ground, but I couldn't help it, I was furious. Didn't he know it was dangerous to let a child swim unattended?

"But he was nice to me today. We had to walk all the way back from San Francisco."

I stared at the man whose reappearance I'd spent a lifetime waiting for. "Go see if you can find your clothes," I said to Steven. "I'll wake him up."

While Steven rummaged around the patio for his underwear, I stood next to the sleeping figure and looked him over. I could see something familiar in the way the skin had settled on his face—a groove by his mouth where the smile went, the slackness of the lips that held my childhood stories. I sat down on the cement beside the chair and watched his chest and stomach, covered with damp gray and black hairs, rise and fall with each breath. Then I touched his arm.

"Daddy?"

I had meant to be stern with him, but when I saw his eyes flicker into wakefulness, my resolve melted. He blinked and then sat up, his mouth springing into its customary half-cocked smile.

"Julia! Where have you been all my life?"

I blew hot and cold on the drive back to my apartment. I was glad to see my father but furious at him for leaving; grateful that he'd been a friend to Steven but livid that he'd let Steven nearly drown himself. I was uncomfortable with both of them, individually and combined, and jealous that they seemed to have more ease with each other than either of them did with me. They told me about their adventures on the Bay Bridge, and I made appropriate reaction noises even though my stomach was churning.

"So you dragged Steven all over Oakland on foot?" I said to my father when they were done with their story. "Haven't you ever heard of taxicabs?"

"I didn't mind walking," Steven said, peacemaking. "And I got to rest in the bar."

"What bar?"

My father's bald head grew pink. "We stopped in a bar to use the phone," he said.

"Who did you call?"

"Well, we tried to call your mother, but we couldn't get through." He smiled at me and slouched in his seat.

"They're worried about you," I said. There was something so pathetic about the man that I couldn't keep up the interrogation. He nodded and reached across the seat to pat my arm.

"Your mother tortures herself," he said, as if we were all part of a family that knew one another intimately.

"Sometimes she has help," I replied.

My apartment was chaos, but I couldn't tell how much was earthquake damage and how much was the mess I'd made before I left. The broken mirror was from the earthquake, and the tipped-over dishes in the cabinets, but what about the jumble of cassettes by the stereo and the pile of clothes in my bedroom? I walked through the rooms, pretending to survey the wreckage but mostly wanting to reacquaint myself with home. The arrangement of shampoos and lotions in the bathroom, the tangle of sheets on my bed, the cornflower curtains in the living room—it was all tangible evidence that I'd once known how to manage my life.

"Are you guys hungry?" I asked when I came to the kitchen.

"Starving," Steven said and sat down at the kitchen table.

After four weeks, the refrigerator was a fairly frightening place, but I found some spaghetti and a jar of sauce in the cabinet and served it up to the men in my life with a little grated Parmesan on top.

"I always knew you'd turn out beautiful," my father said. "You look just like your mother did at your age. I could pick you out in a crowd."

I smiled awkwardly. "Thanks."

"You were the most beautiful little girl. When I used to take you out with me, people would stop me on the street to say how beautiful you were."

"I remember walking with you."

"Walk? You were always running, couldn't sit still. I used to joke that you had someplace to be."

"An appointment with destiny," I said dryly, trying to break the spell. "Do you think Steven looks like me?"

"I don't look like you," Steven said. "I look like my father, whoever he is."

"Don't be perverse," I said.

"I'm not, I'm telling the truth. Do you want me to lie?"

He looked down at his plate and shoveled a forkful of spaghetti in his mouth. A strand of noodle slithered over his chin, leaving a red trail.

I glanced at my father. "He's a little mad at me right now. Usually we get along great."

"Don't talk about me like I'm not here," Steven said.

"Sorry."

We ate in silence. My father looked self-conscious, and I noticed he was going to great lengths to get the strands of spaghetti completely wrapped around his fork before he lifted it to his mouth. Despite his care, a plash of sauce had landed on the collar of his shirt.

"Well, Steven, I still owe you a baseball game," he said at last. "We sure did do our best, though."

"*I* owe him a baseball game," I cut in. "I was the one who promised him the game in the first place."

"My mom loves the A's. Especially Rickey Henderson because he has a cute butt," Steven explained. "She knows everything about the team."

I admit I kind of swaggered, as much as you can swagger while sitting down. It was ludicrous to be competing with my father for the affections of my own son, but I couldn't help it.

"You must have inherited your love of the game from me," my father said to me. "Your mother doesn't care a fig for sports."

"Oh my God, you have to call her!" I don't know how I had let it slip my mind. My father wiped his mouth with one of the paper towels I had put on the table for napkins.

"Do you want to call her?" he said to Steven.

"I think Steven's ready for bed." I got up officiously and herded Steven from the table. Seeing my father try to weasel out of calling Carolina was enough to inflame all my old resentments. "The phone's in the living room," I said.

When Steven had washed up and changed into his pj's, I tucked him under the covers and then climbed onto the bed with him. He leaned up against me and shut his eyes.

"Do you want a story?" I asked.

He nodded. I cast about in my mind for ideas, but all I found was air. Usually I told him stories about things he had done during the day, or things I had done when I was apart from him, but I didn't know what he'd been doing and I didn't quite feel up to telling him about my life with Gabriel. I stroked his forehead. His eyes were already closed.

"What do you want to hear about?" I said.

"Spiders."

"Terratarantulan spiders?"

"No, the spiders that live in the Bay Bridge."

I had no idea what he was talking about, but I gave it a shot.

"Once there was a family of spiders who lived on the Bay Bridge. And they were very frustrated because they didn't have enough flies to eat."

"No, it's just one spider." Steven opened his eyes and looked at me accusingly. "And she doesn't eat flies." He scowled and buried his face in the pillow. "You don't know how to tell it."

"Do you want to hear another story?"

"No, I want that one. Grandpa can tell it. Get Grandpa."

Disappointment tightened my throat, but I told myself not to take it personally. I got up and found my father sitting at the kitchen table staring at the phone. He seemed forlorn.

"Steven wants you to tell him a story," I said.

At once he became the maestro. He stood up beaming and led the way to Steven's bedroom. "Have a seat, Princess." He gestured toward Steven's bed with a flourish. I climbed next to Steven and put my head down on the pillow beside his. He snuggled close to me. My father sat at the foot of the bed and cleared his throat. His lips came together and then opened slowly, as if after a kiss.

I woke up in the middle of the night and knew that he had left again. I was still curled up on Steven's bed, with my arms wrapped around his body. The back of his head was nestled under my chin and a lock of his hair had fallen into my mouth. I've come full circle, I thought.

I got up gingerly, so as not to wake him, and went into the kitchen to get something to drink. The house still smelled musty, and even in the dim light that seeped in from the street lamp outside the window, I could see that a grimy dust had settled on the counters. I filled a glass of water and settled down in one of the living room chairs to plot the cleaning regimen I would start as soon as it was light enough. I felt filled with a drowsy goodwill, as if I had somehow triumphed over everything.

As my eyes grew accustomed to the darkness, I saw that my father was lying on the sofa, using one of the armrests as a pillow. He wasn't sleeping. He was watching me, waiting for me to notice him.

"I thought you left," I said.

"I will, eventually."

"You never called my mother, did you?"

"No."

I sat back in my chair and tried to take him in. His voice was steady, and yet his face seemed weak and searching. It was impossible to know what to feel toward him. I felt like he was some gag prize I'd won at a carnival—a big, squishy middle-aged man. You asked for him, you got him.

"I didn't wish for you to come back," I said. "It was Lisa. You belong with them, they need you."

"I'm no good around people who need me."

"Who is?"

"Julia, it was for the best. It was a disaster waiting to happen. I didn't belong with you."

I waited as long as I could before saying, "Why not?" I could tell he was leading me somewhere. Another story.

He sat up and pulled the blue brocade bedspread off the sofa and draped it around his shoulders. "Speaking from experience, my sweet, I think it's better to lose your father than to find him."

I didn't follow. "Find him how?"

My father's voice sank into its lower register. "I don't look anything like my father," he said. "My father was tall and gaunt, a little ungainly. I have my mother's tendency to fat." He patted his stomach. "But I'm more like him than it appears. I have his nature."

"How old were you when he died?" I asked. He was just starting up, the words like the opening notes of a symphony, and I felt like the person in the audience who ruins the moment with an inopportune coughing fit. I was doing it on purpose. I didn't want to be lulled by his cadence once again.

"Not much older than Steven. But I remember him. Sweet as honey and as simple. He didn't have words for things, so he never could explain to me what was happening to him. But I know now."

He folded his hands behind his head and stared off into the shadows behind me. I tried to catch his eye, make him converse instead of orate, but he was off and running. From my chair I could see the darkness outside fading at the edges as it grew close to morning.

"My father had a sadness in him that wasn't like the sadness other people have. When it came over him, it sucked him under like water."

"What was he so sad about?"

"Everything. How our lives are fated to be full of disappointments and there's nothing we can do about it. How we never make the people who love us happy but only cause them more misery and pain. All the wretchedness and loss that is human existence."

I looked away from him and glanced out the window at the dawn lightening the sky and the pale ring of the streetlight. In the bottlebrush tree next door, birds began to chitter.

"You don't want to hear this, do you?" my father said.

I hesitated. It was going too fast, somehow, and I had the sense that he was leading me away from the truth even as he seemed to be leading me toward it. Still, I wanted to understand. I wanted to know the reason knotted to the reason before it that would explain how we had come to now.

"Tell me," I said.

My father drew the bedspread closer around his shoulders. "My father's workshop was in the cellar, and he used to stay there when he was sad. One night I went down there to see if he wanted dinner. He wasn't at his workbench, wasn't sleeping in his cot. I looked behind the bookcases he was making, behind the stacks of wood and the unfinished cabinets.

"I found him hunched in a corner in a lake of blood. He'd taken one of his tools—his chisel, I think—and tried to carve something out of his own limbs. He must have thought he could make himself useful and beautiful that way, like the swans he carved in his tables, but all he did was turn his arm into a sleeve of blood and open up the veins."

"You must have been so scared."

He shrugged and his flexible mouth twisted, working downward before he wrestled it into its lanky smile. "I tried to wake him, but I couldn't, so I fled. I ran into my mother's bedroom and wrapped myself in the bedspread and tried to go to sleep." He spread his arms so that the cloth around his shoulders opened up like turquoise wings. "It took my aunt Colleen a week of scrubbing to get the stains out."

"Why didn't she throw it out?"

"I don't know. Too frugal, I guess." He wrapped the bedspread back around his body and stared at the floor. "Do you understand now why I left?"

I shook my head. "No."

"My father's sadness ruined everything for me. I didn't want to do that to you and Lisa. Once I knew that I was like him, I knew I had to leave."

I shut my eyes, more tired than I'd realized. What was it that he wanted me to say? That I understood, that I forgave him, that his father's blood had washed him clean? But it hadn't, and I didn't. He shouldn't have left us. Nothing he could say would change that.

"Are you planning to leave again today?" I asked at last.

"I bought a ticket to Miami."

"Well, you can't leave until you say good-bye to Steven. I don't think he can handle any more sudden disappearances."

I got out a dust rag and a sponge and my father helped me clean up the apartment. As we straightened and dusted, we joked around a little about our duplicate natures. He couldn't resist kidding me about my disappearance, and I kidded back, although I wanted to ask him something serious. Was it fear of consequences, I wanted to ask, that made you stay away? Were you afraid to see the unholy mess you'd left behind? Instead, I told him the truth about where I'd been. He just nodded, as if it made perfect sense to him.

Steven slept through all the bustle, even the vacuum cleaner. He woke up while I was in the shower rinsing off the last twenty-four hours' accumulation of chlorine, dust, and death. When I came out of the bathroom, he was sitting at the kitchen table watching his grandfather cut a small circle from the center of three slices of bread.

"Ready for eats?" my father said. "I'm making cowboy eggs." He dropped the slices of bread into a frying pan and cracked an egg over each one. "Do you remember why they're called cowboy eggs?"

I shook my head.

"Because we make them at home, on the range."

He winked at me, and I couldn't help laughing. "I hope those eggs didn't come from my refrigerator," I said.

"We walked to the corner market," Steven answered. "None of the houses have chimneys anymore." His face was flushed with sleep and his cowlick was even unrulier than usual.

I went over and tried to sit on a corner of his chair. "Hey, shove over, Mr. Big Butt."

"You shove over, Mrs. Wide Load."

"I would, but there's a big ol' butt in my way."

We jostled each other until I managed to push him aside and perch my left cheek on the chair next to him.

"Help, there's a big fat ass taking over my chair," Steven called out to my father.

"You haven't seen a fat ass," my father said, "until you've tried to share a chair with me." He put down the spatula and nudged his right hip onto the other side of Steven's chair. Steven squealed and bumped against him, but my father merely grinned and hoisted him onto his lap.

"What are you laughing at, Missy?" he said as I tickled Steven's knee. And in a second he had dragged me onto his lap as well. We lay there for a moment, wrapped in his arms, and then my father made a gasping noise.

"You're right, Steven," he said in a choked voice. "She does have a fat ass. Who'd have thought my little daughter could grow so big?"

After breakfast I remembered that I still had to return Gabriel's car. I wanted to go alone so that I could explain a few things to Gabriel in person, but Steven looked so stricken when I proposed going somewhere without him that I let him tag along.

"Whose car is this?" he asked, fingering the dashboard.

"It belongs to the man who took care of me while I was sick."

"Have I ever met him?"

"No."

"Would I like him?"

"I think so."

For a moment I pictured Gabriel and Steven walking side by side, discussing some private thing. Then I shooed the image away. I liked being a single parent. I was good at it. Mostly.

When we got to Gabriel's apartment, I lingered in the car for a moment to see if he was there. The sills of his living room windows were raised, and the shades rocked gently as the air moved into the room and out again.

"Is this where you were when you were sick?" Steven asked.

"Yup. I used to look at that purple tree from my window." I pointed out the purple bougainvillea across the street.

"I want to go in and see."

That seemed like a bad idea. *Hi, Gabe, this is my son, Steven. Oh, I never mentioned that I had a son? Silly me, it must have slipped my mind.*

"We can't. No one's home."

I hoped that was true. Now that I was there, I could see there was no way to explain what I had done. Better to slink back to my old life undetected, like the air slipping out of his upstairs window.

"Can I go pick some flowers from that tree?" Steven said, losing interest in the outside of the building.

"Okay. Just look both ways before you cross the street."

I watched him cross over to the bougainvillea and begin tearing at the coarse, vibrant branches. "Careful, they have thorns," I yelled.

He nodded, intent. I sat down on the front steps of Gabriel's house and leaned a scrap of paper on the top stair. "Dear, Gabriel," I wrote. "Thanks for the car, and for helping me get my soul back. I have to go back to my old life now. I filled up the tank." I hesitated over how to sign it, whether to say *Love, Julia* or just *Julia*. What I wanted to say was something sadder and more permanent, but signing it *regretfully* sounded too formal and *sorry* sounded flip. I was still sitting with my pen poised over the note when Steven came bounding across the street holding a bouquet of purple bougainvillea.

"Here—now you can look at these when you're at home," he said, thrusting them into my hand.

I turned the bouquet around and examined it from all sides. The strands of bougainvillea sprang wildly in every direction as if electrified. "They're so beautiful—they look like purple fire."

Steven smiled and took them back from me while I folded the car key up inside the note and stuck the whole package in the metal mailbox marked *Gabriel Villalobo*. It wasn't until the bus ride home that I remembered I'd forgotten to sign it.

My father was gone when we got home, but he returned a little later with the rest of the family. Aunt Simone held me in her bird-like embrace for a long time, and then she pinched my chin between her thumb and forefinger and said, "For a while I thought I'd lost you."

She smelled different, like perfume and honey, and I saw that a few black plaits of hair were missing their usual coating of silver lacquer.

"I thought I'd lost *you*," I said. "Where were you yesterday?"

She gave me a vague smile. "I wasn't at home just then," she said, and the fingertips jumped from my chin to my lips, sealing them as I started to ask more. "We've been blindsided by fate, you and I. Keep it to yourself, for now."

We settled in the living room and watched earthquake damage reports on the television, while Carolina explained that earthquakes were caused by an imbalance of air on the surface of the planet.

"It all has to do with wind. When the wind rushes from one region to another, it creates a pressure on certain regions, a weight of barometric pressure," she explained. "That's why it gets so still before an earthquake."

"I thought it was caused by that trampoline competition they were having in China," my father said with mock solemnity. He winked at me. "One billion people jumping up and down on the other side of the world, it makes things slide around."

"Shut up, Bill, I'm trying to explain something serious," Carolina said, pouting. "You think you know everything. Julia, I had hoped to keep this from you when you were a child, but your father's full of shit."

I was pleased to see them flirting with each other, even if it was a bit stagy. I snuggled further into the chair I was sharing with Steven and looked over at Lisa to see how she was reacting. She grimaced and eyed the door to the kitchen.

"I'm going to make a pitcher of lemonade," I said. "Lisa, do you mind giving me a hand?"

While I used a corkscrew to chip the can of frozen juice out of the snowbank in my freezer, Lisa filled me in on the past few weeks of family life.

"I loved it at first, but now I'm sick of it," she said. "I feel like I'm ready to leave the nest, except that it's my own damn nest. What I really want is to kick out the mommy and daddy birds."

I withdrew my head from the inside of the freezer. She looked good—robust, as if she'd spent a week or two in the country. She was wearing a gray-and-white jumper with a black T-shirt underneath and a pair of black high-tops.

"Do I look like I'm twelve?" she said, looking down at her thick torso.

"You look nice. It's been a while since I've seen you in a dress."

"I think Mitch and I are going to get back together."

She lifted her chin and folded her arms, as if waiting for me to contradict her. I felt a pang of jealousy. Her face had the heady, sweating look of someone whose skin has turned painful from too much touching. "I'm glad you guys are working things out. You should bring him over, I'd like to see him."

"He was going to come over today, but he's volunteering at the shelter for earthquake victims. I'm going to go over there in a little while and help out, too." She picked up the spatula from that morning's breakfast and began scraping bits of egg white from the side of the frying pan.

"You know what?" she said suddenly. "I never liked family life. When Mitch left, I thought that's what I was missing, but guess what, it wasn't. Dad and I don't have anything in common really. I don't even think he likes me that much."

"Do you like him?"

"No, not really. He's okay. He doesn't appreciate good food. I made a roast lamb and he put ketchup on it." The pan was now thoroughly scraped, so she carried it to the sink to rinse it out. "You've been using soap on this pan, haven't you, Julia?" she said in a hurt tone. "How many times do I have to tell you that you ruin the seasoning that way?"

"It can't just be the ketchup," I said. "What else don't you like about him?"

"We just don't connect. I'm just a relationship to him—youngest daughter. He's different with you. I can see it already in the way he looks at you." She put the pan back on the stove. "You know, I was wondering if he could move in here for a while. My apartment's getting kind of crowded."

I was surprised at how little I liked that suggestion. I had been looking forward to being alone with Steven, the way we used to be. "What about Mama?"

"What about her? She's sick of him, too. They don't even sleep together anymore."

My heart sank a little. "They seemed to be getting along fine," I said lamely.

"Here's the thing," Lisa said. "Yesterday, when the earthquake happened, the first thing I thought about was Mitch. I thought, His house collapsed and he's lying in a pile of rubble, dying slowly of suffocation. It was just like old times. Did I ever tell you that about me, about how I worry?"

"No." I decided against mentioning my conversation with Mitch.

"Well, I do. Mitch used to hate it. So there I was, in a total state, and when I tried to call him, I got a recording saying the circuits are busy, try again later. I was frantic."

"But he's okay?"

"He's fine, but that's not the point. The point is that I thought Daddy coming back would end all that for me. But it didn't, so fuck him. I survived it anyway."

I stirred the frozen lemonade around in a pitcher, trying to break up the ice with the spoon. "I think Steven and I need some time alone," I said. "I don't want Dad to come stay with us just yet. I have a lot of loose ends I need to tie up."

"All right, fine, I'll move in with Mitch. That's what he wants to do anyway."

With that she grabbed the pitcher and marched into the living room.

I kept waiting for my father to leave, but he didn't. He visited me and Steven every day, and after a while he became part of our routine. He even started contributing his own stories about Terratarantula. Steven illustrated them with drawings of spiders battling one another from their intricate webs. I took the warlike nature of his pictures as a sign that my disappearance still rankled. He was clingy, and when we talked about the time I was sick, he always asked about the person who took care of me.

"I think I should meet him," he said once when we were rocking side by side on the rubber-seated swings at the neighborhood park.

"Why?"

"I just should. It's only fair. I don't like you keeping secrets."

I thought about getting in touch with Gabriel, but each time I was tempted I thought better of it. I looked back on those lion-colored days as if they were an addiction I had freed myself from. At first I craved him, especially at night. I thought about his smooth chest and brick-colored nipples, and the nip of his swimmer's waist. His voice, laying out the structure of his reasoning stone by stone. But I'm used to sleeping alone, and it didn't take long for me to reacquaint myself with the pleasures of stretching out across a wide plain of sheets, untrammeled by anyone else's limbs. And so I loosened my grip on the memory of Gabriel, and after a time it slipped out of my hands altogether.

A few weeks after my return, my mother called and asked if I would go with her to the doctor. "I've decided to get a biopsy," she said. "Would you mind keeping me company?"

The hospital waiting room was painted pale blue with violet trim. The only other person in it was an elderly Russian woman wrapped in an immense black coat that looked as if it had sheltered her entire family during both world wars.

"Do you like her scarf?" I whispered to Carolina. My mother took note of the woman's head scarf, which was patterned with red and blue monkeys.

"Cute," she said, but she didn't giggle the way I had expected. The skin around her eyes was bruised with sleeplessness and creased with worry lines. "I bet that woman's coat embarrasses her children, just like my mother's clothes always embarrassed me."

"Do you still think she's trying to kill you?"

She shrugged. "I could have been wrong. My mother and I never understood each other very well. What do I know about why she does anything?"

Her voice sounded so sad that I seized her hand and held it. "I'm glad you've decided to do this," I said. "And I'm glad you asked me to come along."

"Well, who else would I ask?" She gave my hand a squeeze and then slid out of my grip. "Your father and I just don't have that kind of relationship."

"What kind of relationship *do* you have?"

Carolina crinkled her brow for a minute before answering. "We're intimate strangers. And we have too much history to get to know each other any better."

"Why not?"

She shrugged and folded her arms over her chest. "You can't go home again, that's what I keep telling him. Look at my mother. She spent her whole life trying, and she never got farther than Central Square."

"But you can't just forget about everything that's happened between you."

I meant between her and my father, but Carolina misunderstood. "I haven't forgotten," she said. "She won't let me."

A moment later, the receptionist called her name.

$\mathscr{T}$he Undiscovered Country   (Simone)

After the call came, she got up, put on her purple sombrero, gathered her things. I watched her, a little sad, a little jealous. I would like to go there, but my fate keeps me here. My fate—and Martha, who was outside tending herbs on the veranda as I watched Carolina in my cup of tea. Gardening like a pagan, without her clothes, even though the November fog is chillier than snow. I could see her through the sliding glass door, squatting down by the planters, her pointed breasts no doubt horrifying any street-level passersby who happened to gaze skyward. Fate is a humorist, I often tell her, to pair sweater-clad me with someone impervious to cold.

Martha is my opposite—she believes in magic, not in divination. "I'll tell you your fortune," she says each morning when I reach for the bookshelf. "You will live a long life in the company of women." She grins slyly.

We tut-tut each other. When I come into the bedroom and find her cross-legged, eyes shut, I know she's cooking up some spell, and

I purse my lips and sigh loud enough for my breath to break her trance. More than once I've considered making her leave altogether and take her meddlesome charms and incense with her. But I don't. We complement each other, like mismatched teacups.

She knows to stay away from me when I'm scrying, though she teases me about it later. "It's worse than soap operas," she says. She thinks it's prying. It's no use explaining that every life needs an audience. We all suspect we're being watched, and it's comforting to think that someone might be making sense of it all. You can't see a life in close up any more than you can make sense of a painting with the lumpy brush strokes mounded under your nose. Take a few steps back and the shape becomes clear: a bowl of fruit, a winter landscape.

The day Carolina put on her hat, my fortune spoke of openings. This was the phrase: "An occurrence at the door intervened." A strange one, neither here nor there. I mulled it over while I sipped my tea, stumped. At last I understood that it summed up everything that had happened, and would yet. This going in and out of doors they had been doing. Even me, allowing Martha to intervene when I lost my ability to scry. Thinking of that night, I had to slip past the sliding door and find her in the open air. Touch her soft flesh, ridged with cold.

I didn't predict her. She slipped in through the fissures of the present when my link with time was broken, a wild weed rooting itself in pavement. Glimpsing Julia in the arms of her swain, I had seen how love can make a place for itself in the most unpromising soil. Even so, I thought I knew the future too well to be surprised. I don't mind being wrong, just this once.

And yet it's strange to be a novice at my age. Letting the tide of her body lift me up is like learning to surrender to fate all over again. She washes my hair for me at night, scrubs my scalp with her sharp nails. "You need to be reminded of the actual," she says as she rinses. "Too much time gazing at the future and you'll fade out of reality altogether."

Yet the stories won't stop telling themselves. Even as I stood behind her on the balcony and wrapped my arms around her naked waist, Carolina's face veered into view. Neither sad nor smiling. Determined. She was the occurrence at the door, intervening in the long waiting of her life.

I was proud of her. She was frightened of her future, but she'd taken a peek at it anyway. I don't know why she asked a doctor instead of me; I could have told her whether she had cancer, and a whole lot more besides. But Carolina always had to do things her own way. She certainly isn't the first to choose the white-coated fortune-teller over the one in robes.

I remember her in the gift shop in Cancún near the end of her cruise. Serapes done in Escher patterns. Nylon hammocks in pink and blue and red and yellow strung from the ceiling. Ceramic pigs, black pottery, and painted copper plates stacked on the floor. Carolina, poking about in her white muslin cruisewear, spied a purple sombrero and put it on. Cocked her head at the mirror in the corner, smiled winsomely, twirled. The hat slunk over her eyes and the teenager behind the counter grinned shyly, not sure whether it was permissible to laugh.

Underneath the shadow of the hat, Carolina was afraid. All week she had been feeling death push against her chest. There in the gift shop, she had a craving for some souvenir, something of Mexico, something to take home. Our mother's ancient yearning twisted in her misunderstanding mind, and purple millinery was what she walked away with.

Now an occurrence at the door intervened. Turned her around, set her back on that same path. Lifted the hat, stared her in the face. The prognosis is excellent when you catch it early, the doctor said. What Carolina heard was: *You don't have much time.*

She and Bill had made themselves quite at home in Lisa's spare bedroom, converted it into a marriage bed of sorts. Food stains on the bedspread and the pillow, outfits strewn over the backs of the chair. Her things intermingled with his, like old times. Now she began separating. She picked up her bra from the floor and shook out a pair of his socks that had nested in the right cup. She unstrung her lace nightgown from the edge of the door but left his terry-cloth bathrobe underneath. Gathered up high-heeled shoes and her ruffled white dress, a turquoise belt, three pairs of size-five slacks, and stuffed them all into the suitcase she had dragged out from under the bed.

In the bathroom, her cosmetics were arrayed on top of the toilet tank. She gathered them one by one and tucked them in her bag. Shampoo, conditioner, deodorant. Toothpaste and toothbrush, floss. The black razor and shaving cream were his, the pink razor hers. The mint mouthwash and deodorant soap belonged to him, the perfumes were hers. She packed two bottles of scent, one floral, one citrus, and sprayed herself with the spicy one she'd left on the edge of the sink. That was the one she used to wear the most, and she liked to think of him smelling it after he found her gone, his nostrils dusted with remembrance.

I was glad then that she'd chosen against foreknowledge, because I knew he would disappoint her. "He won't think of smelling it," I murmured to Martha, my face burrowed in her neck.

"Go inside," Martha said, shaking me off. "If you're going to be with them, I don't need you all over me." She reached behind to squeeze my thigh before I wandered back to the kitchen and my tea.

Before she left, Carolina took off the hat and bent over to brush the underside of her hair. She brushed until the black strands shivered with static. When she righted herself, she was almost dizzy, and her hair gleamed. She was dressed for traveling. Comfortable shoes, with only a two-inch heel. A skirt, so she wouldn't feel confined. Layers for the changing weather: a silk T-shirt under a cotton sweater, under a linen blazer. Layers to shed, one by one, as she headed south.

"You'll need an umbrella," I said to my teacup. But she couldn't hear me, and anyway, she didn't care about the rain. Her chest was filled with electricity like her hair. Nothing could dampen that.

She almost didn't leave a note, but sometimes taking the high ground is the best revenge. She knew he'd remember that when he left, he hadn't bothered. So she wrote up an elliptical explanation and left it on the bed. Then she went downstairs, where the cab was waiting.

"Symmetry," I said to Martha when she came in from the veranda.

"Tsk," she said and cast a disdainful eye at my cup of tea. "Let's go for a walk."

I put on my long wool coat, and Martha put on jeans and a flannel shirt. We walked arm in arm down to Lake Merritt and circled it in silence. The fog threaded through the trees in wet wisps that reminded me of my lover's hair. Businesspeople were out walking on their lunch breaks; they scurried past us, chilled. The lake smelled faintly of brine and mud, its main ingredients. As we walked, I thought about my fortune and the importance of doorways. The lake was artificial, a tidal swamp dammed up by the city fathers and fed by creeks now culverted and hidden under concrete. The tide lost its escape route, but the trapped water made a fine home for birds. They bobbed along its edge: duck, egret, pelican, goose. If the water had roamed, where would they be?

That's my own prejudice: I prefer staying put. But Carolina was in a taxi with the windows rolled down, and the gray salty air stinging her eyes. Soon she'd be landing, like the splat of guacamole, in the city of Oaxaca, just miles away from Mitla.

On a map Mexico looks like a snake that has eaten a large rat. Its rattling tale is Baja California; its raised, inquiring head is the Yucatán, eyeing the Caribbean Sea. Mitla lies in the throat of the nation, like something that could be coughed up or swallowed, like something unsaid. I knew Carolina would soon be wandering up the long road that led to the ruins, like our mother did with a basket of fruit balanced on her head. She would come in the afternoon and be a little disappointed by the dusty town, the doors of its shops clamped shut for siesta. Even so, she keeps walking. Past the river where the women bathe, past the one open store selling hammocks and Coca-Cola. The road curves a little, swivels. Stones and sand slip through Carolina's sandal straps and lodge beneath her heel. She sweats, and lifts the heavy fall of her hair to fan her neck.

The buildings by the road are square concrete structures, not the wood-and-mud homes of my mother's time. The doors are curtained with faded fabric. Curious, Carolina thinks of pulling a corner of the cloth aside, just to see the people sleeping. It's shady inside, she can tell that already, and she knows somehow that flies are circling in the middle of the rooms, and that the people resting in hammocks are sleeping a sleep they would wake from in a moment if a middle-aged woman, half gringa, half Indian, should stick her curious face into their home.

Do they know that she looks like them? Carolina has dressed herself to be at home here, in her ruffled skirt and embroidered blouse, but it is her face that she thinks should remind them of the woman who left long ago with the tall blond anthropologist they called Goose. A few children kick a soccer ball along the street, and she waits for them to stop and stare at her. They don't. The air is heavy, muggy. The sun flares in the sky. Along the edge of the road are agave plants and spiny cactus, and terra-cotta pots spilling a few rangy crimson flowers.

When she reaches the top of the road, she is at the center of a green bowl made of mountains, and she feels the thirsty sky might tilt her back and swallow her. The ruins are there, low and gray. At the market next door, a few wakeful women are selling stone ashtrays and wooden letter openers and white blouses painstakingly crocheted. She is the only stranger to come off this bus from Oaxaca, and the women surround her, offering their wares.

"*Cinquenta mil pesos; es muy barato.*"

"*Es muy bonito, Señora. Le gusta? Quatro cientos.*"

She takes an ashtray made of carved lizard faces. Turns it over in her hands. The woman selling it has high cheekbones and a broad forehead. She wears her long graying hair in a braid down her back. She is squat, square, and her muscular arms look strangely vulnerable peeking from the sleeves of a blouse stretched to its maximum by her heavy bosom.

"*Le gusta, Señora?*" the woman prompts.

Carolina says, "*Momentito,*" a word she learned from the clerk at her hotel. She feels she has lost her breath. There is a reunion to be had here somewhere, but it will take time. For now she can only smile at the woman who looks like her mother, and fumble in her pocket for bills she has trouble distinguishing. When the ashtray is hers, Carolina walks to the edge of the market and sits down on a concrete ledge. From here she can see the ornate church the Catholics built atop a portion of the ancient city. The past running under the present, like water. She lights a cigarette and smokes it down to the filter, looking out over the valley that was her mother's home.

"What do you see in that murky lake?" whispered Martha. I blinked my eyes, and the reflections of trees and buildings closed over Mitla. A duck with a sheeny head of green and blue capsized in front of me, head dropping down, bottom rocking up. A moment later he came up clapping his beak.

"This is when they all head south," I said. Martha tossed a crust of bread into the water and a strange flock came paddling up—three soft brown females, and a gawky pelican with dirty white wings.

"They don't head south," she said. "It's perfectly warm here." She pulled another corner of bread out of the breast pocket of her flannel shirt. "If you were talking about the birds," she added.

But I wasn't. "I've gone to Mexico to find my roots," Carolina had written. Now that he had an excuse, it wouldn't take long for Bill to take wing himself. He thought the women in his life would anchor him, but they were pulling out of port one by one, following the current of their destinies. He would follow, soon enough. He'd run from woman to woman all his life. No reason to stop now.

"He's traveling solo now," I told Martha. I thought of Bill lying awake at night, waiting for the ghosts to slip in through the window and take up their wakeful posts at the foot of his bed. Where had they gone? He imagined them wandering the streets of Oakland like a pair of stray dogs, restless and virulent, chasing the deer that grazed on the hilltop rosebushes and the blanket-clad figures that slept in the doorways of downtown. In truth, they were closer to

Bill than he realized. He had seen the face behind their faces, and now they would only show themselves in dreams.

Martha dusted the crumbs from her hands and slung her arm through mine. "Bon voyage to all of them," she said. "I can't say I'll miss them. I was hoping you and I could go out to dinner. Maybe talk about other things."

She kissed my cheek, as if we were no more than fond old ladies. The birds by her feet heaved themselves into the air, beating back gravity with their frantic wings.

The House with the Purple Tree   (Julia)

When Lisa finally decided to speak to me again, she told me about a job at a resource center for homeless people. She heard about it when she was volunteering at the earthquake shelter and thought of me because it had something to do with books. "Homeless people?" I was ungrateful. "I'm practically homeless myself."

"Don't sneer at me." Lisa sighed into the phone. "I'm just trying to help."

I was desperate and it was bringing out the worst in me. I had already run through my meager savings in the short time it took to discover that I wasn't qualified for any of the jobs I wanted. To buy myself a little more time, I had been working temp, but the money was dreadful and the work was worse. For the past week I had been marooned in the windowless file room of a gigantic health insurance company with eighteen cartons of processed claim forms. Each form had a twelve-digit number in the upper right-hand corner, and my job was to file them sequentially in one of the room's nineteen file cabinets. Naturally I spent more time quantifying the dreariness of the task than completing it.

"Nineteen file cabinets! That's seventy-six drawers of files! It's death by a thousand paper cuts!" I whined to Lisa.

"Then get yourself a real job," Lisa said and hung up.

Good advice, but I was losing my momentum. I had started my job hunt with plenty of vigor, but the monotony of filing was making me feel sluggish, not to mention deranged. After my third day at the insurance company I had begun filing forms that started with 101 in the same drawer as ones that started with 110. By Thursday the sloppiness had escalated into full-scale sabotage, and I was stuffing handfuls of forms into random file drawers, laughing maniacally all the while. That Friday I walked over to the homeless resource center after work.

The center was in the library of an old luxury hotel that had fallen on hard times and been converted into a homeless shelter. I fell in love with the room as soon as I pushed open the door. The walls were paneled with dark strips of walnut and lined with bookshelves and wooden tables. Tall casement windows exposed the fog-white sky and the ragged, silvery buildings below. You could see half of downtown from those windows, and even make out a gray-blue swath of the Bay.

The room smelled of paper and old hallways and the acrid odor of a bag lady working at a computer in one corner. It was the smell of a public library, and it swamped me with nostalgia. I thought of Aunt Simone at her desk in the Boston Public Library, stamping due dates in the back of my Pipi Longstocking books. All at once I wanted to spend my life in that room, with all the answers at my fingertips and books stacked close and tight as bricks.

Sitting next to the bag lady was a woman who clearly ran the place. She looked up when I approached and pushed her chair back from the computer.

"Can I help you?" Her voice was crisp, but there was sweetness in its lower register, like honey at the bottom of a glass.

"I'm here to apply for the job." I held out my resumé.

"Let's take a look," she said, standing up. "I'm Monique Patterson. I'm the center director." As she came toward me, I had the sudden impression that the room had compressed itself into human form and I was looking at the result. Her skin was as brown and shiny as the walnut panels, and her eyes were as full of light as the casement windows. She was wearing a crimson jersey dress that rolled over her body's curves and reached almost to her ankles.

"You look like you were born in this room," I said without thinking. My lips snapped shut around the final *m*, wishing they could reel the whole sentence back in. No one wants to be told they look like an office, no matter how lovely an office it may be. But to my surprise, Monique just nodded.

"I practically was born here," she told me, leading me over to a table in the middle of the room. "Back when this place was a hotel, my papa used to play trumpet in the house band and my mama used to wash linens in the laundry room. Sit down."

I did, smitten. Everybody who meets Monique Patterson falls in love with her. She's as strong and graceful as a snake, and like a snake she moves with her hips rocking from side to side. But snakes are supposed to be devious, and Monique doesn't have time for subterfuge. It's the quality of hers I envy most, the way she figures out exactly what she thinks in plenty of time to say it.

"Let me tell you about the job." She leaned across the table and fixed me with her oval brown eyes. "This is a resource center for homeless people. We have books and computers and training manuals as well as application forms for all the different kinds of social services that are available. Most of our clients don't have the best reading and writing skills in the world, so we provide tutoring for them and help with the various forms. We also teach them how to use computers and help them find the information they need in the books. As my assistant, you would do everything from shelving books to tutoring the clients. Does that interest you?"

In Monique's mouth, words like *computer* and *training manual* sounded juicy as berries. I nodded and she broke her gaze away from me and scanned my resumé.

I looked over at the homeless woman who was still sitting at the computer. She was a bony creature with thin blond hair, and when she noticed me looking at her, she bowed her head closer to the keyboard. The deftness with which she flinched away from inspection reminded me of something, but I wasn't sure what.

Monique laid my resumé flat on the table. "This isn't going to make me hire you. Enhancement Press? What in the Lord's name is that?"

"They publish self-improvement books." I was daunted by her candor and by my inexplicable hunger for a place at her feet. I noticed that the outer semicircle of her left ear was punctured by a row of gold studs that went all the way up to the cartilage. The ear listened, its gold rivets glittering. Say something, I thought. It's waiting.

"Look, why don't you let me volunteer here for a day or two and you can see what you think of me," I burst out. "Teaching is sales, after all, and I spent two years at Enhancement Press selling people on books. I can persuade people to read, I can motivate them, and I can make complicated things comprehensible. I know how to pick out each person's special interest and use it to make them want what I have. That's what good teachers do, isn't it?"

I grinned at her, sure that I sounded brash and insincere, but meaning every word of it. Somehow the huckster that had come out at the Psychic Fair was making a reappearance. My tongue felt loose and agile, slick with salesmanship.

Monique leaned back. I'd intrigued her, I could see that much, but she wasn't as easy a mark as the seekers at the Psychic Fair. *"Part* of teaching is sales," she corrected. "And *part* of this job is teaching. But it's also job counseling, and answering the phone, and paperwork. Forms, filing. Writing grant applications, if you know how."

"I've done every secretarial chore under the sun," I said, trying not to think about all the misfiled forms at the insurance company. "I worked temp before I worked at Enhancement Press, so I know how to learn on the fly. Nothing fazes me."

"That's a plus. There's plenty to faze a person around here. Ever worked with homeless people?"

"No."

"Ever done any counseling?"

"No."

"Have you done any work with low-income people, elderly people, people in need? Any volunteer work? Anything for anyone besides yourself?"

She folded her arms across her chest and tilted her head, cocking her gold-rimmed ear toward me. I stared at the short plush of her hair, the smooth skin of her neck, not sure whether I should lie.

I wanted this job, and some superstitious inclination was telling me I shouldn't lie to get it.

"I have a kid," I said lamely. "I used to volunteer at his pre-school when he was younger."

Monique smiled at me. "Next time you should put that on your resumé," she said. "Every bit of life experience counts. That's what I tell our clients all the time." She put my resumé into a folder on her desk and then stood up. "I have to get back to work. If you're serious about volunteering here, follow me and I'll give you some things to do."

I followed her, stuck to her heels like a puppy, and she seated me next to the homeless woman at the computer.

"Mrs. Knox, would you mind if Julia here gives you a hand with that letter while I make a few phone calls?"

The woman looked up from the screen and gave a tiny, cob-webby shrug. I watched her eyes following Monique's retreating back-side and suddenly understood why she looked familiar. She's like me, I thought. Too timid even to seek. Too afraid of being disappointed.

Late in January my father came to visit me at my new job. I looked up and saw him standing in the doorway of the resource center, watching me. My student, Conrad, was busy following the trail of my fingers as I went over the letters in the literacy workbook. He was a gaunt black man with a gray beard that he was nervously twisting into points. This was only his second lesson, and he didn't know how to act with me.

"Could we start from the beginning?" he whispered. "I know I should know these, but I can't seem to get a handle on them." His spindly hands spun his beard into three prongs and then scratched it bushy again.

I traced the letters in the book with my finger. The lower-case *b* on the page was outlined over a drawing of a little b-shaped bird, its tail flying up to the left and its head bobbing down at the right.

"This is a bird. Say *bird,*" I said to Conrad.

The phrase was the beginning of the little catechism I used to teach letters. When Monique first taught me how to do it, I would come home chanting it to myself. The idea is to teach people to recognize words as well as letters, but what I like about it is the way each of the letters assumes an identity. I've always thought of letters as characters: double-breasted, brazen capital B, cowering, fetal-positioned C.

"This is a bird. Say *bird.*"

"Bird."

"This looks like a bird. Say *bird.*"

"Bird."

"This is the word *bird.* Read *bird.*"

"Bird."

"The word *bird* begins with the letter *B.* Say *B.*"

"B."

I peeked over the edge of the book to where my father was standing. He was familiar to me now. The shiny-scalped, slack-skinned father had taken over the place in my memory where the old black-haired, baby-lipped one used to be. He stood with his hands in his pockets, looking embarrassed. He hated coming to the shelter to visit me. I think he was afraid of being mistaken for one of my clients.

I pointed to my watch and flashed ten fingers at him to tell him I'd be done in ten minutes.

"That's my father," I said to Conrad.

"Hello, Juney's father." Conrad's shy voice was too soft for my father to hear from across the room. I could barely hear it and my face was nearly touching his. He called me Juney because he said I was too sweet to be named after July. "July's my unlucky month," he told me the first time he came in. "July 1969 I was drafted. July 1976 my wife was killed by a drunk driver. July 1985 I lost my job at the cannery. July 1988 I started sleeping on the street. After that, every month was a bad month." He laughed then, a low chuckle punctuated by squeaky breaths, and squeezed my arm. "Maybe you'll change my luck, Miss Julia, but for now I'm going to call you June."

Sometimes when I'm talking to my clients at the resource center, I imagine telling them about Shantra Maloney. "Everything that happens to you is your complete responsibility," I could say. "The reason you have to sleep in a doorway is that you've been indulging in negative languaging. Say 'poor me' enough times, and eventually you end up poor."

Conrad wouldn't see the humor. He laughs at his own jokes but not at mine. Anyway, he believes that most things really are his own fault. "If I knew then what I know now, I'd do things differently," he says.

"Too bad we're not born wise," I tell him. "Instead we have to learn from our mistakes."

It's a funny kind of religion I dish out here, sort of a reformed branch of the Church of Aunt Simone. I tell them about learning things from books, and sometimes, when we're talking about their lives, I mention that things happen for no good reason. But I steer clear of fate. Half the time willpower is all they have to live on.

They are drifters, all of them, in one way or another. I think that's why we get along. They've come from Dallas or Detroit or Portland or they've lived here all their lives, but somehow things have always happened to them, and not the other way around. Who's to say if it was bad choices, bad intentions, or bad luck? There's no religion for the poor, as Gabriel understood.

After I introduced Conrad to *b, c, d,* and *f,* I read him a story. Monique believes that hearing words read aloud helps people learn to read. Not all of my clients are as good at listening as they are at talking, but Conrad was everything I could ask for in an audience. As soon as I started reading the words aloud, his face went slack, his eyes soft as gravy.

The story was about a man whose wife has left him, and as I read I began to think about Gabriel returning home to find his car keys and my unsigned note. Did he still think of me, veering between outrage and nostalgia like the man in the story? Or had he accepted my departure with the same grace that greeted my arrival? I wished I could slip into his apartment invisibly, like a ghost, and see how he was doing.

I looked over the edge of the page to see how Conrad was liking the story. He was sitting with his hands gently resting on the table, no longer twisting his whiskers into tufts. His face was somber. I began to read without hearing the words I was speaking, wishing that I'd chosen a story about happiness, if such a story existed. The man had had a life of sorrow; didn't he deserve ten minutes of escape? I read with my mouth refusing the words, as if they were a food I was already full of. I could feel my father's eyes on me from across the room. He had put on his boots and walked out of the house rather than tell me a single sad story.

"I know how it is to be hurt like that," Conrad said when I was finished. "They say time heals all wounds, but some wounds are just there to stay."

"I didn't mean to make you think about your troubles." I touched his hand. It was knobby with calluses.

He squeezed back with a passion that made me flinch. "Don't you worry. I think about my troubles anyway." He gave my hand another squeeze and then took it in both of his. "You're a good girl, Juney. I bet your daddy's proud of you."

I felt my face go hot. Conrad had put his finger on it. I wondered if my father had heard me reading the story and whether he liked the inflection of my voice. I wanted him to be proud of me, to see that I was like him. It was childish, but I hoped that when he saw me with Conrad, he noticed that I was kind.

"Kind of a sad sack, wasn't he?" my father said when Conrad had left and we were walking through the streets of downtown in search of lunch.

"He's had a tough time of it." I began to tell him about Conrad's Julys.

My father shook his head at me. "I couldn't do what you do, Princess. Listen to hard-luck stories all day. Worse than sitting in a goddamn bar."

"I like hearing stories, even sad ones." I turned to him, wanting to meet his eyes. "Always have."

He was striding, hands in his pockets, the collar of his jacket turned up against the wind. He looked out at the run-down, vacant buildings of the neighborhood instead of at me. "You're tenderhearted," he said. "When I hear tales of woe, all I want to do is run or crack jokes, one or the other."

"I already know about your tendency to run."

He shrugged, and the half-grin yanked at one corner of his mouth. "Everybody's got to be good at something. Tell me something, Jules, are we going somewhere or just walking?"

I stopped. Of course we were just walking. I had never gotten the hang of figuring out where I was going before I set out.

"Sorry, I was just walking nowhere out of habit. What do you feel like eating?"

"Whatever you feel like. I'm not really hungry."

I wasn't hungry either, suddenly. The air was cold and alive on my cheeks, and the city streets looked empty and appealing. "We could just walk, if you're really not hungry."

"Lead the way."

He put his arm around me, a little awkwardly, and we began walking along the edge of downtown, through Chinatown. The produce markets had set crates of bok choy, onions, apples, and gingerroot on the sidewalk, and there was barely enough room for us to pass without dropping our arms and going single file. But we didn't. I walked on the edge of the curb and we maneuvered around bins of hot peppers, dried mushrooms, and cloud ears. My father gripped my waist and I rested my head on his shoulder.

"Have you heard from your mother?" We had turned onto a wider street, packed with restaurants instead of markets, and my father had his head turned a little to the side, as if he were addressing the trussed chicken in the store window instead of me.

"She sent us a postcard. She sounded like she's having a good time."

"Is she still in Mitla?"

"She was when she wrote."

I felt a tremble in the soft roll of fat where my hand was resting. It could have been laughter or a sharp breath in. Whatever it was, it didn't show in his face. He just nodded.

"It's quiet in that apartment without her and Lisa."

"Maybe you should come stay with me and Steven."

I felt uneasy offering, but I couldn't stand the thought that he was lonely. Every time I saw him in that apartment, surrounded by the remnants of Lisa's decor, it stung me. I pictured him at night, lying on the beige sofa bed she had left behind. The window open, blowing in fog and regret.

"That's okay, sweetheart. You're crowded enough in that apartment. But thanks for the offer."

The street was widening now, rimmed on both sides by boxy warehouses. Without either of us seeming to let go first, my father and I dropped our arms from around each other and walked unencumbered. I let my arms swing. My father stuck his hands in his pockets again.

"I guess things didn't work out too well with me and your mother or your sister, but I'm glad I've gotten to know you and Steven. I always thought you and I were alike in some way."

"We could almost be related," I said to deflect the little swell of joy that rose up at those words.

The sidewalk had fallen away and we were walking in the street now, stepping over railroad tracks and around the ruts in the decaying asphalt. We had come into the scabby warehouse district that tapers off from downtown. The street was clumped with weeds and trash and soggy cardboard boxes. Beside me, my father seemed to be turning out the pockets of his mind, looking for a story to tell.

"Hey, I didn't tell you what happened on my way over to your office. I'm standing right in front of your building and a man comes over to me and he asks if I want to buy a pair of pants. I shake my head without really looking at him, because the man had a bit of a perfume to him and it wasn't Chanel number 5. But then I look down and I catch sight of two bony little knees. And when I look up a little higher, I see that Mr. Pants Salesman is standing there in his skivvies. The man was trying to sell me the pants off his ass! Now, that's entrepreneurship!"

I had to laugh. My father was standing with his knees half bent, imitating the bare-legged pants vendor. "That was James, I'll bet you anything," I told him. "He's completely nuts. He comes into the resource center sometimes and starts screaming that he's the head librarian and Monique and I have to leave."

"I'm glad you like your job, Princess. You can keep it."

"Thank you, I think I will."

My father rubbed his head, and I could see that there was something he wanted to talk about but wasn't sure how to raise. "Listen, your mother left before I could make things straight with her the way I meant. Financially I mean. I have a little money saved, and I wanted to give some to all of you, but I didn't want it to seem as if . . ." He trailed off and stuck his hands in his pockets. "You know. As if that would make it up."

I stared at him. I had spent November in the worst financial panic of my life and he hadn't said a word about this. I could have killed him, and myself for being so accommodating that I hadn't even asked him for help paying the rent.

"How much money are we talking about here?"

"Don't get your hopes up, I'm not a millionaire. But I thought with fifteen thousand you might be able to do something you couldn't do before." He had his eyes fastened on the pockmarked ground. I tried to think about all the things I could do with my windfall, but I kept suspecting that there was about to be a quid pro quo.

My father quickened his step and I lengthened my stride to match him. We were almost racing. "Look," he finally blurted. "If I leave, am I leaving again? You know, even fathers who stuck around go on a trip once in a while."

So that was it. We came to the edge of Jack London Square and began walking across the cobblestones toward the water. I couldn't speak. The Bay was the color of pale pea soup and flecked with whitecaps. I imagined a crowd of runners digging up the surface of the water with their heels. They came at us in briny gusts, spattering us with their sweat, and it seemed that they howled something in my ears as they hurtled past.

Say it, I told myself. After all this time, you can say it.

"Don't go."

The wind was making my father's eyes tear. He squinted them and hunched his shoulders. "Aw, don't say that. Come on, Julia. You're a big girl now."

"So?" We stood at the railing, with the antsy sea below us. I looked out at the tankers at the edge of the channel and the ugly little pleasure boats moored in the marina on the other side. I didn't feel like a big girl at all. I felt like I was seven years old and one of those ungainly container ships was pulling itself out of the harbor of my chest. "I don't want to do this again. Why did you come back if you were just going to leave again?"

He leaned his elbows on the railing and wedged his head between his hands. I could see his miserable posture from the corner of my eye, but I wouldn't look at him. Who was he, any-way? A phantom, who had missed all the years that bridged this moment to the one twenty-two years before, when I had woken up to find him gone.

"Oh Christ, don't cry. It would just be a little trip. I'll be back."

So I *was* crying. I stood looking out at the port, with the wind slicing past my cheeks, murmuring in my ears, making the tears hot against its cold.

After a moment my father put his arms around me and drew me to him. I sobbed into his jacket collar, all the sobs that had nothing to do with now and everything to do with then. They rolled out of my throat, round and hard and bruising as hard-boiled eggs. I hunkered down into his chest and let the wails erupt one after another like years passing, until I felt myself coming back to the present and I sniffled.

"Okay, sweetheart?" I felt him kiss the top of my head. Then one of the hands around me drew back and he rummaged in his pocket. He tilted my head back and began dabbing at my face with a handkerchief.

It was such an old-fashioned, old-man thing to do that I had to smile. And it was so like my father to want to mop up my face right away, to end the embarrassing moment and wipe away all traces of it. It was enough to start me crying again.

"I'm sorry." I took the handkerchief from him and blew my nose.

My father met my eyes, and his face, for once, was still. I could see the groove on the side of his face that his smile had etched, but he didn't smile. I wanted him to explain himself to me, but maybe there was nothing more to explain.

"I'll stay in touch," he said. "I'll call." Then he turned back to the gray-green channel of the port and let the wind whip his face as if meting out some tiny punishment.

The night after my father left, Steven woke up crying. I was sitting in the kitchen paying bills and listening to the radio. I didn't hear him at first. Thanks to my father's gift, we had money in the bank and it was a pleasure to be able to write the long-delayed checks to the phone company and Pacific Gas & Electric and make the first payment on the used Honda I bought to replace the one that had been stolen. I sang along with the radio's sappy soul ballads and wrote the checks out in my most extravagant handwriting. My life. Maybe at last I was getting a handle on it.

"Mom?"

Steven's voice was sleep-drenched and quavery, a low moan that sounded like it still had bits of dreams stuck to it.

"Mom?"

When I went into his bedroom, he was sitting up in his bed with his arms wrapped around himself.

"What is it?"

"I dreamed you were gone again. I dreamed you went back to that room." He blinked hard, fighting off the pictures.

I sat down beside him and leaned against the headboard so he could climb into my lap. "It's okay. I'm here. I'm not going anywhere." I pulled the blankets over both of us and rocked him. He smelled crumbly and sweet, like cookies. My love for him was too big to fit inside my body. It was stretching me, hollowing me out. And just under the taut balloon-skin of my chest was the nubby, rankling memory of having left him. It was always going to be there, a piece of glass, a sharp shell. Maybe it would dull with time, but

I thought that the best I could hope for is that I would learn to go around it. Memory would take the long way home, bypassing those weeks when I failed at the only thing I ever tried to be good at.

"Do you want to tell me your dream?" I whispered into Steven's hair.

"I got out of bed and the house was empty. You weren't in your room or anything. I looked for you, but I couldn't find you, and I knew you were in that house, but I didn't know how to get there."

"What house?" I held him tighter, feeling his warmth soak through my wool sweater.

"The house you went to when you were gone. The one with the purple tree." He struggled against me a little, impatient. How could I be so slow?

"So what did you do?"

"I walked outside, but I didn't know where to go, so I was crying." He sighed an airy sob.

"And then I came, didn't I? I heard you crying and I came." I stroked his forehead. It was gripped with worry.

"How come I've never met the man who lives there?"

"You mean the man that I stayed with when I was sick?"

He nodded, and burrowed closer into the hollow of my chest.

"Well, I haven't seen him since I got better. I haven't needed to see him."

"What if you get sick again?"

"I won't get sick like that again." I made my voice resolute, determined that this time he would believe me.

"But what if you do? How will I find you?" He rubbed his eyes. "I wish I knew that man. Then I could find you if you were there."

When would the repercussions end? No matter how many times we talked about what had happened, I couldn't seem to win his trust back. We were fine during the day, but at night the fear kept slipping into bed with him.

"Oh, honey, I'm sorry I didn't call you when I was there. That was wrong. But you don't have to worry, I'm not going anywhere now, and if I did go somewhere, I would call you. Remember how we talked about this?"

He nodded.

"And remember how I promised that I would never go any-where again without talking to you first?"

I felt him folding himself into a tight ball. When I squeezed him, my arms met knees and elbows, no softness.

"I don't see why you don't want me to meet that man. It's not fair. Why can't I meet him?"

Because I want it to be over, I could have said. Because I'm tired of everything leading into something else. Because every reason has a reason. Scarves tied together, pulled out of a magician's hat. Paper dolls linked at the wrist.

Instead I said, "All right."

Steven was silent, scrunched into a hard ball in my lap.

"You can meet him. We'll go to his house. Okay?"

The ball unfolded, loosening like crumpled paper, and I felt him nod. "I'm thirsty," he announced. "Can I have something to drink?"

I led him into the kitchen and he sat down at the table, squint-ing in the light and swiveling his shoulders to the music on the radio. "Juice or milk?" I asked him.

"Juice."

I poured us each a glass of cranberry juice, with ice. As he gulped his, he looked over the envelopes on the table and began humming along with Whitney Houston. He was waking up. I could see him throwing off the layers of sleep.

"I'm going to be a little shy." He slapped his fingers on the edge of the table, tapping out the rhythm of the song.

"When you meet Gabriel? Well, he's shy, too, so you can stare at each other for a while and not say anything."

"I don't want to do that. I think I'll talk to him about baseball. Does he like baseball?"

"I don't think so." It was hard to remember many details about Gabriel, but I knew that he hadn't shown any interest in the World Series.

A hip-hop song came on the radio and Steven got up and began dancing around the kitchen. He rocked back and forth from foot to foot, looking cooler than he knew in his baggy pajamas. I leaned against the sink. The window behind me was open halfway and I could smell the night seeping in. It smelled of plants surrendering their last green stench as they crumbled into earth.

"Let's go now," I said. "Do you want to?"

Steven glided over to the table to finish his drink. He watched me over the rim of his glass, appraising. "Okay," he said, sucking the last ice cube. "Let's go now."

Not preparing was part of it. I didn't want to spend the next day thinking about what to say and what to wear. I wanted to dress simply, like a penitent. While Steven changed from his pj's into jeans and a sweatshirt, I looked at myself in the mirror. I had on a pair of black jeans and an oversized men's Shetland sweater that I'd bought to replace the blue-green one I'd lost. I thought the big sweater–small jeans combination made me look like a marshmallow on toothpicks or pregnant, or both, but there was nothing to be done about it, so I stuffed my hair inside a gray beret and rattled my car keys so Steven would know I was ready to go.

The sleepy plaintiveness had left him, and he was back to being a light-footed little boy with eyes so big and green you wondered if he had special sight. We drove with the windows rolled down and the radio blasting. After a while I snapped off the radio so I could hear the sound of the engine parting the wind.

I tried to imagine how it would be to see Gabriel. I remembered his skin, smooth and penny-colored, and his way of looking at me from under his dark eyebrows. I ran my tongue over my palate, thinking of his mouth with its taste of tea and chiles and his inquiring hands. His stomach, hairless except for a small tuft below the naval, just behind the top button of his pants. But it wouldn't be like that. He would be angry at me for disappearing, or hurt, or indifferent. He would have forgotten about me, or concluded that I was just a stray lunatic. At best he would be wary, at worst furious.

"I don't know if he'll be glad to see us," I warned Steven. "It's late at night and I haven't seen him for a long time."

"Okay."

"Will you be upset if he isn't friendly?"

Steven thought about that. He shook his head. "I just want to see him."

"We'll see him."

I parked under the purple bougainvillea. When we got out of the car, faded purple blossoms were scattered under our feet. I looked up at Gabriel's window and saw the disk-shaped glow of his reading light. He was awake. He was up there on his rattan couch, seeking. I had to smile.

The future was so close to me, I could touch it with my fingers. It was the color of night, blank as a blackboard. It felt like air, cold on my face, reeking of nature and the changeful sea. It was coming toward me, ready or not. The story after the story after the story.

"Let's go knock," I said and took Steven's hand.